Tides

SHERIDAN FAMILY TREE

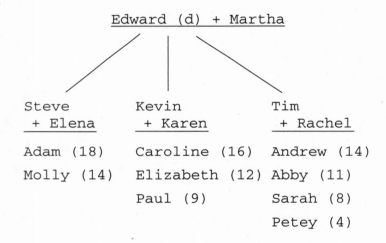

Edward (d) + Martha

Steve + Elena	Kevin + Karen	Tim + Rachel
Adam (18)	Caroline (16)	Andrew (14)
Molly (14)	Elizabeth (12)	Abby (11)
	Paul (9)	Sarah (8)
		Petey (4)

Tides

V. M. Caldwell

illustrated by Erica Magnus

MILKWEED EDITIONS

Published 2001 by Milkweed Editions
Printed in Canada
Cover painting and interior illustrations by Erica Magnus
The text of this book is set in Electra.
01 02 03 04 05   5 4 3 2 1
First Edition

Milkweed Editions, a nonprofit publisher, gratefully acknowledges support from the Elmer L. and Eleanor J. Andersen Foundation; Bush Foundation; Faegre and Benson Foundation; General Mills Foundation; McKnight Foundation; Minnesota State Arts Board through an appropriation by the Minnesota State Legislature; Norwest Foundation on behalf of Norwest Bank Minnesota; Lawrence and Elizabeth Ann O'Shaughnessy Charitable Income Trust in honor of Lawrence M. O'Shaughnessy; Oswald Family Foundation; Ritz Foundation on behalf of Mr. and Mrs. E. J. Phelps Jr.; John and Beverly Rollwagen Fund of the Minneapolis Foundation; St. Paul Companies, Inc.; Star Tribune Foundation; Target Foundation on behalf of Dayton's, Mervyn's California, and Target Stores; U.S. Bancorp; and generous individuals.

Library of Congress Cataloging-in-Publication Data

Caldwell, V. M., 1956–
     Tides / V. M. Caldwell. — 1st ed.
          p. cm.
     Summary: While spending the summer with her new siblings and cousins at their grandmother's house by the ocean, Elizabeth begins to feel that she belongs to her adoptive family.
     ISBN 1-57131-628-0 (cloth) — ISBN 1-57131-629-9 (paper)
     [1. Family life—Fiction. 2. Adoption—Fiction.] I. Title.

PZ7.C127435 Ti 2000
[Fic]—dc21   99-051671

to
RGC
with gratitude
and love

Before the Beginning

In *The Ocean Within*, Elizabeth Lawson, orphaned at age five, spends the next six years building emotional barricades as she bounces from one foster home to another. Intelligent and introspective, she is sustained only by her dream of seeing the ocean.

At age eleven, Elizabeth is placed for adoption with Kevin and Karen Sheridan. Although she has no reason to believe they will be her forever family, upon learning they spend the summer at the Atlantic shore, Elizabeth agrees to live with them.

When they arrive at the oceanside home of Kevin's mother, Elizabeth finds that she must contend not only with new siblings Caroline and Paul, but with Mrs. Sheridan's six other grandchildren as well. Elizabeth's new cousins are boisterous, affectionate, and utterly overwhelming. Certain that Elizabeth is a permanent addition to the family, eldest grandson Adam grows ever more impatient with her unwillingness to act like a sister or a cousin.

Worst of all for Elizabeth is Mrs. Sheridan. Loving but strict, Grandma insists that Elizabeth participate in family life. Elizabeth silently dubs her "Iron Woman" and does everything she can to avoid her.

Despite the Sheridans' efforts to include her, Elizabeth manages to maintain her distance—from everyone but four-year-old Petey. He nicknames her "Turtle" and, against her will, earns a place in her heart. When she inadvertently hurts Petey, Elizabeth realizes in despair that she has come to care about the whole family.

At the end of the summer, Elizabeth must face leaving not only the ocean, but—she believes—the Sheridans as well. During a painful but ultimately tender exchange with Grandma, Elizabeth finally admits that she wants to be part of the family and takes her first tentative steps toward believing it is possible.

In November, Elizabeth's adoption is made final. Eight months later, *Tides* begins. . . .

Chapter One

Less than twenty-four hours!
Smiling to herself,
Elizabeth Sheridan began
to transfer piles of neatly
folded clothes from her
dresser to her suitcase.
Underwear? Check.
Shirts? Check. Shorts? Check. Sweatshirts?
She made another trip to the dresser.
Check! Bathing suit?
She pictured the ocean's waves, shivered, and
smiled again.
I can swim now . . .
Elizabeth folded the navy blue bathing suit as
neatly as the slippery nylon would allow and tucked it
next to the sweatshirts.
Personal stuff?
She unzipped a plastic case and rechecked its
contents.

Brush, comb, toothbrush, nail clippers, deodorant.
She wasn't really sure she needed the last item—
she didn't think she smelled—but she was almost thirteen. It was better not to take chances. She zipped the bag and added it to the suitcase.

Presents.

Paul's birthday present, a regulation soccer ball, would have to go in a separate bag. Adam's high school graduation present, a how-to book about wood carving, fit easily. It had been chosen as a companion to the engraved pocketknife her parents were giving him.

What if he thinks it's dumb?

Elizabeth pressed her lips together and shrugged. She hadn't been able to come up with a better idea. She felt better about Petey's birthday present: a clear plastic paper weight in which a strand of mermaid's hair was suspended. Seaweed wouldn't be of interest to most five-year-old boys, but she thought that Petey would like it.

"Elizabeth!" Paul hollered up the back stairs. "Dinner!"

"Coming!"

She closed the suitcase, set it next to her desk, and trotted down to the kitchen. Caroline and Paul were at the table, napkins already in their laps. Her father was energetically tossing lettuce and peppers. Her mother was leaning over the telephone, her auburn hair a motionless curtain.

"Do I *have* to wear my blazer?" Paul screwed up his face. "I'll broil!"

Elizabeth smiled at her sister. There were advantages to being female. In late June, cotton dresses were among them. Caroline grinned back.

"Paul," his father said quietly, "you're whining." Kevin placed the salad bowl on the table. "And the answer is, yes, you do."

Paul scowled and began to swing his legs back and forth. "Great way to turn ten," he muttered. "Roasting alive and listening to blah, blah, blah."

"Adam didn't choose to graduate on your birthday," Kevin said evenly. "The ceremony will be over by noon, and we're going to Grandma's from there. You'll be in the water by two. Two-thirty, at the latest."

"*Promise?*"

"Promise."

The lines disappeared from Paul's forehead and Elizabeth's chest grew warm. Their parents didn't make promises they couldn't keep.

Karen put her hand over the telephone receiver, whispered, "Caro? Please?" and pointed to the stove. Caroline scooped up two pot holders and pulled a steaming casserole from the oven.

Karen rested both elbows on the counter. "He didn't even pick up his yearbook?"

Kevin glanced at Karen and then turned his attention to the casserole. He lifted the lid and the kitchen was filled with the spicy aroma of onions and gravy.

Elizabeth's mouth watered as she watched him ladle stew onto plates.

"Oh, Elena. We're sorry, too." Karen squared her shoulders. "All right, then. We'll see you tomorrow. Drive safely." She tipped the receiver onto the phone. "You can have the whole day to swim, Paul."

Four pairs of eyes swiveled toward her.

"Adam's not going to his graduation." Karen sighed. "So neither are we."

"What do you *mean*, he's not going?" Kevin demanded.

"Just that." Karen slowly pulled out her chair. "His parents have argued with him until they're blue in the face, and he refuses to go."

"But *why?*" Caroline sputtered.

"He says it's a waste of dry cleaning."

Kevin's eyes narrowed. "That's absurd."

Karen nodded sadly. "And when Elena suggested that he might want to see his friends one last time, Adam said that *his* friends are dead. He doesn't want to have to listen to . . ."

Elizabeth wondered what phrase her mother was choosing to edit.

". . . tributes to Jimmy and Nate."

"I understand that would be painful," Kevin said. "But milestones are times to celebrate. As a *family.*"

"Steve pointed that out."

"And . . . ?"

"And Adam said we were welcome to go without him."

Elizabeth's stomach knotted.

I thought he was getting better!

"What did Mom say?" Kevin asked very quietly.

"She thinks it needs to be Adam's decision."

That sounds like Grandma.

There were several moments of wordless communication between Kevin and Karen.

They're going to talk about it later.

"So what are we doing?" Caroline mumbled.

Karen reached for the salad. "We're all still going to Grandma's."

Paul bounced. "When?"

"Whenever we want, I guess." Karen smiled sadly. "Aunt Elena said they'll meet us there, and do their best to celebrate your first double-digit birthday."

"If we're not going to the ceremony," Caroline spoke to her plate, "does that mean we shouldn't give Adam his presents?"

Karen's eyebrows drew together. "Let's take them with us and see."

Maybe she doesn't want to talk about it.

Elizabeth bit her lip. Caroline seemed so grown-up lately. She'd gotten her driver's license and a part-time job, and she'd been made head of volunteering at school. Half her phone calls were from boys, and she was already thinking about college. But when she'd asked about giving Adam his presents, Caroline had looked like a friendless six-year-old.

Elizabeth gently knocked on her half-open door. "Hi."

"Hi." Caroline looked back to the wrapping paper in her hand. The sweater she'd made for Adam lay on her desk.

"I hope you get to give it to him," Elizabeth stammered. "It's beautiful."

"Thanks." Caroline smiled briefly and shook her head. "It's not the present I'm upset about. There's always his birthday." She set the wrapping paper on top of the sweater. "It's Adam still not being *Adam*."

Elizabeth nodded.

"Not wanting us to see him graduate." Caroline's gaze drifted to a collection of snapshots. "And take his picture in cap and gown, and all that."

Elizabeth nodded again. The Sheridans were a clan of picture-takers, and family portraits held places of honor in each of their homes.

"Like last fall, when you were adopted," Caroline said wistfully. "It was even *more* special because the whole family was there."

Elizabeth's throat was suddenly full. She couldn't have imagined that day without Grandma, or Petey, or Adam, or . . .

"I suppose it's not the end of world." Caroline

shrugged. "We'll all be together anyway, for Paul's birthday."

"Grandma's making three cakes." Elizabeth gave her sister a quick smile. "Chocolate, and cherry, and lemon."

"That's *one* thing that never changes." Caroline grinned back. "We can always count on Grandma!"

Alone in her room, Elizabeth contemplated the family portraits that stood on her desk. The one in the center had been taken two months ago, on the one-year anniversary of her arrival. Caroline and Paul looked back at her with nearly identical blue green eyes. Their hair was the same rich reddish brown as their mother's, and they shared their father's radiant smile. Dark lashes framed Karen's sparkling green eyes. Kevin's eyes were a discerning clear blue, and his hair was dark brown.

Elizabeth looked nothing like any of them. Her eyes were the dark tan of November leaves, her blond hair was free of red highlights, and her smile was nervous and small above her pointed chin. Elizabeth sighed. Being part of a family wasn't about physical resemblance, but did she have to look so *horribly* pasted on?

The family portrait on the left matched the one in their front hall: the one taken last summer, on Grandma's porch. Fifteen Sheridans and Elizabeth

Lawson. The family portrait on the right had been taken in November, just after the judge had signed her adoption decree. Sixteen Sheridans. Adam looked like Adam in that one: black hair, intelligent dark brown eyes, determined chin, and Sheridan smile.

If only Jimmy and Nate hadn't gone to that party . . . if only there hadn't been any beer . . . if only someone had taken Nate's car keys . . .

"Finished packing?" Her mother smiled at her from the doorway.

Elizabeth nodded. "Except for my pajamas."

Karen glanced at the photographs and stepped into the room. "Were you thinking about Adam?"

Elizabeth nodded again. "Is he still depressed?"

Karen shook her head. "I'm not sure. I know he stopped taking the medication, and he hasn't been to the counselor since March."

"But," Elizabeth protested weakly, "at Easter he seemed O.K."

"The best that he's been since the accident, at least." Karen hesitated. "But leaving high school is a big step, especially for someone who doesn't like change. Graduation might be forcing Adam to confront the fact that he can't go kayaking with Nate, and that he can't be roommates with Jimmy this fall. He could be facing their deaths all over again."

Elizabeth sighed.

"Maybe being at the ocean, and with the family, will help." Karen smiled. "You getting excited?"

Elizabeth grinned and nodded. "About seeing everybody," she stammered. "And swimming!"

"Me, too! But I've got to get Paul packed and edit the rest of that book before we can go." Karen kissed her cheek. "Good night, sweetheart."

"Good night, Mom."

Elizabeth's eyes wandered back to the picture, back to Adam.

Maybe being at the ocean, and with the family, will help.

She fell asleep hoping it would.

Chapter
Two

Kevin slammed the rear door of the station wagon. "First shift, Red?"

"Second, thanks." Karen yawned. "I'm not in gear yet."

Kevin slid behind the wheel. "All set, Caro?"

"The doors are locked, the lights are off, and I double-checked every appliance we own." Caroline fastened her seat belt. "There are seventeen of them!"

Karen laughed. "Thank you, sweetheart. I'm glad *you're* on top of things."

"I wasn't *up* until three," Caroline scolded.

"Deadlines are deadlines." Karen yawned again. "Which reminds me . . ."

"I know." Kevin started the car. "Post office first."

Paul scowled. "How long will that take?"

"Two minutes."

Elizabeth grinned. The launching of a family trip was reassuringly familiar now.

Seat belt check, Mom.

Karen looked over her shoulder. "Everyone buckled?"

"Yes!"

Your turn, Dad. "Let's get this show . . ."

"Then let's get this show on the road!" Kevin backed the station wagon onto the street.

Still smiling, Elizabeth rearranged the bags at her feet and rolled down her window. By lunchtime, the car ride and motion sickness would be behind her.

And the whole, wonderful summer will still be ahead.

Walks into town and ice-cream cones on the way home. Fireworks on the Fourth of July. Italian sausage from Mr. Ciminelli, grilled to perfection by Adam. Grandma's pancakes: melt-in-your-mouth golden brown. Reading with Petey. Playing chess with Andrew. Listening to Molly's exaggerated stories about things that had happened at school.

Things wouldn't be *perfect*, of course. For starters, there was having to wear a bathing suit. Elizabeth looked down at her angular knees and frowned. She wasn't Sheridan-slender, she was out-and-out *skinny*. At the community center, even the girls had teased her about it. And, unlike the rest of the family, she wasn't athletic. She hated gym class and anything to do with a ball. But she could ride a bike. And maybe

Grandma would take her back to the tide pools. She sighed happily.

The ocean.

Elizabeth's heart began to beat faster.

And this year, I'll be swimming with the others!

For the rest of the family, being at Grandma's meant being in the water. Every time Elizabeth had attended a swimming lesson, she had been conscious of preparing for the ocean, of doing something quintessentially Sheridan.

A year ago . . .

Elizabeth shook her head. A year ago, she hadn't been a Sheridan. A year ago, she couldn't have imagined she'd ever become one. She contemplated her parents and wondered for the millionth time why they had adopted her.

Kevin and Karen. Dad and Mom.

Kevin, who challenged her with chess and math problems, and who beamed when she solved them. Who teased and called her pet names. Whose strong arms had supported her until she'd figured out how to float . . .

"Dad?" Paul pulled a piece of gum from his pocket. "Can people really set stuff on fire just by looking at it?"

Kevin laughed. "Special effects, Paul."

Karen looked over her shoulder. "What *have* you been watching?"

Karen. Mom.

Just being near Karen was soothing. She spoke softly, and when she listened, it was with her undivided attention. Karen often knew what Elizabeth was feeling, even when Elizabeth couldn't find the words to explain it. On the outside, Mom was gentle.

But Dad always says she's the strong one . . .

"Elizabeth? How's your tum holding up?"

"Pretty well, Dad."

Kevin smiled at her in the rearview mirror, signaled, and pulled onto the highway. Elizabeth checked her watch.

One hundred forty minutes to go.

Two hours and twenty minutes, and they'd *be* there. She pictured the weathered shingles on Grandma's house and the wide swing on the porch. The stone fireplace in the front room. The dining room's enormous dark table. The large cheerful kitchen: blue-and-white canisters on the counter, strawberry print curtains at the windows. The picket fence of unpainted wood, the pine trees near the barn . . .

"I wonder what Grandma is doing!" Paul chirped.

Caroline grinned. "Probably frosting your cake."

"But I wanted to lick the spatula!"

"She'll save it, Paul," Caroline assured him.

She always saves the spatula.

Elizabeth grinned.

Even for grown-ups!

Grandma. A year ago, during the train ride to

Grandma's, Caroline had tried to describe her. "Grandma's amazing, Elizabeth. She's smart, and she's funny, and she really listens." All of that was true, but there was so much *more*. What else had Caroline said? "She always knows who needs a hug."

Elizabeth wrinkled her nose. She'd gotten used to being kissed—*sort* of, anyway—but being hugged still made her tense. To Grandma and the rest of the Sheridans, physical displays of affection were like breathing.

But she hasn't pushed me . . .

Grandma had asked for a hug only once, and then changed her mind. "When you're ready," she'd said. Elizabeth wondered when that would be and almost started to laugh. A year ago, before she understood the caring behind Grandma's strict enforcement of rules, Elizabeth had thought of Kevin's mother as "Iron Woman"—and had done everything she could to avoid being *near* her.

"That's disgusting!" Caroline said sharply.

"Paul." Karen's tone was serious. "We've talked about using that language."

"Sorry," he mumbled.

"Say that in front of your grandmother," Kevin warned, "and you'll have a sore bottom."

Paul squirmed and Karen resolutely stared out the window.

Mom really hates it that Grandma spanks.

As far as Elizabeth knew, it was the only thing

Karen didn't love about Grandma. But while
Grandma was strict, she was fair.

She doesn't spank unless we deserve it . . .

"What time are the others arriving?" Kevin asked.

"Elena didn't say, but I'm sure they'll be there before dinner. Rachel said Tim was aiming for ten, but
not to call 911 before noon."

The others.

Diplomatic Uncle Tim and optimistic Aunt
Rachel. Andrew, a chess whiz with kind hazel eyes.
Abby, athletic and determined — "Sheridan stubborn," Grandma called it. Sarah, pigtailed and
enthusiastic.

And Petey.

Elizabeth's smile began at her toes. Almost five.
The family's tender-hearted, pint-sized philosopher.
Sandy hair, penetrating eyes of dark blue, and an
ability to empathize that was positively frightening.
When Grandma had explained to Petey that Elizabeth
needed time to come out of her shell, he had begun
calling her "Turtle."

. . . Hey!

"Hurry up, Elizabeth!" Paul pointed to the door
lock. "I have to go *bad!*"

"Sorry." Elizabeth lifted the lock and quickly
climbed out. Paul scrambled after her and raced toward the gas station rest rooms. At a more leisurely
pace, Kevin and Caroline headed toward a take-out
window.

"Elizabeth?" Karen asked. "You've hardly said a word since we got into the car."

"Just thinking." Elizabeth smiled. "I'm O.K."

"Dad and Caro were hungry, and I need some coffee. I know you travel better if you don't eat, but how about something to drink?"

"No, thanks, Mom."

"Then will you guard the presents?" Karen's eyes twinkled. "Your brother's just *itching* to peek."

Elizabeth grinned. "I won't let him."

Two minutes later, Paul emerged from the rest room. Drying his hands on his pants, he hurried toward her. He skidded to a stop, looked over his shoulder, and pleaded.

Elizabeth shook her head. "They're supposed to be a surprise."

"You sound like Caro." Paul scowled. "Dumb *girl* rules about presents." He turned his back and kicked the rear tire until the others returned.

"Everyone set?" Kevin handed his car keys to Karen and a cellophane-wrapped pastry to Paul.

Caroline fastened her seat belt and mumbled, "We should be at graduation right now."

"Maybe it's best that we're not." Karen started the car. "It wouldn't have been much of a celebration if Adam didn't want to be there."

Caroline sighed.

"Can't be undone, Caro." Kevin gave her a sympathetic smile. "Let it go."

I hope Uncle Steve has "let it go."

Elizabeth was still a bit scared of Kevin's older brother. Steve was almost as intense as his mother, but he laughed a lot less and seemed to worry more. He thought things through in advance, and he was *always* prepared: cameras, Band-Aids, maps—anything that was needed. But of the three brothers, he seemed quickest to anger.

Adam's sort of that way. So is Molly.

But if Adam and Molly had inherited their father's tendency toward impatience, they had also inherited Aunt Elena's graceful dark beauty. Molly—Magdalena, in full—shared her mother's effortless elegance. She was impulsive, and her wit was sarcastic, but even at fourteen, she had *style.*

And then there's Adam.

Whenever Elizabeth thought of her eldest cousin, she felt confused. He had been angry at her for most of last summer, mystified by her reluctance to interact with the family. But he had rescued her from rock-throwing strangers, and when her adoption had been finalized, he had written her a tender letter of congratulations.

The fearless leader of the Sheridan brat-pack.

A year ago, Adam had been referee, safety warden, mediator, and lifeguard to his younger cousins. Grandma had gratefully relied upon him, and the others had looked up to him.

So did I. Even when I couldn't admit it . . .

"I see Vermont!" Caroline pointed to a pickup truck with green license plates.

"That red car's from Ohio," Elizabeth offered.

"Come *on*, Elizabeth!" Paul argued. "I called Ohio an hour ago!"

Chapter Three

"The ice-cream parlor has a new awning," Karen observed.

"And they painted the pavilion!" hollered Paul.

The pavilion—we're almost there.

Elizabeth breathed a mental sigh of relief. Although she had taken her motion-sickness pills, her stomach had been restless for most of the three-hour trip.

"Ugh!" Caroline said. "What a gross shade of yellow."

Elizabeth nodded. Why hadn't they repainted it white? The way it *belonged*?

The third stop sign marked the end of "downtown" South Wales. They turned left, turned right four blocks later, and pulled into the driveway.

Grandma waved to them from the porch. She was

wearing gray shorts, a short-sleeved white shirt, and her Sheridan smile. As usual, she wore neither makeup nor glasses, and her only jewelry consisted of a wrist-watch and a narrow wedding band. Her dark hair was combed casually back, framing the laugh lines at the corners of her eyes.

"Welcome, everyone! Happy birthday, Paul!"

"Hi, Grandma!" He barreled up the steps and threw his arms around her.

We're here.

Elizabeth sniffed the hot, pine-scented air, vaguely wondered why she could not smell the ocean, and slowly drank in her surroundings. She had missed too much of last summer to want to miss a minute of this one.

The trees . . .

Four pines stood between the house and the road. Last year, there had been six. A storm had felled the two in the middle and part of the porch had gone with them. In the bright sunlight, against the silver gray of the rest of the house, the new shingles looked offensively orange.

But the swing is still there, and the fence, and the same bushes need trimming . . .

A burst of laughter drew her attention to the porch. Kevin was grinning and protesting his innocence to his clearly skeptical mother. A horn beeped twice and another car pulled into the driveway.

Petey!

Uncle Tim brought an overloaded station wagon to a stop and his family tumbled out. Aunt Rachel looked rumpled and relieved. Andrew's expression was one of eldest-child forbearance. Abby waved enthusiastically and shouted to Paul. Sarah looked hot and sulky, and Petey's brow was furrowed. He raced across the lawn, slipped through the mob, and pounded his way to the second floor. A door slammed, a thudding sound peculiar to the bathroom, and Elizabeth smiled.

He's still pretty little.

The air began to vibrate with Sheridan noise: top-volume greetings, bursts of laughter, and hundred-word-a-minute efforts to catch up with each other. Elizabeth stood to one side of the porch watching the parade of exuberant hugs.

Before last summer, I didn't even know these people existed . . .

"Hi, Elizabeth!" Sarah skipped toward her. "Guess what?" She grinned and pulled back her pigtails.

"You got your ears pierced!" Elizabeth smiled. "They look great, Sair!"

Sarah beamed and ran off.

"Hey, Elizabeth!" Andrew appeared at her side. "Got a chess question for you: what did the bishop say to the frivolous knight?"

He's started to shave!

Elizabeth tried hard to think, but her mind remained stubbornly elsewhere. "I give up."

"Quit horsing around!" He grinned down at her. "Awful, right?"

Elizabeth wrinkled her nose. "Terrible."

"The chess club had a joke contest," Andrew explained. "Can you believe that was the winner?"

She shook her head and stammered, "I learned two new gambits."

"All *right*, Elizabeth! A game before dinner?" She nodded.

"Andrew!" Caroline opened her arms and he leaned down to hug her.

Last year, they were the same height . . .

Petey came back through the door and raced down the steps. "Hi, Turtle!" With trusting abandon, he jumped. Holding her breath, Elizabeth caught him.

He's gotten so heavy!

"Hi, Petey!" Elizabeth carefully set him down. His sapphire eyes sparkled above a gap-toothed grin.

"Look!" He proudly pointed to the space. "Sarah threw a block, and there was blood all *over*, and the tooth fairy brought me a dollar!"

Before Elizabeth could reply, Petey bounced toward her father. Kevin scooped him into the air and Elizabeth briefly wondered whether the impulse to hug was something genetic.

"Hello, Elizabeth!" En route to the porch, Aunt Rachel and Uncle Tim greeted her warmly.

"Hi, Elizabeth!" Abby grinned. "I brought you *five* books, and one of them's three hundred pages!"

"Thanks, Abby." Elizabeth smiled. "I like your earrings."

"You should get *your* ears pierced." Abby tipped her head. "But you never wear your hair back, so they wouldn't show much."

"C'mon, Abby!" Andrew called. "I can't carry your stuff *and* Petey's."

The hubbub began to subside and Elizabeth climbed the steps to the porch. Grandma's slate-colored eyes sparkled brightly. "Hello, Elizabeth!"

Her hair is grayer!

"Hi, Grandma." Elizabeth smiled.

Her grandmother kissed her cheek and examined both sides of her neck. "Just checking for gills." She winked. "Kevin says you've become quite a fish!"

Elizabeth blushed. "I made Intermediate Swimmer on the last day," she said shyly. "Thanks again for the lessons, Grandma."

"You're welcome." She grinned. "I can't wait to see what you've learned!"

Elizabeth carried her suitcase into the house and past the beach whistles that hung from a hook in the hall.

One tweet for "too far," two for a head count, and three for "time to go home."

"Hurry up, Elizabeth!" Paul raced down the stairs. "I'll be *eleven* before you get changed!"

She trotted up to the second floor. Karen stepped into the hall wearing a new bathing suit.

What was wrong with her old one?

Kevin came up the back stairs and whistled. "*Nice,* Red!"

Karen rolled her eyes. "Kevin, you are incorrigible!"

"Thoroughly!" He grinned and leaned forward.

Kissing time—outta here!

Elizabeth ducked into the front bedroom and quickly shut the door. She was relieved to see Abby's clothes on the top bunk and Sarah's on the bottom one: she would again have the single bed by the window.

"Elizabeth?" Caroline called. "You ready?"

"Almost!" She flipped her suitcase onto the bed.

Swimming, swimming, swimming . . .

She wrestled the nylon straps over her shoulders.

Hope the water's not super cold.

Elizabeth pulled on her sneakers and hurried down the stairs. The porch was full of people and noise. Sunscreen and towels and beach toys in hand, twelve Sheridans swarmed onto the lawn. Elizabeth reached the road before the smells of seaweed and salt sent an icy cascade down her spine.

A year ago, I'd only dreamed of seeing the ocean . . .

Elizabeth's mind leapt backwards. She was once again six years old, and another change in foster homes meant another change in schools—and leaving behind a teacher of whom she had been very fond. Elizabeth could see very clearly the expression on Mrs. Miller's face as she said good-bye.

"You're a special girl, Elizabeth." She tucked a small package into her hand. "I won't forget you."

Elizabeth hadn't opened the gift until bedtime. Alone in the bathroom of her newest foster home, she had unwrapped a delicate seashell—a sand dollar. From that moment on, she had been determined that, one day, she would see the ocean.

Her mind vaulted forward nearly five years, to her third preplacement visit with the Sheridans. It was a muggy day in May, and Kevin was explaining that the family spent July at his mother's home near the Atlantic shore. Unwilling to meet his direct gaze, Elizabeth had been staring at Karen's shoes when she realized what Kevin had said—that her dream was within her reach.

The following day, and for that reason only, Elizabeth had agreed to live with Kevin and Karen. Then she'd held her breath for two months, hoping they wouldn't send her back before she'd had a chance to see the ocean. She had never imagined that they were serious about adopting her, that they intended to keep her . . .

And now they're my parents.

A seagull squawked loudly and Elizabeth looked up. Kevin and Karen were walking in front of her, holding hands.

Kevin Thomas Sheridan and Karen Granger Sheridan. Parents of Caroline Leigh, Paul Edward . . .

She shook her head.

. . . and me.

"Race you, Andrew!" Paul shouted.

They took their marks, Uncle Tim hollered, "Go!" and they sped toward the waves. Paul reached the water ahead of Andrew and dove. He surfaced and raised his arms over his head.

Laughing and screaming, the others followed him into the water. Elizabeth watched them for several moments, and then lifted her eyes to the horizon. A haze, or some trick of sunlight, blurred the distinction between ocean and sky.

It goes on forever . . .

A strong breeze blew Elizabeth's hair from her shoulders. The scents of seaweed and fish filled her nostrils and her intestines convulsed.

No!

She jerked her gaze downward. Breakers roared toward her and crashed onto the sand, obliterating retreating waves as they fell. Her heart pounded as she watched the foam writhe and vanish.

I can't do it!

Her breathing grew rapid and shallow.

I can't!

She could not touch the ocean, much less go swimming.

But I swam in the pool!

Her mind wailed.

Even over my head!

Tears stung her eyes.

And last year I went in! Up to my knees . . .

Her rational mind thrust the facts toward her, but to no avail. Panic had paralyzed her lungs, and icy terror was rippling its way through her limbs. Her knees shook as she stared down at the sand.

"Sweetheart?" Karen asked. "Are you O.K.?"

Help me!

Karen laid a hand on Elizabeth's arm. "You're *freezing!*" Her voice rose. "And you haven't even been in the water!" She snatched up a towel and wrapped it around Elizabeth's shoulders. "Whatever's the matter, you need to warm up." Karen pulled on her sneakers. "Let's get you into a hot bath."

Karen spoke briefly to Kevin and hurried back across the sand. They stepped onto the road and Elizabeth pulled the salt-filled air an inch deeper into her lungs. A block later, her knees felt less stiff. By the time they reached the driveway, she no longer felt cold — she felt merely nauseous.

Although she knew a bath would not help, that there was no longer a need, Elizabeth dutifully climbed into the tub. Twenty minutes later, she climbed out. She was sitting on her bed, fighting to keep her thoughts and emotions at bay, when Karen appeared in the doorway.

"Feeling better?"

Elizabeth nodded.

"Do you know what happened?" Karen's green eyes were filled with concern. "Why you got so cold?"

Elizabeth shook her head. If some part of her knew, it wasn't a part that had access to words.

"Maybe just too many people, and too much excitement, after such a long ride?"

Lying is better than having her worry.

Elizabeth nodded. Her stomach twisted, but relaxed as the lines disappeared from Karen's forehead.

"I'm sorry, Mom."

Karen gave her a puzzled look. "About what, sweetheart?"

"You didn't get to go swimming."

"Not to worry." Karen gave her a gentle smile. "The two of us can have a swim later."

Elizabeth listened to her mother's footsteps echo on the stairs.

No, we can't, Mom.

Tears spilled down her cheeks.

No matter how much I want to.

Chapter
Four

"Adam has decided to attend college locally, at least for a year." Aunt Elena's words lilted softly. "And to keep living at home."

Elizabeth loved Aunt Elena's Spanish accent, still present after twenty years in the United States.

Karen tipped her head. "How do you feel about that?"

Although she was sitting in plain view of her aunt and her mother, Elizabeth felt as though she were eavesdropping. Not wanting to interrupt their conversation by getting up from the picnic table, she continued to nibble her hot dog. The others had finished their dinners and were playing capture the flag. His hands in his pockets, Adam stood alone by the fence.

Aunt Elena rested her arms on the table. "I think it is a good idea." She sighed. "But Steve is afraid Adam's decision was strictly financial. Adam knows Steve took a cut in salary when he began working for Tim."

"Have they talked about it?" Karen asked gently.

Aunt Elena shook her head. "Adam simply *announced* his new plan. He had already made the arrangements. Admissions, registration—" She waved one hand. "Everything! He'd even found a work-study job. It was frightening to have him be so independent." She turned to look at her son. "But I could not help being proud."

Karen smiled.

Aunt Elena smiled back and ran her fingers up and down her glass of ice water. "I hope he can find time to be a *kid* this summer." Her black eyes grew bright. "This year has been so hard on him . . ."

"Hard on *all* of you," Karen said softly.

"Time for dessert!" Grandma called from the porch. "Elizabeth? Will you give me a hand?"

"Coming, Grandma!"

In the front room, Elizabeth paused. The blue chairs were in their places by the porch window, and the sofa built for six people was where it belonged. Photograph albums still lined the bottom bookshelf, and bits of sunlight flickered onto the stone fireplace in the way she remembered . . .

This room's the same.

She glanced up.

Except for the painting.

Elizabeth couldn't decide whether she was embarrassed or pleased that Grandma had chosen to hang her Christmas present over the mantelpiece.

Was that only six months ago?

A cupboard door banged and Elizabeth hurried through the archway. Two piles of presents waited on the window seat. Plates and cake servers lay on the dining-room table. In the kitchen, window curtains flapped wildly.

"We'll have to do cake inside." Grandma grinned. "Or Paul won't have a *chance* to blow out his candles!"

Elizabeth smiled. "He keeps changing his mind about what to wish."

Grandma laughed. "Good thing birthdays come around again!"

Elizabeth carried three trays to the dining room and then carefully arranged ten candles on the fudge cake. Grandma handed her a box of matches and went to call the others.

The back door banged softly. Footsteps passed the mudroom and came up the steps to the kitchen. Adam paused in the doorway, nodded to Elizabeth, and strode to the telephone counter. He scribbled a note, taped it to the big refrigerator, and retraced his steps. The door banged again, and Adam was gone.

Elizabeth tiptoed across the room.

"To town on an errand. Back by 9:30. Adam."

Sheridan noise swelled as the throng moved toward

the dining room. Kevin poked his head through the doorway. "O.K., candle lady!"

Elizabeth struck the match four times before it caught fire.

How could he just leave?

Her hand trembled as she held the flame to the wicks.

When it's time for Paul's cake?

She dropped the match into the sink.

Now everyone will be mad!

She bit her lip and picked up the cake. Waxy smoke stung her eyes.

Maybe they won't notice right away . . .

She stepped through the doorway. Past the glow of the candles, she saw Paul grin.

"Happy birthday to you . . ." Everyone sang very loudly, few voices on key. ". . . dear Pa-u-u-u-l . . ." Elizabeth set the cake in front of her brother and stepped back from the table. ". . . Happy birthday to you!" The chorus howled the last note and broke into applause.

"Make a wish!" Molly called.

Paul nodded eagerly, took a deep breath, and blew out all the candles. Everyone cheered and he took several theatrical bows.

"Elena, will you cut the lemon? Rachel, the cherry?" Grandma turned to Karen. "Birthday Mom, you're on chocolate!"

Kevin took orders for juice and for milk. Uncle

Tim handed out scoops of vanilla ice cream and Uncle Steve dispensed raspberry sherbet. Grandma poured coffee and tea. Children swarmed among adults and each other, cheerfully marking their passage with crumbs.

"If you'd put candles on all of the cakes," Paul lamented, "I'd have gotten *three* wishes!"

The room erupted in laughter.

"Here, greedy." Caroline grinned and held a box toward her brother. "Maybe it's something you wished for."

"Thanks, Caro!" Paul licked his fingers and accepted the package.

So far, no one's noticed that Adam's not here . . .

Paul ripped the paper from a model rocket kit. "Awesome!" He gave his sister an enthusiastic hug.

"You're welcome!" Caroline smiled and wiped a smear of frosting from her cheek.

"Adult supervision on that one, Paul." Kevin pointed to the warning on the box. "Promise?"

"O.K., Dad!"

"Happy birthday, Paul!" Abby handed him something wrapped in plaid paper. He continued to open gifts until only one box remained in his pile.

"Who hasn't had a chance to give Paul a present?" Aunt Rachel asked.

No one moved toward the package and the room grew very quiet.

"It's from Adam!" Sarah proudly read from the tag.

Uncle Steve's eyes swept the room. "And where, exactly, *is* Adam?"

"In town." Elizabeth spoke without having intended to, and she blushed as people turned toward her. "There's a note in the kitchen."

Uncle Steve strode toward the back of the house. Grandma and Kevin exchanged a quick look and Kevin turned to Paul. "How about trying out that new soccer ball?"

"It's your birthday, so you choose the teams," Andrew said quickly. "Petey and I will set up the net." He led the pack toward the porch.

"Can I be goalie?" Abby begged. "Please, Paul?" The screen door banged.

Uncle Steve stepped back into the room. In a tight voice, he read Adam's message.

"Elizabeth?" Aunt Elena turned toward her. "Did you see him leave the note?"

She nodded.

"*Qué?* Did he *say* anything?"

Elizabeth shook her head.

"Let's take our coffee out to the porch," Grandma suggested quietly. "It's a beautiful evening."

The grown-ups refilled their cups and drifted toward the front of the house. Elizabeth remained where she was, relieved that Adam's message was no longer a secret, but uncomfortably certain that a confrontation lay ahead. She checked her watch: 8:24. Adam might not be back for more than an hour.

If he comes back when he said he would.

She shook her head. Adam had already committed two crimes: missing the party, and failing to leave a number where he could be reached.

He won't risk disaster by being late, too.

Elizabeth took refuge in a mechanical task, and found solace in warm, soapy water. Half an hour later, the dining room was spotless, the kitchen gleamed, and the dishwasher was humming. She dried her hands wishing something else needed cleaning.

The banging of the back door was followed by the clink of glass against glass. "Grandma said there were *six* jars," Abby complained.

"Five's enough," Caroline answered. "I'm helping Petey, and Andrew said he'd help Sarah." The door banged again.

Elizabeth turned off the kitchen light and looked out the window. Near the barn, a hunt for fireflies was underway. As she climbed the back stairs she heard Petey call, "Look, Molly! We *got* one!"

Elizabeth wandered down the hall wondering why Grandma hadn't seemed more upset about Adam. Maybe she wanted to keep things calm. Her grandchildren would be staying for more than a month, but the adults were all leaving tomorrow. They wouldn't be back until the first week in August.

It'll be awful if they leave feeling angry.

Elizabeth sighed and flopped onto her bed.

Sheridans didn't yell very often, but there were consequences for breaking the rules.

"He's eighteen, Steve." Kevin's voice floated up through the dusk to the window. "And he did leave a note."

"Which said next to nothing," Uncle Steve snapped. "And what does being eighteen have to do with caring, or manners? Pretending his graduation didn't matter was bad enough. There's no excuse for missing Paul's birthday."

Someone said something brief. The voice came from the far end of the porch and Elizabeth wasn't sure who had spoken.

"He's known the rule about leaving a phone number since he was Petey's age," Uncle Steve answered flatly.

He must be exaggerating. Petey won't even be five until Thursday.

The air below the window grew suddenly still.

"Where have you been?" Uncle Steve's voice was harsh.

"The note said I'd be back by nine-thirty," Adam replied. "It's only twenty-five after."

"Where *were* you?" his father demanded.

Elizabeth tiptoed to the window and peered down through the screen. Adam stood at the bottom of the steps, straight-backed and still. When he spoke, nothing moved but his mouth.

"The bait shop."

"*No te gusta* —" Aunt Elena sputtered. "You *hate* to fish!"

Uncle Steve put his hands on his hips. "Ludlow's closes at six."

"I had an appointment with Mr. Ludlow."

"That couldn't have waited? That was more important than Paul's *birthday?*"

A note of defiance crept into Adam's voice. "He had to show me the shop and give me a key." There was a brief pause. "He wants me to open, Sunday through Thursday. Five-thirty sharp." Adam looked toward the road and then back to his father. "I start tomorrow."

Chapter Five

The firefly hunters swarmed around the corner of the house, glowing trophies held high. Each collection was admired, lids were removed from their jars, and the little lights vanished. Bedtime was announced and footsteps thundered up the stairs. From her post at the window, Elizabeth watched Grandma walk toward the fence with Uncle Steve.

I wonder what she's saying to him . . .

The light went on overhead.

"Hey, Elizabeth!" Abby grinned. "Did you see how many we caught?"

"Me and Andrew got six!" Sarah's pigtails bounced.

Elizabeth smiled. "That's great, Sair."

"Did you *hear*?" Abby's voice dropped to a stage

whisper and she closed the door. "Adam got a *job*. At the bait shop."

Little puckers appeared on Sarah's forehead. "Who's gonna lifeguard us, then?"

"Grandma," Abby said quickly. "Like always."

"But Adam watches us when Grandma's not there."

Abby shrugged. "Then Caro will. Or Molly, or Andrew."

Sarah's forehead relaxed. A moment later, her eyebrows drew together again. "But it won't be the *same* without Adam."

"He can't work *all* the time, Sair," Abby assured her. "He'll still come swimming."

Someone knocked.

"Girls?" Aunt Rachel opened the door and frowned. "I *thought* the line for the bathroom was a bit short."

They scurried to find their pajamas and Aunt Rachel withdrew.

It won't be the same without Adam.

Elizabeth brushed her teeth slowly.

I hope Uncle Steve isn't still mad.

She followed her roommates down to the front room in time to see Adam hand his present to Paul.

"Happy birthday."

"Thanks, Adam!" Paul eagerly tore the paper from a fluorescent green squirt gun. The box claimed it could shoot thirty feet. "Coo-*oool!*"

"Glad you like it." Adam gave Paul a brief smile. "I'd better get to bed. C'mon, Petey."

Adam waited on the landing while Petey collected kisses from his mother and father, both aunts, and both uncles.

"Now, scoot!" Grandma smiled at Petey and pointed to the stairs. Sarah yawned loudly and Paul rubbed his eyes. "The rest of you, too. I'll be up in a minute."

Elizabeth crossed the room to her parents.

"How are you feeling?" Karen asked.

"I'm O.K., Mom."

Karen gave her a kiss and smoothed her hair with both hands. "Sleep well."

Kevin grinned. "Dibs on morning swim!" He leaned down to kiss her.

Did he have to say that?

"Night, Mom. Night, Dad."

Elizabeth hurried up the stairs and climbed onto the bed by the window.

"You sure you want that bed again?" Abby was perched on the top bunk, swinging her legs over the side. Below her, Sarah seemed not to mind the fact that the whole structure was swaying.

Elizabeth gave Abby a weak smile and nodded. Bunk beds were not for the faint-of-stomach. Footsteps came down the stairs from the Crow's Nest, the third-floor room shared by Adam and Petey, and crossed the hall.

"All set, girls?" Grandma gave each of them a kiss and a smile. "Sleep tight. You've got a whole day of swimming tomorrow!"

The light went off, the door clicked closed, and Elizabeth's eyes filled with tears.

How can I stay out of the water without hurting their feelings?

This afternoon, her parents had *handed* her an excuse not to swim. "It would be smarter to wait," Karen had said. "The water *is* cold, and your resistance is down."

"Mom's right," Kevin had added. "You don't want to risk getting sick and being dry-docked for a week!"

How about five weeks?

Elizabeth's temples thudded into the darkness. She knew with absolute certainty that she could not go into the water. She didn't know *why*, but there was no doubt in her mind: she could not go into the ocean.

But what am I going to say?

She had no idea. She didn't want to lie, but if they asked for a reason, she had none to give. Heat snaked from her chest to her throat.

And they were all so happy about my being able to swim . . .

Kevin had cheered each new accomplishment at the pool, and Karen had promised to take her skin diving. Paul was dying to teach her how to play shark bait, and Grandma couldn't wait to see what she'd learned . . .

And Adam won't even be there.

Elizabeth silently choked back a sob. In just over twenty-four hours, the summer to which she'd looked forward had all but evaporated.

Thin gray light crept around the edges of the window shade. Elizabeth lifted her head from her pillow and listened.

Adam's awake.

Bare feet tiptoed past her room and down the front stairs. The screen door squeaked but closed without banging. Elizabeth crept to the window. Adam dropped his sneakers onto the lawn, shoved his feet into them, and headed for the driveway. Pale early morning fog hovered by the fence. It parted and swirled as he walked through it.

Like the end of a movie . . .

She lost sight of him and looked to her left. Last summer, the taller pine trees had blocked the view to the ocean. This morning, only fog kept her from seeing the water. But she knew it was there, waiting for her.

What am I going to do?

Her stomach twisted upward. She tried to distract herself with a book, but her insides continued to churn. By the time breakfast was served, her throat was almost too narrow to swallow. She managed one sip of juice and gave up.

Aunt Rachel nudged her arm. "Elizabeth, would you please pass the butter?"

Wondering whether it was the first time she'd been asked, Elizabeth quickly complied.

"Thank you." Aunt Rachel turned to Aunt Elena. "We *have* to go. There's never anything like it near us."

"Absolutely." Aunt Elena nodded and addressed the group. "Rachel and I would like to drive up to Lewiston to see the Floral Bonanza. Would anyone else like to come?"

Molly rolled her eyes skyward and Abby pretended to gag. The politer members of the family shook their heads or mumbled, "No, thanks."

"May I go?" The words leapt from the back of Elizabeth's throat.

Aunt Elena's black eyebrows shot up. A moment later, her face melted into a smile. "Of course you may, Elizabeth." She turned to Karen. "It's all right, isn't it?"

Kevin and Karen exchanged puzzled glances.

"It's a long ride, Elizabeth," Kevin said slowly. "Lewiston's an hour from here."

"That's O.K., Dad. I'll take my pills, and I haven't eaten very much . . ." Elizabeth's cheeks grew warm. She hadn't intended to call attention to her untouched plate.

"Why do you want to look at a dumb bunch of flowers," Paul demanded, "when you could be *swimming?*"

Elizabeth shrugged. "We did botany in science this year," she mumbled. "It's interesting."

"Bravo, Elizabeth!" Aunt Elena lifted her chin. "Botany *is* interesting, not to mention beautiful. If these nincompoops do not appreciate God's bounty," she waved one elegant hand, "we shall leave them behind!"

Everyone laughed and Elizabeth looked down at her lap.

I'm a nincompoop. And a liar.

She'd hated botany—pistils and sepals and stamens—a bunch of boring words to memorize and tedious diagrams to label. But being car sick and bored was better than . . .

"Gentlemen!"

Elizabeth jerked her head up. Grandma was glaring at Uncle Steve and Uncle Tim. With competitive gleams in their eyes, they were each reaching for the last sausage. Midlunge, they both blushed and sat down. There were giggles all around the table.

"Andrew, would you care for another sausage?"

"Thanks, Grandma!" Grinning impishly, he helped himself.

Grandma folded her napkin and smiled. "You may all be excused."

Elizabeth quickly began to clear serving dishes from the buffet. When she returned to the dining room, Karen gently corralled her and led her to the porch. "Are you sure about going?"

Elizabeth's stomach flip-flopped. She was longing to blurt out the truth, but how *could* she? When they'd be so disappointed? When she didn't know *why?* She looked at her sneakers and nodded.

"All right, sweetheart." Karen gave her a quick kiss. "I hope you enjoy it."

"Found them!" Aunt Rachel jingled her car keys.

Aunt Elena looked at Elizabeth with twinkling black eyes. *"Chuleta?"*

Wondering why "pork chop" was a term of affection, Elizabeth followed her aunts to the car.

"We've got to be on the road no later than four," Uncle Tim called to them from the porch.

"Back by one-thirty!" Aunt Rachel started the car.

Not that *soon!*

Elizabeth had hoped they'd be gone for most of the day, that they would *miss* the afternoon swim. She locked her door, slumped against the window, and closed her burning eyes.

Chapter Six

"Elizabeth?" Aunt Rachel patted her shoulder. "We're here."

Where?

Elizabeth sat up and blinked. Even inside the car, the midmorning sun was painfully bright. She stumbled from her seat, shaded her eyes, and took a deep breath. A warm, inland breeze blew toward them. As they crossed the shimmering blacktop, the scents of fertilizer and flowers mingled with those of tar and exhaust.

"*Mira!*" Aunt Elena put her hands to her cheeks. "The impatiens!"

"And the *size* of those azaleas!" Aunt Rachel moaned with delight.

Which is which?

Elizabeth's eyes darted from one bonfire of color to another. To her left were mounds of bittersweet orange, raspberry pink, and rose-tinted ivory. To her right lay banks of cobalt blue and a velvety-looking plum. Straight ahead, blossoms spanned the spectrum from salmon to azure.

As she followed her pleasure-dazed and babbling aunts, Elizabeth tried to identify the odors she encountered. Something like cinnamon, but not quite. A peppery tang. An air-freshener sort of smell—lemon and pine? Something honey sweet and cloying that made it difficult to swallow.

Hey!

Elizabeth jumped to her left, shocked by cold water.

"*So sorry!*" someone twittered.

Elizabeth turned around. A freckle-faced woman in a wide-brimmed pink hat was trying hard not to laugh. She hoisted a dripping hose nozzle into the air. "The catch doesn't always stay," she apologized. "You're all right, aren't you?"

Scared out of a year's growth, thanks, but fine.

Elizabeth wiped the water from her cheeks and hurried after her aunts. She found them between a group of rose-covered trellises and a building made of stone. Greenhouses jutted from the back of the structure.

"*There* you are!" Aunt Rachel smiled.

The smell of sunbaked roses was overpowering and Elizabeth began to feel dizzy.

"In ten minutes there will be a talk about pruning."

Aunt Elena offered her an apologetic smile. "We would like to listen, but you might find it boring . . ."

"Can I go see what's in there?" Elizabeth pointed to the building. She hoped there would be a drinking fountain inside.

Aunt Elena nodded. "Meet us by the gate in an hour?"

"Take good notes." Aunt Rachel smiled. "With everything there is to see out here, I doubt we'll make it inside."

A loudspeaker began to blare a lengthy request to the grounds-keeping staff. Elizabeth nodded her assent, set her watch alarm, and trotted toward the stone building. Inside the heavy oak door, she paused to get her bearings. The foyer was soothing, quiet and cool. When her eyes had adjusted to the dim light, Elizabeth stepped toward a brass plaque. "Welcome to the Nosolkoff-Finkenbinder Memorial Botanical Garden."

And I thought "Elizabeth Sheridan" was a mouthful!

She glanced around. Two slender windows, easily ten feet tall, began at the floor. Between them, a shorter glass door led to a greenhouse. It opened with surprising ease and the smell of warm, wet earth enveloped her. She stepped into a grove of palm trees.

It's so dark!

She looked up. Rectangular leaves the size of crib sheets blocked the light from above.

If you sewed the edges together, you'd have a canoe.

Brown-edged triangles ringed the trunk. Had leaves fallen off? Another palm was speckled and gray. Its leaves grew straight up, like the fingers of praying hands.

Plop!

A drop of water splashed to the floor, emphasizing the stillness around her. On tiptoe, Elizabeth made her way forward. More palms, large and small, stood in the center of the room. She scanned their tops, disappointed to find neither coconuts nor bananas. Along the room's perimeter, reaching toward sunlight, were hundreds of ferns. There were unexpected splashes of color in pots, plants with heart-shaped pink-and-white leaves, but Elizabeth's overall impression was of a room bathed in green light.

She turned a corner into a room full of flowering plants. She resisted touching a tangerine-colored blossom with a drop of water in its center, but when she passed a cactus, curiosity got the better of her. She poked one of its spines, yelped, and sucked the blood from her finger. Cursing her stupidity, and hoping the plant wasn't poisonous, she turned another corner. The air was suddenly hot and so thick with moisture that she had trouble breathing.

A rain forest . . .

Elizabeth listened for the sounds of animals but heard only the trickle of water. She located the stream and watched it slide into a pool covered with lily pads. Vines looped from one tree to another and mosses flourished on rocks. Shoots of burnt orange and lime green erupted from nests of black leaves.

Elizabeth's nose grew accustomed to the dampness. As she wandered forward, the scent of vanilla was replaced by a flinty mold and a pungent ginger. She turned another corner, took a deep breath of air that now seemed too dry, and checked her watch.

I still have twenty-five minutes.

The air was now cool and tasted faintly of salt. In front of her were three stunted palm trees. To her right was an easel bearing a sign hand-lettered in blue marker: "Sisters from the Sea."

Huh?

Below that, in much smaller letters, was written, "Courtesy of the Monroe County Aquarium Association."

Elizabeth followed the bubble and gurgle of water to the center of the room. Seven aquariums of various sizes were dotted with small typewritten labels. She gave a cursory glance to the shrubs that lined the walls and turned back to the tanks. These weren't the first aquariums she had seen, but they were the first ones without animals in them — fish, or crabs, or sea horses. She shrugged.

It is a plant museum . . .

In the tank closest to her, thickly matted, yellow-brown seaweed floated on top of the water.

Looks sort of like holly, but smaller.

The wrinkled leaves had spiky points, and little

grapelike balls clung to the stems. Elizabeth stepped back to read the first label: "Sargassum Weed." It certainly *was* a weed. Compared to the flowers she had seen, it was positively ugly.

Why are they displaying this stuff?

She leaned down to read the next label. "Sargassum weed is almost the only macroscopic plant found in the open ocean."

"Macroscopic?" Must be the opposite of "microscopic."

"The structures that look like berries are air bladders. They keep the seaweed afloat."

Elizabeth looked at the little balls with new respect.

"The Sargasso Sea is nearly four miles deep. An estimated ten million tons of sargassum weed floats above it."

Ten million tons?

Elizabeth slowly exhaled.

"Sargassum weed supports an astounding variety of life. Among its inhabitants is a crab which, as an adult, cannot swim!"

Elizabeth scowled.

Petey should call me "Sargassum Crab" instead of "Turtle."

She shook her head and continued to read. Other creatures lived on the seaweed: tube worms, sea squirts, barnacles, and something called a hydroid. Shrimp camouflaged themselves among its leaves, and flying fish deposited their eggs there for safety.

Pretty useful, for a weed!

In the next tank, Elizabeth recognized strands of brown kelp and discovered that she had been mistaken about the absence of animals. The blades in front of her were barely a foot in length, but they were covered with tiny crustaceans. She read another small sign.

Kelps are algae? *I thought algae were tiny!*

Elizabeth continued to read and explore, encountering plants that looked like spun glass, dandelion leaves, and lobster claws. She discovered that algae grew in a variety of colors, as well: golden ochre, livid red, purple, even pale pink.

What's this?

Although the seventh tank's filtration system bubbled merrily, the water was a murky yellowish green. Elizabeth couldn't see any plants, but the tank's title proclaimed it "The Ocean's Grassland."

Looks more like a wasteland!

"This tank contains microscopic plants known as *phytoplankton*. They are the plants upon which all ocean life depends."

Elizabeth blinked, reread the label, and suddenly recalled a videotape she had seen in which plankton had been magnified hundreds of times. They had looked like glass ornaments with little specks of green inside. The specks were called *chloroplasts*, and photosynthesis took place inside them.

"The mass of phytoplankton in the world's oceans

is equivalent to the mass of the world's land-growing plants."

No kidding?

"To receive sufficient sunlight for photosynthesis, phytoplankton must remain close to the ocean's surface. Holes make their silicon shells lighter. Hairlike structures help them float in the water, as milkweed seeds float in the wind (see diagram to the right)."

Elizabeth walked around the end of the tank. Something called *Chaetoceros* was shaped like a pillow. From each of four corners, a threadlike structure extended several times the length of the rectangle.

"Try it yourself!" the sign urged. "Is it easier to float with your arms and legs close together, or spread apart from your body?"

Elizabeth clenched her teeth.

I came on this trip to get away from that topic!

But the example rang true. At her swimming instructor's suggestion, Elizabeth *had* tried floating both ways. It was *much* easier with arms and legs spread apart. She had managed pretty well in the pool, but the thought of floating in waves made her lightheaded.

Beep-beep! Beep-beep!

Elizabeth clicked off her watch alarm and hurried toward the lobby.

Good-bye, phytoplankton — and good riddance!

Chapter
Seven

"You're back in business, ladies!"

"Wonderful!" Aunt Rachel handed a bill to the man who had replaced her front tire. The operator of the tow truck, a brown-skinned man with grizzled gray hair, made change from the drawers of an ancient cash register and wished them a safe journey home.

"Thank you." Aunt Rachel returned her wallet to her bag.

"*Muchas gracias*," Aunt Elena added. "It would have been a long walk!"

Elizabeth climbed into the backseat and watched the car's clock glow to life: 4:48. Everyone would be back from the beach by now, and they'd have heard the message about the flat tire.

You're off the hook for today.

Elizabeth fastened her seat belt and sighed.

But what about tomorrow?

She brooded all the way home.

Minus Adam, the entire family was gathered on the lawn. Aunt Rachel's overnight bag lay at Uncle Tim's feet. The car pulled to a stop and all three men checked their watches. There was a flurry of haphazard good-byes and promises to call. Kevin and Karen each gave Elizabeth a hug and a kiss. She swallowed hard.

Don't! Don't ask if you can go with them.

"Bye, Mom. Bye, Dad." Elizabeth said quickly. "I'll miss you."

"We'll miss you, too, sweetheart." Karen smoothed her hair.

"We'd better get going." Kevin gave Elizabeth another kiss. "The *minute* we get here in August, we'll go swimming, O.K.?"

Elizabeth tried to smile and discovered that her cheek muscles were frozen. Paul and Caroline barreled across the lawn and Elizabeth gratefully backed away from her parents. There were more hugs and kisses and three cars drove off.

"Hey, Turtle!" Petey raced toward her. "Want to *see* something?"

Elizabeth smiled. "I sure do."

He led her to a wasp nest near the barn and asked far-ranging questions until Abby called them to dinner.

Thank you, Petey.

The dining room looked soothingly familiar: red-and-white napkins on the dark table, seagull plates stacked on the buffet, the cushion on the window seat faintly pink in the late-afternoon sun . . .

Adam's graduation presents are gone.

Wondering what had happened to them—Elizabeth doubted that he would have opened them in his mother's absence—she filled her plate and sat down.

"Who'd like to start 'bests'?" Grandma glanced around the table. "Molly? You look like you've got good news."

"There's going to be a bonfire party. On the beach, on the Fourth of July." Molly gave her grandmother an imploring look. "Mom and Dad said it's O.K. with them if it's O.K. with you . . ."

Grandma smiled briefly. "We'll see."

Molly hesitated, as though trying to decide whether to say something more, and then passed her turn to Andrew. He smiled at his brother.

"My best is that Petey learned to hold his breath when a wave is coming."

Petey proudly grinned back.

"My second best is this chicken!" Andrew toasted his grandmother with his fork. "I pass my turn to Adam."

A fleeting look of annoyance crossed Adam's face. "Work." He finished chewing and swallowed. "I pass my turn to Sarah."

"But what is it *like*, Adam?" Abby asked. "What do you have to *do?*"

Adam shot a dark look in Abby's direction and addressed his empty milk glass. "Unpack things. Wait on customers." He scowled the length of the table. "Your *turn*, Sarah."

Sarah's eyes were bright above a small, round mouth. Grandma gave her a quick smile. "It's your first day in a new job, Adam," she said quietly. "We'd like to hear about it."

"I told my best," Adam muttered, "and I passed my turn." He put a quarter of a baked potato into his mouth with a gesture of finality.

Sarah stared down at her plate.

"Was the raft your best, Sair?" Caroline prompted in an encouraging tone.

Sarah lifted her head and nodded. "The new raft." She looked at Elizabeth with wide eyes. "It feels like you're floating!"

"You *are* floating," Paul argued.

"Until you wipe out," Abby added morosely, "and get sand up your nose."

A burst of laughter told Elizabeth that Abby wasn't alone in having had that experience. Sarah nodded energetically and passed her turn.

"Swimming!" Paul said loudly. "I pass my turn to Grandma."

"Having all of you here." She smiled at each of them. "I pass my turn to Elizabeth."

Not having to go to the beach!

"The botanical garden," she stammered. "They had aquariums with sea plants." She took a quick breath. "I pass my turn to Petey."

"This!" He pulled something from his pocket and grinned.

"Petey!" Molly complained. "That's gross!"

"No, it's not," he said stubbornly. "It's a *crab* leg."

Laughter filled the room and Petey's chin quivered.

"It *is* a crab leg, Petey, and it's a beautiful specimen," Grandma assured him. "But perhaps we could look *after* dinner?"

"O.K." Petey returned his prize to his pocket. "I pass my turn to Caro."

"My best is that the Tiny Theater is showing *Gone with the Wind.*"

"Not that again," Paul groaned. "You've seen it ten thousand times!"

"Only on video. I want to see it in a theater, the way it was meant to be seen." She glowered at Paul. "And no one's forcing *you* to go."

"Frankly, my dear," he said in a falsetto voice, "I don't—"

"That's enough, Paul," Grandma warned.

"I pass my turn to Abby."

"My best is that the Friedmans are staying an extra week this year."

"Wonderful," muttered Andrew. "*Two* weeks of Lauren."

"You don't have to be so mean about it, Andrew," Abby snapped. "Anyway, Lauren doesn't like *you* anymore. She likes Ben Manzella."

"Poor Ben." Andrew grinned and ducked beyond Abby's reach.

"Everyone had a turn?" Grandma asked. "Then let's talk about Thursday. Have you decided, Petey?"

"The naval park!" Paul pleaded.

Sarah bounced up and down. "The aquarium!"

Grandma held up her hands. "Petey's birthday, Petey's choice."

Petey looked around the table and back to his grandmother. "I pick the boats."

"The naval park it is, then!" Grandma smiled. "We'll have plenty of time to explore if we leave after lunch. What time do you finish work on Thursday, Adam?"

"Six." He spoke without looking up. "Mr. Ludlow is having some medical tests. I told him I'd work the whole day."

Not again!

A hush fell and Petey's dark blue eyes clouded over. Elizabeth turned toward the head of the table. Grandma was gazing intently at Adam, but the rest of her face was without expression.

"You're not coming?" Petey said softly.

Adam shook his head.

"Even for cake?"

"What if we do cake and presents at dinner,

Petey?" Grandma suggested. "That way Adam can still be part of your birthday."

The lines disappeared from Petey's forehead and he nodded.

"Good." Grandma stood up. "Popsicles for dessert. Whose turn is it to clear?"

Most of the group milled toward the kitchen. When Abby removed Adam's plate, he abruptly pushed himself to his feet and strode through the front room. A moment later, the screen door banged.

Why is he so angry?

Elizabeth bit her lip.

Grandma didn't even argue about Petey's birthday . . .

"Elizabeth?" Caroline called from the kitchen. "You want dessert?"

"No, thanks," she called back. Deep in thought, she wandered upstairs. She was dabbing toothpaste on her brush when Andrew's voice came through the window.

"Can't someone else work?"

"No."

"Then couldn't you at least tell Petey you're sorry?" Andrew demanded. "He doesn't understand about jobs, or medical tests. His *feelings* are hurt."

"Fine. I'll tell him I'm sorry." Adam's voice was weary. "Satisfied?"

"What is *with* you, Adam? Why are you being such a jerk?"

"I don't have to answer to you."

"When you hurt Petey, you do!"

"Stuff it, Andrew! Save the 'big brother' act for someone who *cares*." Adam wheeled away and stomped toward the fence.

It's like he hates the whole family!

Elizabeth felt suddenly chilled.

"I adore my family, Elizabeth. Every person in it, and the times we're together most of all."

Adam had said that last summer, and she had known that he'd meant it.

Doesn't he feel that way anymore?

Chapter Eight

 The ocean and Adam haunted her dreams, and Elizabeth woke up with a headache. Breakfast was full of laughter and teasing, however, and she was distracted enough to eat half a piece of French toast.

Almost time for Grandma's report card ritual.

Last year, Elizabeth hadn't known what was coming. She still felt funny about having the others see her grades, but she hoped that Grandma would be pleased: her third and fourth quarter marks were all A's.

At least I know how to do school.

The only discordant note in the room was the empty chair at the foot of the table. Once again, Adam had left the house in the dark—well before he was due at the bait shop.

Is he still depressed?

Elizabeth pictured Adam in the kitchen and decided that he looked almost the way he did before the car accident that killed his two closest friends. He had regained most of the weight he had lost, and his dusky skin was again more pink than gray. His ebony eyes were no longer dull, but neither did they sparkle. Adam seemed reluctant to look at people directly, and when he did so, it was through narrowed lids.

The table erupted in noise and Elizabeth was pulled out of her musings. Grandma was wearing an expression of feigned innocence, and the others were laughing.

Adam doesn't laugh anymore.

Elizabeth recalled meeting him, her instant recognition of a Sheridan in his radiant smile. That was gone, too. Since they had arrived, his few smiles had been tight-lipped and brief. Someone nudged her and she looked up again.

"You'll have to work harder, Elizabeth," Grandma admonished. "This sort of thing simply won't *do.*" Her eyes twinkled as she offered Elizabeth's report card to Molly.

"Geez, Elizabeth!" Molly smacked her forehead with the back of her hand. "You make the rest of us look like delinquents!"

A five dollar bill and three singles made their way to Elizabeth's place. She blinked in surprise, but a second later she nodded.

That's right — I'm in eighth grade now.

"Thank you, Grandma," she stammered.

Grandma winked and picked up Andrew's report card. She read his, and then Molly's, and finally Caroline's. There was a brief pause before she slipped the bank envelope back into her pocket.

The envelope can't be empty. Adam's turn should have been last.

"Next year, Petey!" Grandma smiled. He grinned back and nodded.

A year from now he'll be in first grade!

Elizabeth lost track of the conversation as she tried to imagine Petey at six, at ten, at thirteen . . .

". . . a royal pain to redo the whole thing!" Andrew tossed the job list onto the table and sat down hard.

"Adam to a T," Molly said bitterly. "Mister Consideration."

"Magdalena." Grandma's eyes flashed and Molly dropped her gaze to the table.

"All I'm saying . . ." Andrew folded his arms. ". . . is that he could have mentioned that he wouldn't *be* here for chores."

"He probably didn't know you were putting together the job list," Caroline said.

"He knew," Andrew muttered. "He came through here right before dinner. I'd already finished the grid."

"He may have been thinking about something else, Andrew," Grandma said quietly.

Andrew sighed. "All right. I'll take care of his job this morning and figure out the rest later."

"Thank you, Andrew." Grandma turned to Caroline. "Since Adam's not coming on Thursday, it looks like we'll need you to drive." She smiled. "How about a practice session before lunch? My station wagon's a bit longer than yours."

Caroline swallowed hard and nodded.

"Good." Grandma smiled again and stood up. "You may all be excused."

Elizabeth folded T-shirts and shorts with precision, aware that the others were racing through chores. She stacked the clothes and checked the empty dryer again. Unable to think of an alternative, she climbed the stairs and put on her bathing suit.

"Thanks." Elizabeth accepted the towel that Abby offered her, set it on the bed, and retied her sneakers. At the bottom of the stairs, she took a deep breath and pushed open the door.

"What *takes* you so long?" Paul leapt from the porch and the tribe followed him onto the lawn.

Elizabeth walked to one side of the group, suddenly tired, barely conscious of the chatter around her. She was exhausted from wondering why she had panicked, numbed beyond planning what she would do once they reached the sand. She heard the waves and her stomach muscles grew tight.

I shouldn't have eaten.

They came to the patch of stony ground that separated the road from the beach.

"I call first on the raft!" Molly ran toward the water.

"I call second!" Paul yelled.

"I call third!" Abby and Andrew shouted together.

I call never.

Elizabeth dropped her towel, pried off her sneakers, and forced herself to look up. The ocean was there, and most of the family was already in it.

"It's freezing!" Sarah hollered happily as a wave rolled past her knees.

Elizabeth shuddered and looked back to the sand.

"It's not *that* cold, Turtle." Petey peered up at her. "Are you O.K.?"

Elizabeth nodded.

Petey's brow became furrowed. "We can hold hands if you want . . ."

Elizabeth shook her head. Petey remained where he was and she finally glanced sideways. His dark blue eyes were filled with questions and sadness.

He knows I can't go in!

Despair mingled with relief.

Don't tell. Please don't tell the others.

Petey contemplated his sand pail. "Want to build a castle or something?"

"Come *on*, you guys!" Abby shouted to them.

"Go ahead, Petey," Elizabeth said quickly. "I'll start. You can do the towers after you swim." She tried to smile, but her lower lip began to twitch and she was forced to bite it.

"O.K." Petey handed his purple bucket to her. Abby called to them again and he shuffled toward the water. Elizabeth dropped to her knees, dragged the pail through the sand, and dumped it beside her.

How many buckets would it take to empty this beach?

She refilled the pail.

Depends on where the beach ends.

She dumped the sand out.

It ends at the water.

She jerked the bucket toward her again.

But the water keeps moving. There are waves, and currents, and tides.

She poured slowly this time, squinting as the breeze blew the lighter grains toward her face.

The beach keeps changing size.

She dug into the damp sand at the bottom of the hole.

So there's no answer . . .

She took a quick breath and pulled hard with both hands.

. . . to the question.

She dumped the damp sand onto the mound. As she patted it into place, hating the grinding of the grains against her skin, she became aware of the sun on her back and the soft crashing of waves. Involuntarily, her eyes moved toward the sound.

"Andrew?"

The breeze carried Petey's voice across the sand. He was standing waist deep in water.

No one's carrying him. He goes in by himself now.

Petey's ball rose and fell several yards from the shore. Andrew dove. A moment later, he surfaced and tossed his brother the ball. Grandma was standing near the water's edge, listening to a bald man with a beard. Sarah was wading and the others were playing tag. Elizabeth's throat swelled. She turned toward the boulder that had been her refuge for most of last summer. It looked smaller than she remembered.

But I might as well still be up there.

She twisted around to her right. A small black-and-white boat was bobbing a quarter mile from the shore. It might have been a fishing boat, but neither nets nor poles were visible, and it appeared to be anchored. A shirtless man raised a walkie-talkie to his ear. Elizabeth followed the man's outstretched arm to the end of the beach. A van was clearly visible against the rocks.

Cars aren't allowed on the sand.

Elizabeth shaded her eyes. Someone wearing a baseball hat was affixing a box to a tripod.

Too big for a camera . . .

"Elizabeth?"

Grandma was walking toward her. Elizabeth snapped her eyes back to the sand.

Hurry! Before she asks . . .

Elizabeth scrambled to her feet and brushed her hands together. "Hi, Grandma!" Her voice squeaked. She cleared her throat and pointed to the boat. "Do you know what they're doing?"

Grandma shook her head. "No idea."

"Can I go find out?"

Squawking loudly, a seagull circled overhead. Its shadow passed between them, briefly dulling the glare from the sand.

Grandma examined her closely, but at last she said, "You may."

"Thanks." Elizabeth flashed a quick smile in her grandmother's general direction and took several steps backward. "I won't be long." She stumbled, caught her balance, and ran.

Chapter
Nine

Elizabeth ducked around a group of teenagers with hula hoops, trotted past two olive-skinned toddlers with shiny black hair, and came to a halt between the van and the waves. She caught her breath and examined the vehicle.

Doesn't look like much.

Where it wasn't crumbling with rust, the van was pale blue. The side and back windows were screened by white fabric. A faded American flag flew from the antenna. A breeze caught it and it waved limply.

Whose is it? And why is it here?

Elizabeth turned toward the water. A stocky figure wearing a navy blue baseball cap was juggling a pair of binoculars, a clipboard, a pencil, and a black walkie-talkie. The figure grunted into the radio and returned it to one of a dozen vest pockets.

"Bastards!"

Elizabeth's eyes widened. The person had pro-
nounced it, "Bas-*tids*," but there was no mistaking
the oath or the venom behind it. The figure turned
to its left.

Female.

The clothing and the haircut were unisex, but
neither the vest nor the objects that jutted from it
could conceal the woman's shelf of a bosom. She
waved one arm in a circle over her head. In an oily
cloud of smoke, the boat's engine sputtered to life.

What . . . ?

The woman read some numbers from the box on
the tripod, entered them on the clipboard, and hob-
bled to the van. There was a metallic screech as she
yanked the door open. The boat began to putt-putt its
way along the shore, maintaining a course parallel to
the beach.

"Got hands?"

Elizabeth looked to her right and behind her.

Is she talking to me?

The woman's biceps rippled as she pulled a large
cooler from the van. "Save me a trip." She jerked her
head toward a cardboard box at her feet.

Elizabeth hesitated.

She's a stranger . . .

"Never mind," the woman said gruffly. She put
down the cooler, set the box on top of it, and hoisted
the containers into the air. Cardboard slid across

plastic and Elizabeth leapt forward. She caught the box with both hands and looked up. The woman's deeply tanned face was lined with wrinkles, and her eyes were mere slits beneath the brim of her cap. She gave Elizabeth a brief nod and lurched toward the water. Carrying the box, Elizabeth meekly followed her.

"Ugh!" Glass rattled as the cooler thudded onto the sand. The woman put a hand to her back and straightened her spine. "Know what diatoms are?"

What?

"Phytoplankton?" The woman grunted and reached for the box. "Course not."

"They're plants," Elizabeth stammered.

The woman's head snapped up. She squinted at Elizabeth for a moment and then nodded. "Something's killing 'em." She knocked the lid from the cooler with her foot and set the box on it.

Elizabeth stepped forward. The cooler contained hundreds of test tubes sealed with rubber stoppers and dozens of plastic bottles with milky white caps. The woman filled several pockets with bottles, pulled some wooden sticks from the box, and waded into the waves. When the water reached her knees, she filled one bottle and capped it. When she returned, she wiped the outside of the bottle with a rag, slapped a label on it, and scribbled duplicate numbers on the label and on one of the sticks.

"High water?"

Elizabeth nodded. The woman thrust the stick toward her, her thumb just below a band of orange paint.

"This deep."

Elizabeth accepted the stick and trotted toward the line of seaweed that marked the high tide. She poked the stick into the sand and turned around.

O.K.?

The baseball cap bobbed once. Its owner scribbled on the clipboard, hoisted the cooler onto one hip, and limped forward. Elizabeth picked up the lid and the box and followed her. They repeated the process three times before the woman spoke again.

"Shells dissolving." She looked out to sea. "Something chemical." Two samples later, she held up a collecting bottle and muttered, "Probably not in this far yet."

This far yet?

"Where is it coming from?" Elizabeth asked.

The woman lifted her chin toward the boat. "That's what we're finding out." She labeled another stick. "Could be a time bomb. Barrels rusting." Her eyes narrowed. "Could be a flush."

A flush?

"E-*liz*-a-beth!" Caroline uncupped her hands from her mouth and waved. "*Lunch*-time!"

It can't be!

Her watch read 11:55. "Sorry." Elizabeth looked down at the box. "But I have to go."

"I'll manage."

"If you're here this afternoon . . ."

"I'll be here."

The woman picked up the cooler and Elizabeth trotted toward her sister.

"What were you doing?" Caroline asked. "And who was that guy?"

"Collecting water samples." Elizabeth paused to look over her shoulder. "She's not a guy, she's a woman. But I don't know her name."

"Better check with Grandma," Caroline warned. "South Wales isn't exactly a hotbed of crime, but you still don't *know* her."

"You may continue to help, if you'd like," Grandma said during lunch. "But I'd like to meet her and find out her name."

Elizabeth nodded.

"And under no circumstances are you to *leave* the beach." Their eyes met. "Understood?"

Elizabeth nodded again. "Promise."

"Good." Grandma stood up. "Then let's get the dishes out of the way and go get some books!"

Fifteen minutes later, nine Sheridans ambled past the fence.

"Hi, Turtle!" Petey said brightly. "Will you help me pick?"

Elizabeth cringed.

That's your game with Adam . . .

She forced herself to smile. "Sure, Petey."

The tribe chattered happily on the way into town. Elizabeth listened with interest to the morning's adventures with the raft, to the catalogue of friends who had arrived, and to another of Paul's far-fetched tales about aliens. This time they were flesh eaters, disguised as seagulls, and they had invaded South Wales.

"That's not *true*, Paul!" Sarah wailed. "They're just plain *birds*." She reached for her grandmother's hand. "Aren't they, Grandma?"

"Just plain birds," her grandmother assured her. "All of the aliens are inside of Paul's head."

"Oh-h-h-h!" Molly cried. "*That* explains Paul!"

Paul launched a zombie attack and everyone laughed.

When they reached the library, Petey took Elizabeth's hand. Inside, he released her fingers, closed his eyes, and slowly turned in a circle. On the third time around, he staggered and stopped. His eyes popped open and he grinned.

"I see it!" He scurried forward and pointed. "The red one." Elizabeth reached up. "No. The one with gold letters."

Elizabeth moved her hand three books to her right and looked down. Petey nodded. She pulled the volume from the shelf and winced.

How does Adam handle this sort of thing?

"What's it say, Turtle?"

"The Concise Columbia Encyclopedia." She hesitated. "Do you know what an encyclopedia is?"

Petey nodded happily. "Books that tell about *everything!*" He pointed to the reference section. Three sets of encyclopedias spanned two entire shelves and he suddenly looked doubtful. "How'd they fit it all in one book?"

Elizabeth tipped back the cover and turned several pages. "The print is really tiny and they only wrote a little bit about each thing." She held the book toward him. "But these are awfully big words. Maybe we should choose something else?"

Petey shook his head vehemently. "It's the *rule.*" His chin quivered.

"O.K." Elizabeth shoved the heavy volume under one arm. "This one's your surprise book. Next we pick a chapter book for bedtime, right?"

Petey nodded. "One about mouses, O.K.?" He grinned. "Me and Grandma found two mouse nests in the barn!"

Elizabeth searched her memory. *Stuart Little* met with approval and they made their way to the picture book aisle. Petey made three selections and then waited patiently while Elizabeth chose two books about ocean food chains. One cover was adorned with an octopus, the other with a cold-eyed, open-mouthed shark.

Petey beamed. "Cool books, Turtle!"

Why are little boys so bloodthirsty? Even sweet ones, like Petey?

Elizabeth swallowed a giggle.

And I'm going to read about plants!

Her chest began to shake and she pinched herself—hard. If she started to laugh, Petey would want to know why.

Chapter
Ten

"Martha Sheridan." Grandma took off her sunglasses and extended her hand. "Elizabeth's grandmother."

The baseball cap levered herself off the floor of the van. "Marion Papinchak." She gripped Grandma's hand firmly, pumped it once, and sat down again. "They call me Pap."

Who are "they?"

"Elizabeth tells us that plankton are dying."

Pap nodded. "Someone's dumping." She squinted at the water and her chin jutted forward. "We're not sure what. Or where."

"Who are 'we'?" Grandma's blue gray eyes flickered from Pap to the van.

"Water Minders." Pap tipped her head toward the cooler. "Watchdogs. Nonprofit. Mostly volunteers."

"Like Greenpeace?" Elizabeth asked.

Pap nodded. "Sort of." The trace of a grin hovered near her mouth. "No protests. We leave 'headlining' to them." She grunted. "Make near as many enemies, though."

"How?" Grandma had replaced her sunglasses and Elizabeth couldn't read her expression.

"Ain't the *testing*." Pap jerked her thumb toward the water. "It's the results." She sat up taller. "Our stuff holds up in court."

Grandma nodded slowly. "Big fines. Enemies with financial grudges."

"We don't advertise where we are." Pap cocked her head in Elizabeth's direction. "She wants to help, no one'll know."

Grandma turned to Elizabeth.

Please?

"Then I'll let you get on with your work." Grandma smiled at Elizabeth, nodded to Pap, and walked up the beach.

"Done collecting for the day." Pap rummaged behind her on the floor of the van. "Next part's tiresome." She squinted. "But critical."

Elizabeth nodded and Pap explained. The Water Minders sent duplicate samples to different agencies. When results from two independent labs were the same, courts considered the evidence solid.

Elizabeth's eyebrows drew together. "Isn't that expensive?"

"We got us a philanthropist," Pap admitted. "*Pompous* little idiot, but his checks don't bounce."

Elizabeth's task was to transfer water from collecting bottles to pairs of test tubes. To insure that they remained sterile, their tops were the sort that couldn't be removed. She would fill them using disposable syringes, a fresh one for each sample. Once they were labeled, she would sort them: gray-topped samples for one lab, orange-topped test tubes for the other.

Pap watched her fill the first pair, nodded her approval, and began to copy numbers onto a map. When Elizabeth dropped the last syringe into the sharps container, a thick plastic bottle labeled "Biohazardous Waste," Pap looked up. "How old are you?"

Why?

"Twelve."

Pap grunted. "Better'n that graduate student they sent me. All chatter, he was. Sloppy, too."

Did she just give me a compliment?

Pap pointed to the test tubes. "Express mail. Should have numbers by Wednesday." She rocked herself to her feet.

Elizabeth placed the boxes on the floor of the van. "Will you be here tomorrow?"

Pap slammed the rear door. "You take after your grandmother?"

Huh?

"She looks the sort that keeps her word. Finishes what she starts."

Elizabeth hesitated. "I try to."

"Collecting's quick work. *This* eats up time."

Elizabeth nodded.

"More help with the scut work, more time the boat spends out there." Pap turned toward the water. "You in?"

Elizabeth nodded again.

The baseball cap disappeared around the far side of the van. "Tomorrow. At ten."

Elizabeth wandered up the beach wishing there had been more work to do: they wouldn't be going home for at least an hour. She declined three invitations to swim and spent the rest of the afternoon piling sand into a pyramid. Her thoughts alternated between Pap, the polluters, and a growing sense of being distanced from the others. That feeling was cemented by a scrap of conversation she overheard just before dinner.

"She can *too* swim," Paul insisted. "I *saw* her. At the community center."

"Then how come she won't go in the water?" Abby demanded.

"I dunno," Paul said crossly. "Why don't you ask her?"

"I can't. Grandma said not to."

The voices faded.

Grandma knows.

Of course she knew. Grandma always knew.

Then why hasn't she said anything?

Elizabeth brooded until Caroline called her to set the table.

Dinner was strained. Abby and Sarah were fighting and wouldn't look at each other. Molly had been reprimanded and refused to converse. Petey spilled a full glass of milk, and Adam was a sullen, mute presence at one end of the table. Grandma valiantly attempted to lighten the atmosphere by asking questions as each person reported his best.

"When is this soccer clinic, Paul?"

"Just one day, Grandma. The eighth. Can I go? Pleeease?"

"We should be able to work something out."

"Thanks, Grandma! I pass my turn to Adam."

"Work," he said brusquely. "Elizabeth's turn."

"You can do a little better than that, can't you, Adam?" Grandma's voice contained a warning.

Ignoring his grandmother's question, Adam continued to fork salad into his mouth. Grandma watched him swallow a third oversized bite before she addressed him again.

"There are rules in this house, Adam." Her tone was icy. "Civility is among them."

"May I be excused?" Adam spoke to his plate through clenched teeth. "*Please?*"

There was a terrible moment of silence.

"You may."

In three long, angry strides, Adam left the dining

room. The back door banged and frightened eyes turned toward the head of the table.

"What's *wrong* with him, Grandma?" Sarah asked.

Grandma shook her head. "I don't know, sweetheart."

"*I'll* tell you what's wrong." Molly slammed her napkin onto the table. "Adam's being a selfish little brat!" She got to her feet. "You've only had to put up with it since we got here, but it's been going on for months, and I'm *sick* of it!"

Molly stormed through the front room and onto the porch. Grandma took a deep breath, excused herself from the table, and followed her.

"It's Molly's night to clear." Caroline sighed. "Please bring things out when you're done." She carried her plate and Adam's to the kitchen.

By the time Elizabeth finished helping Caroline with the dishes, Molly had come in from the porch and was playing Scrabble with Andrew and Abby. Grandma came through the kitchen and went out the back door. Through the window, Elizabeth watched her walk toward the barn.

I hope Adam's calmed down . . .

Grandma found Paul instead. She stood over him while he collected something from the lawn and then followed him back to the house. The door banged and heavy feet climbed the stairs. Quick feet came into the kitchen. Grandma tipped Paul's rocket kit onto the top of the dish cupboard and returned a box of matches to the stove. Elizabeth winced.

Uh oh . . .

Paul got spanked, the Scrabble game ended in a fight, and the evening continued its downward spiral. The dishwasher backed up onto the floor and Elizabeth spent ten minutes mopping. Caroline went to look for Adam. She came back in tears, refusing to speak, and Sarah's hand got caught in a drawer.

Won't this day ever end?

Elizabeth pulled a bag of ice from the freezer. When Sarah could wiggle her fingers, Elizabeth put the ice away and went to brush her teeth. As she stepped into the hall, Grandma called up the stairs to the Crow's Nest.

"Petey is sleeping down here tonight." Without waiting for a response, she closed the door.

Poor Grandma.

Elizabeth crawled onto her bed, picked up the book with the shark on it, and put it back down.

I don't remember days this bad last summer.

Grandma knocked, smiled bravely, and gave them each a kiss. "Sleep tight." The light went off. "Tomorrow will be better."

Elizabeth buried her face in her pillow.

It has to be!

Chapter
Eleven

Tuesday morning was better. Breakfast, without Adam, was fairly cheerful. Although the breeze was cool, the sun was shining. The trip to the beach was filled with Sheridan noise and the illusion that things were as they should be.

Elizabeth spent a productive two hours packaging and labeling samples that had been collected at sea. Pap was uncommunicative, but she swore only twice and waved briefly when Elizabeth left.

During lunch, Grandma announced her wish to deepen the family's appreciation of nature in general and of flowers in particular. She had purchased two dozen marigolds, a dozen begonias, and a flat of petunias. Would anyone like to earn some money by planting them?

Abby astonished them all by saying she would. She

dug and watered with enthusiasm, and by the time they set off for the afternoon swim, the area below the porch had been transformed. Petey called it "a mixed-up rainbow," and even Paul acknowledged that it was pretty.

Disaster struck just before dinner. Elizabeth and Petey had just come down from the barn where, to Petey's delight, they had discovered another mouse nest. Abby pounded past them, Paul and Andrew in tow. She rounded the corner of the house and began to shriek. Seconds later, Grandma hurried through the screen door.

"What's wrong? Who's hurt?" Her eyes darted from one frozen face to another. Caroline followed her grandmother onto the porch. Abby continued to howl.

"Abigail!"

"Look, Grandma!" Abby pointed to the flower bed. "Sarah ruined them! She ruined them *all!*"

Grandma came down the steps. Her lips became a thin line as she surveyed the damage. "How do you know Sarah did this?"

"She *told* me to go see my flowers," Abby wailed. "And she was laughing!"

Grandma looked again at the uprooted and broken foliage. "Andrew? Please tell Sarah she needs to come to the kitchen."

He nodded and reluctantly set off toward the barn.

"Abby?" Grandma folded her arms. "Is there any reason Sarah might be angry with you?"

Abby blushed and looked down. "Paul and I were doing secret codes," she sulked. "I told her she was too little."

Grandma spoke very quietly. "I seem to remember *your* feeling left out once or twice." She raised one eyebrow and went into the house.

"C'mon, Abby. Maybe we can save some of them." Caroline began to gather the broken flowers together.

About half were worth replanting, and five pairs of hands fell to work. When they assembled for dinner, Sarah sniffled an apology. Abby's reply was cool but polite, Adam managed a sentence and a half during bests, and Elizabeth allowed herself to hope that the rest of the evening would remain conflict-free.

At bedtime, Petey announced that he itched. Grandma examined the watery blisters on his legs and sat back on her heels. "You went behind the barn, didn't you?"

"Only for a minute," Petey protested. "I heard a woodpecker . . ."

"Hands off of Petey, everyone." Grandma sighed and got to her feet. "He's got poison ivy." She pressed her lips together. "And we're out of calamine lotion."

"Baking soda?" Caroline suggested. "Oatmeal?"

"Those will help in the bath," Grandma acknowledged. "But if he's going to sleep, at *all*, he'll need calamine." She turned to Paul. "Please call Adam."

Adam came down the steps slowly. "I've been up for sixteen hours, and I'm *tired*. Why can't Caroline go?"

"She's driven my car only once," Grandma replied

evenly. "It's almost dark, and you know she isn't licensed to drive at night."

Adam scowled.

"I would go, but I don't want anyone else to give Petey a bath."

Adam rolled his eyes, wrenched himself from the wall, and plodded down the front stairs. Twenty minutes later, he left the bottle outside the bathroom door and retreated to the Crow's Nest in stony silence.

Elizabeth read three pages about marine photosynthesis, realized that she had absorbed none of it, and closed the book. Grandma's good night was quiet and quick. Wishing her roommates were on better terms, Elizabeth curled up and closed her eyes.

"Abby?" Sarah's voice was very small.

There was a long pause. "What?"

"I really *am* sorry about the flowers."

There was another pause, a brief one, before Abby sighed. "I'm sorry you got spanked, and for not letting you play." The bunk bed creaked. "But next time, just *tattle* or something, O.K.?"

Sarah giggled. "O.K."

Grandma hates it when we tattle!

"Then we'll both be in trouble!" Sarah giggled again.

Oh. Abby said that to be funny.

Elizabeth pulled the blanket over her head. She'd gotten better at recognizing family jokes, but there was still a long way to go.

The following morning was peaceful, on all fronts. After lunch, Elizabeth returned to the van in a good mood. Pap had stopped at the post office. She ripped open an envelope, muttered an oath, and slapped the computer printout into a file folder. "Nothing."

"Isn't that good?" Elizabeth asked.

Pap grunted. "Doesn't help us track the source."

"Could be a time bomb . . . could be a flush."

Elizabeth thought she understood "time bomb": it would take a while for a barrel to rust, for chemicals to begin to leak out . . .

"What's a flush?"

"Dumping directly. No containers. Catch 'em red-handed, the damage is done." Pap used a particularly colorful epithet to describe the followers of such practices and Elizabeth drew her breath through her teeth.

If I ever said that . . . especially near Grandma!

Elizabeth took an immediate vow of silence. Grandma might paddle her for reporting even *part* of Pap's phrase!

And she probably wouldn't let me come back.

When Elizabeth rejoined the others, she found her sister leaning on Andrew's shoulder. Caroline had made a goal-scoring lunge for the soccer ball, but had hurt her ankle in the process. Grandma went home for the car and, with Andrew and Molly's support, Caroline bravely hopped up the beach. Everyone squeezed into the station wagon and they all rode home laughing.

"I'm pretty sure it's only a strain." Grandma settled Caroline on the sofa, wrapped her ankle in ice, and went off to change.

"Does it hurt *lots*, Caro?" Petey asked anxiously.

Caroline shook her head. "Hardly at all anymore." She smiled. "I'm sure I'll be able to drive tomorrow."

Petey's forehead relaxed and he grinned.

"Give me a break, Paul." Adam's low voice rumbled through the window. Petey's grin faded and he scurried toward the back of the house. The screen door banged. "What happened to *you?*"

"I twisted it." Caroline shrugged. "Playing soccer." Adam snorted.

"I'm sorry to have to ask, Adam." Grandma appeared in the archway. "But we're almost out of milk. Would you mind picking up a couple of gallons?"

"Yes." Adam's eyes narrowed. "I *would* mind."

Grandma slowly raised one eyebrow and went back through the archway. She returned with car keys and wallet in hand. "Elizabeth? When the timer rings, would you take the casseroles out?"

Elizabeth nodded. When the car started, Caroline wrenched herself upright, wincing as her ankle dropped from the pillow onto the sofa.

"What is your *problem*, Adam?" Her cheeks grew flushed. "Grandma's got ten people to feed! You're never even here to do your chores. Couldn't you have run one lousy errand?"

"I'm tired of following orders!" Adam spat back. "And if you weren't such a sycophant, you would be, too."

Syco-what?

"I don't grovel to Grandma!"

"Sure you do! *Everyone* does." Adam waved his arms to encompass the room. "She's got the entire family in a mental headlock!"

"What are you talking about?"

"You're pathetic, Caroline." He glared at her. "This whole family's pathetic."

"What's *pathetic* was you walking out on Paul's party." Caroline's voice rose. "Getting everyone all upset because you couldn't bother to *mention* that you had a job interview."

"It wasn't an interview. I already knew I had the job."

"Then why didn't you say so?"

"Have you ever heard of the concept of *privacy?*"

"What's private about having a job?"

"Nothing," Adam growled. "If you live here!"

"What's that supposed to mean?"

"You haven't noticed how everyone in this family knows everyone else's business? With Grandma sticking her nose into everything? Telling us all what to do?"

Caroline stared at him. "You're nuts, Adam."

"Am I?" He laughed, a harsh little yelp. "How many kids our age spend the entire summer with their grandmother? How many of them spend every single holiday in exactly the same place, with exactly the same people, doing exactly the same things?"

"It's called having traditions, Adam."

"It's called doing everything Grandma's way." He fired the words into the air. "*When* she says, *how* she says, and only *if* she says."

Caroline's cheeks grew a shade redder. "That is totally unfair, and you know it."

"The truth hurts, doesn't it, Caro? But it's not our fault that we're puppets. We learned it from our parents." Adam pointed to the porch. "Why do you think my father didn't blast down the roof when I missed the party?"

"I haven't a clue," Caroline said coldly.

Adam's voice became sweetly sarcastic. "Because *Grandma* asked him *not* to."

Caroline threw up her hands. "Grandma's supposed to be a big manipulator because she kept you out of trouble?"

"The point is," Adam spoke very slowly, "that my father does whatever she *tells* him to do. So does yours." His smile was mirthless. "So does Uncle Tim, and everyone else in this family."

"Grandma isn't a dictator, Adam!"

"She's a control freak! We have to do everything *her* way. And if we don't, we get spanked. Like two-year-olds!"

"We get spanked when we break *rules*." Caroline slashed the air with one hand. "What have you got against Grandma all of a sudden? Why are you acting like she's some kind of monster?"

"I've *had* it with being told what to do, I've *had* it with Grandma's rules, and I've *had* it with being her lackey." Adam pulled his key to the station wagon from his pocket and thrust it toward her. "*You* want the job? Fine! It's yours."

Caroline stared at him without moving.

"I'll be at Brian's." Adam dropped the key onto the table. "And the only reason I'm telling you is that I don't feel like having Grandma humiliate me, trying to find out where I am." He stomped to the hall. "As if I were Petey's age!"

The door slammed, the windows rattled, and the color drained from Caroline's face.

Andrew came through the archway and glanced toward the porch. "What was all that about?"

Elizabeth shook her head. If she hadn't witnessed it, she would not have believed it.

"I don't know," Caroline whispered.

"Did Adam have another temper tantrum?"

Caroline looked at the door with brimming eyes. "You could call it that."

Andrew turned to Elizabeth. "What did he say?"

"That we're all pathetic." Elizabeth swallowed. "That Grandma tells everyone what to do, and he'll be at Brian's."

Andrew swore. Loudly.

He never swears!

The screen door banged. "Andrew?" Grandma's voice was cold. "Would you care to repeat that?"

"No." He blushed. "Sorry."

"Then would you explain why you said it?" Grandma lowered two gallons of milk onto a chair. "Why Caroline's in tears and Elizabeth looks like a ghost?"

"It's my fault, Grandma." Caroline sniffed. "I yelled at Adam for not getting the milk, and we got into a big fight . . ."

"And Adam slammed off," Andrew muttered. "For a change!"

"He said that he'd be at Brian's," Caroline continued, "and he was only telling us because he'd be humiliated if we looked for him."

Grandma's charcoal eyes darted from face to face. "What was the fight about?"

"He said . . ." Caroline hesitated. ". . . that he's sick of rules." She looked at her lap and swallowed. "And I said he was nuts."

Talk about editing!

Elizabeth didn't dare to look at her sister.

"What else did he say?"

"I don't know, Grandma." Caroline wiped her eyes. "It all happened too fast!"

Grandma turned to Andrew, who shrugged. "I wasn't there. I didn't come in here until the house shook."

"Elizabeth? Can you remember anything else?"

I can't repeat what he said! Not to you!
She shook her head and took a deep breath.
Something's burning!

"The casseroles! Grandma—I never heard the timer!"

Elizabeth darted through the archway, raced to the kitchen, and yanked open the oven. Squinting and blinking, she scrambled for pot holders. She set the first dish on the counter, the smoke alarm wailed, and her eyes filled with tears.

My feelings, exactly.

Chapter
Twelve

As people carried plates to the table, mumbled questions mingled with whispered replies.

Sounds like a swarm of bees in here.

Paul nudged Elizabeth. "What happened?"

She shook her head, picked up a serving spoon, and pried loose a bit of casserole that wasn't too charred.

We're going to have to sandblast these dishes . . .

Grandma came into the dining room and the whispering stopped. She served herself quickly and sat down with resolve.

"O.K." She looked at each of them. "Let's get it all on the table. Caroline, please tell everyone what happened."

Caroline's eyes grew bright and she looked down

at her hands. "Adam and I had a fight and he left."
She paused. "He said he was going to stay at Brian's."

"There's a bit more to it than that," Grandma said
crisply. "Although Caroline and Elizabeth are unable,
or unwilling, to share the details . . ."

The back of Elizabeth's neck grew warm.

". . . it seems that Adam takes exception to the fact
that this family has rules."

There was a lengthy pause.

"What does that mean?" Sarah asked Andrew.

"Adam doesn't like rules."

"But we *have* to have rules," Petey protested.

"Why?" Grandma put down her fork. "Why do we
have to have rules? Paul?"

"To stay safe!" he hollered. "Like, 'No swimming
alone.'"

"Everyone agree that safety is a good idea?"

There were puzzled nods around the table.

"O.K. What about the rest of the rules? Should we
get rid of them?"

"Like what, Grandma?" Abby asked.

"Respecting other people's privacy. Leaving a
phone number where you can be reached. Telling
the truth. Doing your fair share with chores."

"I get it, Grandma!" Sarah bounced. "If we didn't
have rules, nothing would *work!*"

Molly sat back and folded her arms. "If having
rules is why Adam left, then let's make some *more.*"

Grandma gave her a piercing gray look, but spoke

very softly. "We often regret what we say when we're tired."

Molly's dark eyes glittered and her cheeks grew flushed.

"If Adam hates rules," Paul demanded, "then how come he tells when we break them?"

"He doesn't *always*," Abby argued. "He only tells if it's dangerous."

Paul tipped his head to consider. A moment later, he nodded.

"Grandma?" Petey asked. "When is Adam coming back?"

"I don't know, sweetheart."

Petey suddenly scowled and reached under the table. Grandma leaned over and winced. "Oh, Petey! You've scratched yourself raw . . ."

"But it itches!"

"We'll do another bath right after dinner," Grandma said quickly. "And at least for tonight, you can sleep in my room. We'll make you a nest on the floor."

Petey grinned. "A *mouse* nest!"

Grandma agreed to a mouse nest, and then insisted that each of them think of a best. It was uphill work for everyone and Elizabeth was relieved when dinner ended.

When Petey had finished his bath and had been recoated with calamine, he asked Elizabeth to help him paint with watercolors. They set up shop on the kitchen table.

"You make one, too!" he urged.

Elizabeth smiled as she watched him swirl paint onto paper.

"Look, Turtle!" Petey pointed to where a pool of lemon yellow was sliding into a river of turquoise. "When they touch, it turns green!"

"Try these two." Elizabeth pointed to cobalt and scarlet. As he reached for the water, Molly came into the kitchen and picked up the phone.

"Oh! Sorry, Grandma. I didn't know you were talking." She frowned and replaced the receiver.

"Turtle!" Petey grinned. "I made *purple!*"

Seven paintings later, Petey thanked her and ran off to look for his dump truck. Elizabeth was rinsing the brushes when Molly returned and picked up the phone again.

"Sorry. I thought you'd be finished." There was a pause. "No big *deal*, Dad. Adam's just being a jerk." There was another pause, a lengthy one. "O.K. I'll try. Love you, too. Bye."

Molly hung up the phone, looked at the clock, and muttered her way out the back door.

Grandma's been talking to Uncle Steve for almost an hour . . .

Elizabeth finished her task and wandered into the front room. It was empty of people and disturbingly quiet. Her eyes gravitated to the mantelpiece, to the family portrait taken last summer. Adam had his mother's dark coloring but his father's features.

And Uncle Steve looks like Grandma.

Elizabeth bit her lip. Last summer, Adam had acted so much like his grandmother that she had considered them colleagues.

How could he have changed so much?

Her eyes moved from the photograph to her painting. She had begun with Grandma's initials, woven them into a mosaic of blues and grays. Then she had taken on the challenge of working everyone's name into the design. She smiled very slightly. It had been difficult, but she had done it: Tim, Abby, Molly, Karen, Paul, Rachel, Kevin, Andrew, Elena, Caroline, Petey, Steve, Elizabeth, Sarah, and Adam.

"Hi." Caroline limped through the archway.

"Hi." Elizabeth pointed. "How's your ankle?"

"O.K." Caroline gazed at the sofa. "It was horrible, wasn't it?"

Elizabeth nodded.

Caroline turned to face her. "I *couldn't* tell Grandma."

"Me either."

"He wasn't making any *sense*, was he?"

Elizabeth shook her head.

"You know how close we are, right?" Caroline swallowed hard. "Well, this afternoon it was like he was a total stranger. Someone I didn't know . . ." Her eyes filled with tears. ". . . and didn't *want* to."

Poor Caro!

"Grandma's sure we didn't tell her everything." Caroline took a deep breath. "But even if she asks again, I don't think we should. It would only hurt her feelings, and Adam's done enough damage by leaving."

Elizabeth nodded. Caroline gave her a brief smile and limped toward the front hall.

He didn't even care that she'd gotten hurt.

Elizabeth followed her sister up the stairs, put on her pajamas, and brushed her teeth slowly. She rinsed and watched the bubbles hover near the drain.

All because he wouldn't get milk?

If it all wasn't so awful, it would almost be funny. The last bubble popped. Elizabeth turned the water on and off several times and restlessly walked down the hall. The door to her bedroom was nearly closed.

"It is *not* like last summer!" Abby's whisper was harsh. "Elizabeth just didn't talk. She wasn't *mean* to people." A drawer slammed. "Besides, she had a reason. She didn't think she was staying."

"That can't be Adam's excuse," Molly muttered. "He's been in this family since he was born."

More than eighteen years . . .

"Maybe Grandma is right," Molly continued. "Maybe I'm tired. But I'm still glad he's gone."

I don't want to hear this!

Elizabeth retreated as far as the bathroom. When Molly went downstairs, she walked back down the hall.

"Hey, Elizabeth!" Abby pulled something from the top of the dresser she shared with Sarah. "Want to see Petey's present?"

Elizabeth examined the picture on the box. It was a crane, the kind used to knock down old buildings, with "seven moving parts and a real magnet."

"It's perfect, Abby." Elizabeth smiled. "He'll love it."

"It was pretty expensive," Abby confided. "Me and Sarah went halves."

Grandma carried an armful of clean shirts into the room. "Sarah and *I*," she scolded gently. "But Elizabeth is right." She smiled. "Petey will love it."

Abby's brow became furrowed. "Is he upset? About Adam?"

Grandma nodded. "He is. But he's hoping that Adam will at least come for cake."

Poor Petey.

"C'mon, girls," Grandma said. "Hop into bed. It's been a long day."

Sarah scurried into the room and onto her bunk. Grandma tucked the blankets around her shoulders and gave her a kiss. Elizabeth watched her repeat the process with Abby and then quickly climbed under her own covers.

"Good night." Grandma kissed her forehead and whispered, "We'll get through this."

Elizabeth looked up into reassuring gray eyes.

"Promise." Grandma smiled gently and turned off the light.

Chapter
Thirteen

 Elizabeth rose before dawn, dressed, and tiptoed from the room. The doors on both sides of the hall were still closed.

Even Grandma's asleep.

Aimlessly, Elizabeth wandered out the front door and onto the lawn. A crow cawed and she lifted her eyes from the dew-covered grass.

Pink sky at night, sailor's delight.

Frost crept up her spine.

Pink sky in the morning, sailor's warning.

This sky wasn't pink. It was an inflamed crimson, streaked with maroon and edged by dark gray. The pines near the barn, normally still at this hour, were swaying. Elizabeth shivered.

It's not that cold out.

She shivered again and decided that, regardless of

what the thermometer said, she needed hot tea. She retraced her steps and paused in the archway. The glow from the kitchen light spilled onto the dining-room floor.

"Good morning," Grandma called softly.

Elizabeth stepped into the kitchen.

"I wondered who was up so early." Grandma looked up from her mixing bowl and smiled. "I'm glad that it's you!"

Why?

"We haven't had much chance to talk." Grandma reached for the vanilla. "And I've missed you."

I've missed you, too.

Elizabeth smiled and pointed to a large can of peaches. "Would you like me to open that?"

"Please."

Elizabeth pushed down hard on the handle of the can opener. The whirring stopped and she let the lid drip into the can.

"I've been doing some thinking."

Please don't ask about Adam . . .

Grandma began to sift flour. "How would you like a new roommate?"

What?

"Adam seems to need to be elsewhere. We don't know for how long." Grandma's voice was level, but Elizabeth thought she was working hard to keep it that way. "I don't want Petey on the third floor by himself, and I'd like to keep Paul and Andrew together."

Elizabeth nodded. Andrew was a good influence on Paul.

"Moving up to the Crow's Nest would mean having to change in the bathroom . . ."

"That's O.K.," Elizabeth said quickly.

"Then that's one problem solved." Grandma gave her a gentle smile. "Thank you."

"You're welcome." Elizabeth smiled back. "Should I drain these?"

Grandma nodded. "But please save the juice."

Elizabeth lined the cake pans with fruit and held them steady while Grandma scraped in the batter. The oven door had barely closed when footsteps pattered down the back stairs.

"Our five-year-old is awake." Grandma grinned. "Happy birthday, Petey!"

"Hi, Grandma!" He threw his arms around her. "Hi, Turtle!"

Elizabeth smiled. "Hi, Petey! Happy birthday!"

Grandma examined her grandson from all sides. "*Definitely* older."

Petey giggled.

"Elizabeth?" Grandma winked. "What do you suppose boys who are *five* like for breakfast?"

"Liver," Elizabeth said solemnly. "And horseradish."

"No, they don't, Turtle!" Petey wailed. "That stuff is *yuck!*"

"Onions?" She spread her hands. "Lima beans?"

"Grandma-*a-a!*" Petey spun around and found his

grandmother shaking with laughter. His cheeks grew pink and he stamped his foot.

"I guess we need some help," Grandma finally said. "What *would* you like, Petey?"

"French toast." He glowered at Elizabeth. "And bacon."

Grandma raised one eyebrow.

"Please," Petey added.

Grandma ruffled his hair and gave him a kiss. "French toast, coming up!"

During breakfast, Petey reported Elizabeth's menu suggestions with indignant horror. Everyone laughed and his good humor returned.

Despite the red dawn, the morning was sunny and the tribe bantered cheerfully on the way to the beach. Caroline limped along bravely, claiming her ankle was more stiff than sore.

"Come back *early*, Turtle?" Petey pleaded.

Elizabeth tipped her head. "We're still friends?"

Petey put his hands on his hips and rolled his eyes. *He learned that from Molly!*

"Don't be *dumb*, Turtle!" Petey grinned.

"I'll be early." Elizabeth smiled back and headed toward the van. Pap spied her coming and waved.

Has she got news?

"Heh-hey, Elizabeth!" Pap snapped a piece of paper with her finger. "We're onto 'em!"

"You found out where it's coming from?"

Pap nodded. "To within a half mile. Lab faxed the numbers this morning."

Elizabeth grinned. "That's great!"

"Good," Pap corrected her. "Doesn't look like it's barrels."

"But if it's a flush, you can't *do* anything."

"Stow the long face," Pap grunted. "Lab's closing in on what was dumped. Phospho-methyl something-or-other."

"How does that help?"

"We track six miles of coastline. Twenty-mile radius, only forty-three places with chemical permits." Pap squinted at her.

Elizabeth's mind raced. "If you know what was dumped, you can figure out the ingredients." Her eyes grew wide. "And who *has* them, so who could have *made* it!"

Pap nodded. "Leastways, narrow it down. Keep our eyes on five or six, not the whole forty-three."

Elizabeth threw herself into her work and by lunchtime she had transferred and labeled sixty-two samples. Pap spent the morning poring over a map and muttering at the sky. The sun was still shining, but there was a metallic smell in the air and the breeze had grown strong.

"I can't come this afternoon," Elizabeth apologized. "It's Petey's birthday, and . . ."

"Won't be here myself." Pap sealed the last box. "Weather's shifting. Might get one more set of samples before the storm hits." She slammed the van door. "Might not."

"Then what?"

"We play Sherlock Holmes with the permits." Pap shrugged. "And wait."

Elizabeth watched Caroline negotiate another inter-section and cautiously close the distance between the station wagon and the borrowed car Grandma was driving.

She sure looks *miserable, but she's doing really well.*

"Wasn't the submarine awesome?" Abby said.

"Ugh!" Molly wrinkled her nose. "People stacked like sardines? No fresh air?" She shook her head. "I was claustrophobic the whole time!"

Me, too!

"Caro?" Sarah leaned forward. "How come all the doors had round corners? And handles in the middle?"

Caroline continued to peer through the windshield.

"Ask her later," Abby advised. "She's busy driving."

Sarah examined Caroline's hunched shoulders and nodded. "What did *you* like best, Elizabeth?"

The part that didn't move!

The wind had blown hard throughout their visit to the naval park, and ships had strained against moorings and anchors. Elizabeth had braved the submarine and one fishing boat before retreating to dry land.

"The old maps," she said, "and the telescopes."

"Those *were* cool, weren't they?" Molly agreed. "But the whaling room gave me the creeps." She shuddered. "Those harpoons—even Moby Dick didn't deserve *that!*"

There was a chorus of agreement and then Sarah shouted, "We're home!"

Caroline pulled into the driveway, turned off the ignition, and closed her eyes.

"All in one piece!" Molly clapped her shoulder. "Good job, Caro!"

"Thanks." She smiled weakly.

Grandma crossed the lawn to offer Caroline her congratulations. "You've earned a rest, and you should probably put that ankle up for a while." Caroline nodded, and Grandma turned to Molly. "'Helping' tonight is salad. Romaine and cucumbers, please."

"Honey-mustard dressing O.K.?"

"Perfect. Elizabeth, let's get your things moved."

Elizabeth collected fresh sheets and climbed the stairs. A sharp breeze blew through the Crow's Nest, causing window panes to rattle and bedspreads to flap. Mr. Hum, a corduroy cross between a bear and a monkey, lay on Petey's pillow. The top of a trunk was covered with his beachcombing treasures.

But . . .

Elizabeth's eyes jerked from the dresser to the hooks under the eaves and her stomach congealed. All of Adam's belongings had vanished.

"Beds are really a job for two people." Grandma trotted up the stairs. "*Much* faster that way!" She read the expression on Elizabeth's face, her eyes swept the room, and she pressed her lips together.

Oh, Grandma.

"I was afraid this might happen." Grandma looked at her watch. "But there's not much we can do while he's at work. Let's get you settled, and we'll try to reach Adam later."

When the bed was made, Elizabeth collected her suitcase and spent several uncomfortable minutes filling Adam's empty dresser with her clothes. On her way down the stairs, her stomach growled and she smiled. Petey shared her love of Italian sausage, and she was looking forward to dinner.

Unfortunately, Andrew's inexperience with the grill left the sausage charred on the outside and still cold in the middle. Grandma gamely scraped off the outer layer and finished cooking it on the stove. No one teased Andrew, table manners were impeccable, and people stumbled over each other to say how much they had enjoyed the naval park.

Everyone's trying so hard.

Uneasy glances were exchanged as they waited for Grandma to carry in the dessert. She came through the doorway and everyone sang loudly and cheered. When one slender piece of cake remained on the plate, Grandma quietly set it on the buffet.

"Time for presents!"

Petey turned each package over several times, deliberately removed the ribbon, and slit the paper close to the tape. After an appreciative thank you, he handed each gift to Andrew.

"Thanks, Turtle!" Petey held up the mermaid's

hair paperweight for everyone to see. "It's really neat!" He quickly returned it to its box.

The book about trucks would have been better.

One unopened present remained. "This was in the kitchen, Petey." Grandma held the gift toward him. Petey sat up tall, read the tag, and shook his head.

It's from Adam.

"Come on, Petey!" Paul urged. "Open it!"

"Yeah, Petey!" Sarah added. "Don't you want to see what it is?"

He folded his arms and shook his head again.

"All right, everyone," Grandma said. "Petey will open it when he's ready." She stood up. "Would you please check the windows upstairs? It looks as though it's going to pour any minute."

Elizabeth started to follow the others but was stopped by a hand on her shoulder and a look she couldn't decipher. Grandma squatted down next to Petey. He began to breathe through his nose, little puffing sounds, as though he were a very small dragon.

"I know you're disappointed that Adam isn't here." Petey's eyes narrowed.

"We all are. Maybe something unexpected came up, or maybe Adam just needs some time by himself. But he *cares* about you. If he didn't, he wouldn't have brought you a present."

Petey glowered at the floor and resumed puffing.

"I bet he'd like the chance to say happy birthday. Let's call him and see."

Petey gave Elizabeth a misery-filled glance and followed Grandma to the kitchen.

"Elizabeth? Would you dial? The number's on the counter."

Why is she making me do it?

Grandma began to wrap leftovers. Elizabeth pushed the first three numbers and replaced the receiver. "What should I say?"

Grandma replied without looking up. "Is Adam there, and would he please speak to his cousin Petey?"

Elizabeth dialed seven digits this time, aware of Petey's intense blue gaze and unable to meet it.

"Hello? Um, this is Elizabeth. One of Adam's cousins. And, um, could he please talk to Petey?"

"Hey, Sheridan!" a male voice bellowed. "One of your cousins is on the phone."

"Which one?" Adam sounded far away.

"Sorry." The voice returned to the phone. "Who wants him again?"

Elizabeth took a quick breath. "Petey."

"Petey!" the voice hollered.

"All right." Adam sounded weary.

Elizabeth handed the receiver to Petey. "He's coming."

Petey held it with both hands, close to his ear.

Grandma collected a sponge from the sink and began to wipe the stove.

"Hi."

Shut up, clock!

Every tick underscored Petey's silence. When at last he spoke, he said very clearly, "Why didn't you come?"

Elizabeth caught her breath and looked up. Grandma had abandoned all pretense of cleaning and was watching Petey with wary eyes. Suddenly, he thrust the phone toward her. Grandma's eyebrows drew together and she raised the receiver.

"Adam?"

What did he say? What's going on?

Elizabeth's eyes darted back and forth. Two red spots stood out on Petey's cheeks, throwing his long, dark lashes into relief. Grandma had grown very pale, and when she replaced the receiver, it was with a trembling hand. She swallowed loudly, walked to the hall doorway, and paused.

"Petey? Elizabeth? I'm sorry."

Grandma went down the steps. A moment later, the door to the mudroom clicked closed.

Chapter Fourteen

Elizabeth watched another truck send another line of cars skittering across the floor.

At least he's not pretending that nothing happened.

Eyes almost closed, mouth pursed, Petey pulled another fist full of cars from his box. With little jerking motions, he set the stage for another crash.

But he's not talking, either.

As soon as Grandma had left the kitchen, Petey had stormed up to the Crow's Nest. Elizabeth had followed him, certain her presence was unwanted, but too frightened to care. Petey had glanced at her once and pulled his car box from under his bed. Elizabeth looked at her watch. He had been crashing cars for almost an hour without saying a word.

A flash of lightning was followed by a house-shaking

roll of thunder, and Petey didn't even look up. Elizabeth returned her eyes to her book, but her mind wandered downstairs.

What did Adam say that made Grandma cry?

Caroline had come up to report that Grandma had stayed in the mudroom for half an hour. When she emerged, it was with a laundry basket full of clean clothes. She had said nothing to anyone about the phone call.

"Petey?" Grandma called from the bottom of the stairs. "Bedtime."

Without comment or protest, Petey gathered his cars and put on his pajamas. When Grandma came to say good night, he allowed her to kiss him but did not speak.

"Good night, Elizabeth." Grandma kissed her without making eye contact.

"Good night, Grandma."

The door to the Crow's Nest closed softly.

"Petey? Want me to read?"

He pointed to *Stuart Little* and pulled the blanket over his head. Elizabeth read the chapter in which Stuart captains a boat through stormy seas, and paused. There was no response from her roommate.

Happy birthday, Petey.

Elizabeth tried to lose herself in the complexity of ocean food chains, but the wind's roar was soothing, and scavengers gave way to sleep.

Petey?

Elizabeth was instantly awake. She had fallen asleep with the light on, and the bed across from her was indisputably empty. The windows rattled as rain swept against them.

Where is he?

A muffled *click!* at the bottom of the stairs was followed by cautious footsteps. Elizabeth propped herself on one elbow. Without looking at her, Petey hurried across the floor and climbed onto his bed. "I had to go to the bathroom."

Wondering why he seemed angry about it, Elizabeth turned off the light. Gales ripped through the pines near the fence, carrying shrill threats toward the house.

Even if they come down, the tallest one won't reach the porch.

It was hard not to imagine the wind as alive, hands hurling water in gleeful destruction. As terrifying as it was, Elizabeth was grateful for the distraction. She shivered, conscious of her twisted clothes, the tightness in her chest, and the unfamiliar mattress beneath her.

I wish Dad and Mom were here.

Elizabeth counted the days until she would see them again and drifted into a restless sleep.

No beach today.

Elizabeth peered through the rain-spattered window.

Not this morning, anyway.

The front lawn glimmered dully in the cold pre-dawn light. Elizabeth pulled on a sweatshirt and tip-toed down to the front room.

Power still on?

Experimentally, she flicked a lamp switch. Light spread to the corners of the room. Through the arch-way, against the dark shine of the dining-room table, she could see Petey's presents. The one in red paper, the unopened gift from Adam, was missing.

What happened to it?

Elizabeth shook her head. There was something else wrong. . . . Her eyes found a chair out of place.

No.

Fire swept through her chest.

Oh, Petey!

Six feet from the fireplace, she closed her eyes.

Maybe I can . . .

She opened her eyes and stepped closer.

A magic wand couldn't fix that.

Her delicate mosaic was marred beyond repair by a black oval that could only have been scribbled with five-year-old fury. Where Adam's name had been, the cardboard was shredded and gouged.

Grandma!

Elizabeth's heart pounded wildly. This was worse than what Sarah had done to the flowers. As bad as that had been, plants could be replaced. When Grandma saw this, she would be *livid.*

Oh, Petey . . .

Water ran and the kettle bumped onto a burner.

Do something!

Elizabeth slid two candlesticks in front of the scar and quickly moved the offending chair back into place.

"Morning!" Grandma whispered from the dining room.

Act calm. Act normal.

"Morning, Grandma." Elizabeth stepped through the archway.

"Some storm, wasn't it?"

Elizabeth nodded and followed her grandmother to the kitchen.

"I'm amazed the power's still on." Grandma took two cups from a shelf and set them on the stove. "Petey sleep all right?"

Elizabeth nearly choked. Unsure of her voice, she nodded again.

Grandma pulled the outer wrappings from two bags of tea and stepped on the lever to open the garbage can. The lid did not bang.

What's wrong?

Elizabeth cringed as Grandma pulled Adam's gift from among the remains of last night's dinner. She took it to the sink, wordlessly sponged the exterior, and carried it to the mudroom. When she returned, she addressed the stove.

"That stays between us, please." Although the

kettle was not even steaming, she poured water into her cup and carried it up the back stairs.

Oh, Petey . . .

Elizabeth looked at the clock. It wasn't even six-thirty.

At eight o'clock, Grandma confessed to having a headache and asked Caroline to make sure that everyone had something to eat. Rain continued to fall, and the morning was restlessly quiet. The door to Grandma's bedroom remained closed until noon. Declining offers of help, she made lunch and returned to her room.

"What's wrong with Grandma?" Sarah asked as they sat down.

"I think she's upset about Adam," Caroline said.

"That he didn't come?" Sarah persisted.

Caroline exchanged glances with Andrew and Molly, took a bite of her sandwich, and nodded.

"Can I be excused?" Without waiting for an answer, Petey slipped from his chair.

"What's wrong with *him?*" Paul demanded. "He *loves* tuna!"

Abby pointed to the stack of boxes on the buffet. "And he hasn't played with his presents."

The older kids looked at Elizabeth. Helplessly, she shrugged.

"He hasn't said anything?" Andrew's forehead became furrowed. "Not even last night?"

Elizabeth shook her head.

"Adam's not even *here* and he's making everyone miserable," Molly muttered.

"Then don't *let* him!" Andrew snapped. "Do something constructive."

"Like what?" Abby asked.

"Something to cheer Grandma up." Andrew folded his arms. "Something that has nothing to *do* with Adam."

"Good idea!" Caroline said quickly. "What if we did some cleaning? Stuff that isn't on the job list."

"Spend the afternoon *dusting?*" Paul squeaked.

"Not the whole afternoon," Caroline countered. "How about an hour?"

"We can't go outside," Abby pointed out. "And an hour wouldn't kill us."

"I'll do anything but the bathroom," said Molly. "It was my turn this morning, and I can handle only so much soap scum per day!"

"I'll take the bathroom," Elizabeth said. "I haven't done it in a while."

"Day before yesterday," Andrew said dryly. "But I won't fight you for it."

They divided the chores and began. At the end of the hour, Andrew organized a card tournament. The front room was soon filled with accusations of dumb luck and laughter, and the aroma of popcorn made its way to the second floor.

Elizabeth lingered over the chrome and the tiles,

taking satisfaction in making them gleam, enjoying the sound of the rain against the house, grateful for a reason to be by herself. A knock made her jump.

Grandma?

Elizabeth opened the door. "Sorry," she mumbled. "Have you been waiting?"

"No. I came to tell you dinner's almost ready." Grandma looked at the sponge in her hand and then at the bottle of cleanser on the edge of the tub. "What's this all about?"

Elizabeth blushed. "It was supposed to be a surprise."

"What was?"

"Extra cleaning," she stammered. "Everyone did it. I'm just slow."

"Whose idea was that?"

"Andrew's, and Caro's."

"And how did they enlist the cooperation of a group that drags its feet through regular chores?"

Elizabeth swallowed. "They said it might cheer you up."

Grandma studied the floor until the *ping!* of the oven timer floated up the stairs. "That was very thoughtful. Thank you." She lifted her head. "Time to eat."

Elizabeth stepped into the dining room in time to see Andrew put a full plate in front of his brother. Petey continued to stare at his hands.

He's still not talking?

Chatter was warily cheerful. Grandma listened and watched from the doorway. When the last person sat down, she spoke.

"I understand the good fairies have been at work." Surprised faces turned toward her, and she smiled. "Thank you, everyone. I hope you'll give me a tour after dinner."

"Please, Grandma?" Paul sounded wistful. "Can you please see the hall closet *now?*"

"He worked really hard, Grandma," Molly volunteered. "It's spotless!"

Grandma raised one eyebrow. "The front hall closet, in *this* house, is spotless?"

Paul nodded eagerly.

"Then I'd better come." Grandma grinned. "Something might happen to it during dinner!"

Laughter filled the room.

Thank goodness!

Elizabeth smiled at Caroline. A moment later, Paul bounced back into the room. "Grandma said that it's gorgeous!"

"Good job, Paul!" Andrew gave him thumbs-up.

Grandma appeared in the archway. Her face was stone and her eyes were blazing.

Oh, no!

"Who did this?" She held up the painting.

Why did she have to find it just now?

Six pairs of horror-filled eyes stared at the picture.

Red faced, Petey looked at his lap. Grandma lowered the painting and slowly turned toward him.

She's going to tell him to wait for her upstairs.

Elizabeth's heart pounded.

He knows he's going to get spanked.

Grandma shifted her gaze and spoke in a monotone to the edge of the table. "I will see you all in the morning."

She returned the painting to the mantelpiece and soundlessly climbed the front stairs. The silence lasted until her bedroom door closed.

"Petey!" Abby demanded. "How *could* you?"

"Elizabeth *made* that for Grandma!" Sarah scolded.

Petey continued to stare at his lap.

"Elizabeth?" Caroline's voice trembled. "Is there any way . . . ?"

If only there were!

Elizabeth shook her head.

"Petey?" Andrew leaned forward. "Why did you do it?"

"I *hate* him!" Petey launched himself from his chair. "He didn't even *come* for my birthday," he screeched, "and he made Grandma *cry!*"

His footsteps faded, the clock chimed, and rain began to splash against the side of the house.

Chapter
Fifteen

The wind's still blowing hard.
Elizabeth watched the early morning sunlight fade in and out on the floor.
Please, Petey. Or today'll be another disaster.
Andrew frowned. "You can't stay up here for the rest of the summer."

Petey looked at his brother with brimming eyes.

"C'mon, Petey." Andrew's voice became gentle. "I'll go with you, O.K.? You'll feel better after you've told her you're sorry." He looked over his shoulder. "Right, Elizabeth?"

"Please, Petey?" Elizabeth gave him what she hoped was an encouraging smile.

Andrew held out his hand. Petey slipped off his bed and took it, and they went down the stairs. Elizabeth watched the second hand of her watch complete four circles before she followed them.

Please don't be mad anymore.

"Morning, everyone." Grandma smiled very briefly at no one and set a platter of cinnamon rolls on the buffet.

"Morning, Grandma," several timid voices replied.

"Please begin. I'll join you in a few minutes."

Grandma went back to the kitchen and Elizabeth whispered to Petey, "Are things O.K.?"

He gave her a melancholy look and she turned to Andrew. He glanced toward the doorway and mouthed, "I think so."

Breakfast began quietly, but when Grandma sat down the older kids began to tell rapid-fire stories and jokes. The meal was nearly over before Elizabeth realized that they had done so by agreement. Grandma did not speak at all: not when Andrew gulped his milk, not when Sarah buttered her roll with her finger, not when Paul wiped his mouth with his hand.

Finally, she stood up. "Thank you all, again, for the work you did yesterday. As soon as morning jobs are finished, we'll swim."

She left the room and Molly flopped back in her chair. "*That* was fun."

"Never mind," Caroline said quickly. "We got through it."

"And the sun is out." Andrew pushed himself away from the table. "Another rainy day and we'd all have gone psycho."

True.

Elizabeth was a little ashamed of how much she was looking forward to seeing Pap, to thinking about something other than the family.

On a day when Pap had been unusually talkative, she had mentioned having served in the Navy. She had been widowed shortly after her marriage to a boat-builder. During their courtship, he had founded the group of environmentally concerned citizens that eventually became the Water Minders.

When they reached the sand, Elizabeth salved her conscience by promising Petey that she would help him build a fort later, and briskly walked up the beach.

The sea was still choppy and the waves were topped by whitecaps. Elizabeth felt goose bumps rise as she picked her way among the storm's litter: driftwood, dead fish, shells, a jellyfish, seaweed, a plastic bleach bottle . . .

How can people do that?

Pap's attitude toward anyone who sullied the ocean was contagious. Scowling, Elizabeth scooped up the bottle and hurried toward the van.

"Last batch," Pap said by way of a greeting. "Least for a while."

Elizabeth sat down and reached for the syringes. "How come?"

"Storm stirred everything up."

Elizabeth looked at the water and shivered.

"Settles down, we'll start spot testing again."

"Did you look at the permits?"

Pap nodded. "Four to watch. Seven maybes."

"How do you watch?"

"Stakeouts."

Did she just wink?

Elizabeth would have liked to ask more questions, but Pap pulled out her map and reached for a pen. Half an hour passed before she spoke again.

"You got a brother?" Pap yanked the tape from a new box of collecting bottles. "Dark eyes, at the bait shop?"

"My cousin Adam." Elizabeth swallowed. "Why?"

"Was in there this morning." Pap swore, tossed her pen into the garbage pail, and rummaged in her tackle box for a new one. "Happened to mention I'd found some good help, name of Sheridan."

Elizabeth blushed.

"Ludlow said he'd found the same. That summer help's tricky, and he wouldn't hire any *but* Sheridan, could he help it."

Elizabeth reached for another pair of test tubes.

"Then the dark-eyed fellow up and *quit*. Said he didn't need Ludlow to do his grandmother any favors." Pap shrugged. "Took off his apron and walked out."

Elizabeth's heart skipped a beat.

"Ludlow said he hadn't taken him on as a favor. All he'd meant was Sheridans work hard and they're honest." Pap rocked herself to her feet and took the test tubes from Elizabeth's hand. "He was sorry to see him go. Come Monday, was going to give him a raise."

Should I tell Grandma?

Elizabeth was suddenly dizzy.

Not one more *thing. Not today.*

The slamming of the van door pulled her out of her reverie. "When will you be back?"

"When there's work," Pap replied. "Truck's here, I'm here."

Elizabeth watched the van roll over the sand and bump onto the road. Then she limply walked up the beach. Grandma was sitting by herself several yards from the water. Petey was sifting sand through a strainer, and the others were swimming.

Everything looks normal enough.

She sat down next to Petey. He declined her offer to begin his fort and continued to sift. Elizabeth glanced at Grandma again.

Looks sure can be deceiving.

Elizabeth wedged six peppers between a bag of carrots and a stalk of celery and slid the drawer of the crisper back into place.

Thank goodness there's something ordinary to do. Something we don't have to think about.

She hefted three gallons of milk onto the top shelf and closed the refrigerator.

Caro feels that way, too.

Her sister was humming as she sorted dry goods into cupboards. The telephone rang. "Sheridan residence!" Caroline answered cheerfully. Then her back stiffened.

It's Adam.

Caroline's blue green eyes glazed over and her lips became a thin line.

What is he saying?

The back door banged.

Why isn't she talking?

Grandma stepped into the room as Caroline replaced the receiver.

"Who was it?"

Caroline folded her arms. "Adam."

Grandma looked at her expectantly. Caroline didn't say anything further, and her forehead grew furrowed.

"Where . . . ?"

"He's at Ron's."

At the gas station?

"He moved out of Brian's. Ron's letting him sleep over the garage in exchange for pumping gas. He just wanted to let us know where he'd be, in case of emergency." Caroline took a deep breath. "Wasn't that *thoughtful* of him?"

"Why did he leave Brian's?"

"He didn't give me a chance to *ask*, Grandma! He just delivered his message and hung up." Caroline glared at the phone. "Without bothering to inquire how *we* are."

"I don't think Adam is able to think about other people right now."

"No one could argue with that!"

Caro!

Elizabeth warily looked at her grandmother.

"I'm not sure he should be working two jobs."

Grandma spoke as though she hadn't heard Caroline's outburst. "Maybe I'd better call Steve . . ."

"He's not," Elizabeth heard herself say.

"He's not *what?*" Caroline demanded.

"Working two jobs."

Grandma looked up sharply.

"He quit the bait shop," Elizabeth stammered. "This morning. Pap told me."

Grandma tipped her head. "Did she know *why?*"

Elizabeth shook her head and felt her intestines ripple.

"Would you two mind starting dinner?" Grandma said. "I'll be back in a few minutes." She scooped up her wallet and went through the door to the dining room.

"I'm beginning to share Petey's feelings," Caroline muttered.

Elizabeth sighed.

And you're as miserable hating Adam as he is.

Chapter
Sixteen

 "Grandma?" Elizabeth waited until she looked up from her sewing. "Is it O.K. if I stay home this afternoon?"

Grandma dropped her gaze to the needle and thread in her hand. "If you'd rather, you may."

"Thanks." Elizabeth gave her a small smile and turned toward the stairs.

"Elizabeth?"

She turned around.

"You're not sick, are you?"

Elizabeth shook her head. "I just feel like reading, and it's too bright on the beach."

Grandma returned to her task and Elizabeth slipped up the stairs.

Beaches are for people who swim.

She turned the corner to the Crow's Nest.

Until Pap comes back, there's no point *in going.*

Elizabeth watched the others until they reached the end of the driveway, glared at the haze on the far side of the pines, and flopped onto her bed.

How did everything get to be such a mess?

On the surface, the last few days had been better. Petey's poison ivy was nearly gone, Caroline had stopped limping, and no one else had been hurt. There hadn't been any fights, only minor squabbles over games, and no one had gotten into trouble.

But nothing's the way it's supposed to be.

Elizabeth looked around the Crow's Nest and sighed. For starters, she shouldn't be lying on Adam's bed. But he wasn't here. And since Grandma's silent return from the bait shop, no one had even mentioned his name.

No one's yelled, either.

Everyone was pretending. That it didn't matter that Adam had removed himself from the family. That there was nothing wrong with her refusal to go into the water. That Grandma was herself . . .

Elizabeth sighed again. Grandma *acted* like Grandma. She went to the beach, and she cooked, and she kissed them good night—all of the things she usually did. It was the *way* she did them. More slowly than usual. Mechanically.

And dinner's the worst.

At dinner it was impossible not to notice that Grandma's mind had wandered, that she'd missed someone's best. That she wasn't commenting when table manners were breached. That she wouldn't offer her opinion, even when asked.

Maybe the others haven't noticed, but Petey sure has.

Petey had watched his grandmother with worried eyes. He'd made dozens of efforts to engage her attention, to get her to smile. He had met with limited success, even when he'd presented her with his best moon snail shell.

He was so disappointed last night. . . . Who is that?

An ancient blue pickup truck rattled into the driveway. Elizabeth watched a gray-haired man ease himself, in stages, from behind the wheel. His dark green apron glinted as he crossed the grass. He disappeared from view and Elizabeth heard knocking. Several minutes later, he reappeared on the lawn—minus the envelope that had been in his hand.

Mr. Ludlow?

Elizabeth watched the truck pull away.

Should I have answered the door?

She shrugged. He'd left whatever it was, and he had no reason to suspect that anyone had been home.

Why would he? Everyone knows the Sheridans spend all day at the beach. That they practically live in the water.

Elizabeth glanced at Petey's beachcombing collection: shells, starfish, a crab carapace and two claws, driftwood, the mermaid's hair paperweight.

All the Sheridans but one.

She looked at the triangle of ocean between the

pine trees. Her eyes watered and she turned away from the window.

Maybe the others can pretend that it doesn't matter. But I can't.

"Grandma wants you."

"Hi, Petey." Elizabeth pushed herself off her bed. "Where is she?"

"In the kitchen." He scowled at the floor. "How come you stayed home?"

"I just felt like reading today."

Petey turned away. "Even if you won't swim, you're supposed to *be* there."

"I'm sorry, Petey." Elizabeth sighed. "I'll come tomorrow."

"Promise?"

"Promise."

Elizabeth found Grandma at the sink, her hands full of wet lettuce. She lifted her chin toward an envelope that lay on the counter.

"Mr. Ludlow dropped that off for Adam. It's his pay, for the week he worked." She shook some water from the greens. "Would you take a bike out to Ron's and give it to him?"

Elizabeth swallowed hard.

"He might need the money," Grandma added.

Elizabeth's stomach twisted.

"Please?" Grandma spoke to the lettuce. "I'd feel a lot better if you could tell me you'd seen him." She hesitated. "That he's O.K."

You sure don't want to go . . .

Grandma had driven to Brockport to get gas rather than make the two-minute trip to Ron's Parts & Service. Grandma's cheeks grew flushed and Elizabeth quickly picked up the envelope.

"Thank you." Grandma gave her a quick smile. "Ride carefully."

Elizabeth pedaled slowly, her heart beating fast.

I'm just doing what she asked me to do. Why do I feel like a traitor?

She swerved around a pile of red dirt and a bunch of new sewer pipes.

Maybe he won't be there, and I can just leave it.

Holding fast to that thought, she pedaled the three blocks through town and turned the corner. Adam was wiping the windshield of a little tan hatchback. He saw her and frowned.

Too late to go back.

Elizabeth pulled the bike to a stop between a stack of old tires and a display of motor oil. Adam finished what he was doing, wiped his hands on a maroon rag, and made change from a wad of bills in his pocket. The tan car pulled away and he walked toward her.

He hasn't shaved in days!

Adam stopped six feet in front of her and folded his arms.

Has he showered?

There were rings of sweat-soaked dust around his neck and smears of oil among the stubble on his face. His blue jumpsuit looked as though it had never been washed, and his hands were caked with filth. The contrast to his usual well-groomed appearance was unnerving and Elizabeth stared at him dumbly.

"Well?"

Elizabeth shifted her gaze to her handlebars.

"You come out here for a *reason?*"

Elizabeth snatched at her pocket. "To bring you this."

Adam's eyes narrowed. "What is it?"

"Your pay," she stammered. "From the bait shop. Mr. Ludlow dropped it off."

He reached forward, accepted the envelope, and stepped back. Without looking at it, he shoved it into a grease-covered pocket. "Thanks."

"You're welcome." Elizabeth searched his face quickly and threw her leg over the crossbar. "I'd better go."

"Hey!"

Elizabeth reached for the brakes and looked over her shoulder.

"Everyone's O.K., right?"

Everyone's pretending to be.

Elizabeth nodded.

No one's even close to O.K.

She pushed hard on the pedals.

But I'll pretend, too. If it'll make Grandma feel better, I'll say you seemed fine.

Chapter
Seventeen

"Adam seemed O.K., Grandma. A little dirty, but O.K."

Elizabeth looked into the mirror and sighed.

Academy Award material, that was. I'm getting to be quite the liar.

She wiped her face and hands on a towel and went down the stairs.

And another secret to keep. Whatever happened to this family's rule about telling the truth?

At the end of dinner Elizabeth decided that, whatever her qualms, her trip to Ron's and her lie had been worth it. Grandma hadn't been animated—not by a long shot—but she hadn't missed anyone's best, and during dessert she had suggested they go to a movie. The Tiny Theater was showing a W.C. Fields film.

"Petey?" Elizabeth stepped onto the porch and offered him a sweatshirt. "Grandma says we need two layers."

His shoulders rose half an inch.

"Petey?" She sat down beside him. "Don't you want to see the movie? It's got car chases and juggling."

He put his head in her lap and closed his eyes. "I don't feel good."

You don't look good.

"Do you want to stay home?"

He nodded. "With you."

The screen door banged. "What's wrong with Petey?" Paul asked.

"He doesn't feel well."

"Grandma!" Paul bellowed through the screen. "Petey's sick!"

There were quick steps in the front room, a pause, and more footsteps on the porch. Grandma's eyes flashed a question to Elizabeth. She spread her hands in reply.

"Petey?" Grandma squatted down in front of him. "What's wrong?"

His eyes remained closed.

"He wants to stay home," Elizabeth stammered. She looked up into worried blue gray eyes. "I'll stay with him."

Grandma shook her head. "That's very generous of you, Elizabeth, but if he's sick, I think I'd better stay."

"I'm not sick." Petey sat up. "I'm just tired."

Grandma pressed the back of her hand to his forehead. "You don't feel warm . . ."

"I want to go to bed," Petey said in a small, flat voice. "I want Turtle to read to me."

Grandma contemplated them both. "You really wouldn't mind missing the movie?"

Elizabeth shook her head. "I'm kind of tired, too."

"All right then. Thank you." Grandma smoothed Petey's hair and got to her feet. "I hope you feel better. I'll come up when we get home."

The others swarmed through the door and Grandma looked at her watch. "If we're going to get seats, we'd better hustle."

When the throng reached the end of the driveway, Petey slipped off the swing and silently led Elizabeth up the stairs.

He's not just tired.

Petey put on his pajamas and got into bed without saying a word. Elizabeth considered making him brush his teeth but decided against it. He looked past making the effort. She picked up a book and began to read. Petey sat very still, eyes glazed, Mr. Hum in his lap.

He's not listening.

"Time to turn off the light?"

Petey fingered one of Mr. Hum's buttons and nodded.

Elizabeth clicked the switch and amber light dissolved into damp gray. It had begun to drizzle and the screens on the triangular windows shimmered faintly in the cloud-covered dusk.

"Stay with me, Turtle?"

"Sure, Petey."

Elizabeth crawled onto her bed, pulled the blanket up to her chin, and wondered how long the movie would run.

What if he's really sick?

Rain began to *pop!* onto the roof. Individual drops quickly blended into a spattering hiss.

I wish . . .

Petey sobbed. Not a prelude to relief, the brief shedding of tears, but a drawn-out wail that came from deep, deep inside.

"Petey?" Elizabeth's heart galloped. "What's wrong?"

He sobbed again. She stumbled to his bed, knelt beside it, and put a hand on his shoulder. "Petey? What is it?"

He curled himself into a ball, his chin touching his chest. "She . . ."

"Who, Petey?"

"Grandma." He choked. "She hates me."

Elizabeth was blinded by a surge of red horror. "Grandma *loves* you, Petey!"

His whole body heaved. "Not anymore." His tiny fist rubbed one dripping eye and then an equally wet nose. "Not since the painting."

Elizabeth's mind scrambled after words that might

reassure him. "She was upset, Petey. That's all. Being mad doesn't mean stopping loving," she ungrammatically quoted Karen.

"The painting was different," he slurped. "She didn't spank me, or anything."

"That doesn't mean Grandma hates you."

"But she always spanks when we do something bad. And then everything's O.K. again."

"But you told her that you were sorry."

"She didn't believe me. I could tell." Petey's gasps came in triplets. "And I wanted to fix it, and Caro said she would help." He hiccupped. "But now it's *gone* and we can't even try!"

Elizabeth's mind raced. Even at five, Petey had absorbed the family formula for dealing with mistakes. He had admitted that he'd done something wrong, but he hadn't been punished, he didn't believe his apology had been accepted, and he could not make amends. He was just old enough to understand Grandma's rules and he wasn't able to follow them.

No wonder he's so unhappy!

And, Elizabeth realized with a start, the painting was gone. Had *been* gone, for days.

Petey sobbed again and wrenched himself toward the wall. Elizabeth lay down beside him and wrapped an arm around his trembling shoulders. He pulled her wrist tightly to his chest. The cool night air mingled with the salty warmth of his breath.

Oh, Petey . . .

Elizabeth's hand began to tingle. She tentatively opened her fingers and he clutched her with an intensity that sent chills down her spine.

How could he think Grandma hates him?

Her throat swelled and she closed her eyes.

"Elizabeth?"

A stair creaked and her eyes opened into rain-soaked blackness.

"Petey?" Grandma whispered anxiously.

Elizabeth scrambled for leverage on the edge of the bed. Grandma was poised halfway up the stairs.

"Is Petey all right?"

Elizabeth turned around. His breathing was rhythmic and slow. She pulled up the blanket and crept across the floor.

"He's asleep."

"Did he throw up, or . . . ?"

Elizabeth shook her head. "He's not that kind of sick."

Grandma peered into the darkness, toward Petey's bed. "Sounds as though we need to talk."

Elizabeth followed her grandmother down to the kitchen. Water droned against window panes, emphasizing the quiet.

Where are the others?

Grandma turned on the stove light and Elizabeth looked at the clock.

It's only 8:20!

"I was worried," Grandma carried the kettle to the sink. "So I came home." She turned on the tap, turned it off, and addressed the faucet. "What's wrong with Petey?"

I can't pretend about this.

Elizabeth stared into the pool of light between the burners.

What should I say?

"Did someone hurt his feelings?"

Elizabeth could barely distinguish Grandma's outline from the darkness behind her.

"Was it me?"

Elizabeth swallowed hard. "He thinks you don't believe him."

Grandma set the kettle into the sink. "About what?"

"About the painting." The words came out in a rush. "That he's sorry." Elizabeth took a quick breath. "He thinks that you hate him. Because you didn't spank him for scribbling out Adam's name."

"Because I didn't . . . ?" Grandma whispered.

Elizabeth stole a quick glance at her grandmother and looked back to the stove.

I wish I'd never made the dumb thing!

The sputtering of rain ebbed and flowed against the relentless ticking of the clock.

What is she thinking?

Elizabeth risked another glance. Grandma's head was bent nearly to her hands. In unsteady streams, tears slid down her cheeks and dropped into the sink.

I shouldn't have told her!

Panic pulsed in her chest.

But how could I not?

Grandma's shoulders jerked as she inhaled. Elizabeth's eyes filled and she tiptoed across the linoleum.

"Grandma?"

Several long seconds passed before she turned around.

Oh, Grandma!

Elizabeth opened her arms. They held each other tightly, barely breathing, not moving at all.

Chapter
Eighteen

A burst of laughter floated from the front hall to the kitchen.

"Grandma?" Andrew called. There was more laughter. "We need some help."

Elizabeth let her arms fall and Grandma took a step backwards. Her eyes were unfocused and bright.

"Grandma?" Andrew called again.

She blinked and turned toward the sound. "Coming!"

Elizabeth stood still, her whole body tingling. She shivered and became aware of the icy gale coming through the open windows.

The temperature's dropped . . .

"Good heavens!" More laughter. "Stay *right* where you are!"

The others are home . . .

"We tried to come in the back," Caroline explained. "But the door was locked!"

Quick footsteps came through the dining room.

"Elizabeth? Would you grab a laundry basket?" Grandma scooped up the entire pile of dish towels and hurried back through the doorway. "You'd think they'd been swimming!"

Still feeling lightheaded, Elizabeth emptied the dark load into the washing machine and carried the basket to the front room.

"Good evening, Elizabeth!" Andrew bowed. "*Lovely* weather, isn't it?"

Her mouth dropped open.

It's raining mud!

The others laughed.

"Hey, Grandma!" Molly grinned. "Any film in the camera?"

Grandma shook her head. "And I don't know whether to be sorry or glad!"

They all laughed again.

"All right," Grandma said briskly. "Everything into the basket."

"Even our sneakers?" Sarah asked.

"Even your sneakers."

"But how . . . ?" Elizabeth stammered. "What *happened*?"

"You know those pipes they're replacing?" Caroline asked. "Near Mrs. Davenport's house?"

Elizabeth nodded.

"Well, all the dirt washed into the road . . ."

"And we stopped so Sarah could tie her shoes," Molly interrupted. "So we were all standing still . . ."

"And this truck came by," Paul hollered. "Doing *ninety!*"

"And hit a puddle this deep . . ." Andrew held his hands eighteen inches apart.

"And made a tidal wave!" Abby finished happily.

Caroline grinned and held up two dripping brown socks. "And here we are!"

"C'mon, everyone. Get those things off." Grandma closed her eyes for a moment. "You all could have been killed."

"You're not kidding, Grandma." Andrew pulled his shirt over his head. "That guy was a maniac!"

"All right. *Quick* showers." Grandma picked up the basket. "When you're in your pajamas, come down to the kitchen. I'll make some hot chocolate."

"Petey's asleep," Elizabeth warned, hoping that was still true.

"O.K.," Caroline said. "We'll keep it down." A dozen bare feet scampered up the stairs.

"Elizabeth?" Grandma said quietly. "Thank you. For telling me about Petey."

Elizabeth's eyes flew to the empty spot above the fireplace and then dropped to the floor. "I'm pretty tired, Grandma. I think I'll go to bed now."

"Sleep tight."

"You, too."

Elizabeth gently closed the door to the Crow's Nest and inched her way to the top of the stairs. Petey was snoring softly.

Thank goodness.

Elizabeth pulled her pajamas from under her pillow and forced herself to put them on. She added a sweatshirt and pulled back the covers.

Poor Petey . . .

She crawled onto her bed and felt a wave of exhaustion wash through her.

. . . but at least he's asleep . . .

She dropped onto the mattress and pulled up the blanket.

. . . and Grandma will fix things tomorrow.

She closed her eyes. A portrait of six mud-covered people appeared and she felt herself grin.

Piggies in a puddle!

She wished for a moment that Adam had been there to see it, and then sighed.

He probably wouldn't have laughed.

In the distance, a foghorn blared weakly, and Petey's bed creaked as he turned over. Long, still moments passed before Elizabeth heard the others make their ways to the second floor.

"Good night, everyone." Grandma's voice echoed very faintly.

Good night.

Elizabeth's eyes fluttered closed and instantly flew open again.

I hugged her!

Elizabeth cautiously allowed herself to replay the event, and finally to believe that it had happened. She decided it hadn't been any stranger than the rest of the summer and slipped into slumber.

. . . is someone talking to me?
Elizabeth blinked. The sun had not yet risen and the world around her was gray. Grandma was sitting on Petey's bed, speaking softly.
". . . about it when the others go to the beach." She gave him a kiss and stood up.

Elizabeth snapped her eyes shut. When she re-opened them, the room was full of pale yellow light and the sugar-and-salt smell of bacon. She dressed quickly and went down to the dining room. Petey was already at the table, listening to the events of last night, friendly arguments about who looked better, or worse, covered in mud. Breakfast ended, chores were completed with dispatch, and Caroline led the pack to the beach.

Elizabeth was putting the finishing touches on a sand castle guardhouse when she heard Petey's voice and looked up. Grandma kissed the top of his head and said something. He nodded and took his purple bucket into the waves. When it was full, he carried it to where Elizabeth was working and dropped to his knees.

"Grandma doesn't hate me." His dark blue eyes met Elizabeth's very briefly. "She explained about the painting. That it was special. 'Cuz you made it, and put everyone in." His cheeks grew pink and he sat very still. "I'm sorry I wrecked it, Turtle."

"I know." Elizabeth gave him a small smile.

Petey scooped some sand into the bucket. "She didn't spank me. She said she knows I'm really sorry."

"Are you friends?"

He nodded and began to drip towers. "We hugged."

Elizabeth watched the breeze play with his hair and drops of water sparkle as sand fell from his fingers.

"We hugged" covers a lot.

Elizabeth dipped her hand into the bucket, made two small spires, and glanced to her right. Grandma was watching them, smiling gently.

Chapter
Nineteen

Elizabeth sat on the swing, looking at nothing. The boys had gone fishing with Mr. Ciminelli. Abby and Sarah were at a birthday party. Caroline and Molly had invited her to go with them to a movie, but she had declined. The sky was darkly overcast, the air was heavy, and she didn't feel like doing anything. Weeks of holding her breath had taken their toll, and the weather cemented her desire to stay where she was.

The screen door squeaked. Grandma stepped onto the porch and surveyed the yard. "Quiet, isn't it?" She looked up at the sky and sat down on the railing.

She wants to say something.

Elizabeth felt her pulse quicken.

Something she thinks I don't want to hear.

"Been quite a summer, hasn't it?"

Elizabeth glued her eyes to the railing.

"Not the one I had hoped for." Grandma paused. "Especially for you."

She's finally going to ask.

Elizabeth's throat swelled.

Say it, Grandma. "Why won't you go into the water?"

"Why . . ."

Elizabeth's stomach lurched.

". . . don't we go for a bike ride?"

What?

"To the tide pools. Last summer I promised we'd go back, didn't I?"

Elizabeth nodded.

"My calendar's free." Grandma gave her a small smile. "How about yours?"

Elizabeth nodded again.

"Good." Grandma stood up. "I'll just leave a note."

Five minutes later they pedaled onto the road. Elizabeth couldn't help but wonder what had made Grandma suggest doing this. She kept promises, but why today? When the air was thick and it looked like rain?

When she's still not herself?

Elizabeth shook her head. Grandma was *more* like herself, but she wasn't the person who had greeted them in June. There was something wrong, a flatness . . .

The whole summer's gone flat.

They'd gone to the beach every day, but Pap had not reappeared and Elizabeth had done nothing but dig in the sand. They'd been to the usual places—the ice-cream parlor, the pavilion on the Fourth of July, to the lawn fete—but none of it had been the way Elizabeth had imagined it would be. Everything was less colorful, less intense, less . . .

Stop whining. Just be glad nothing awful has happened.

If there hadn't been any wonderful ups, neither had there been any terrible downs. Adam had been sighted once or twice in town, but there had been no further discussion of him at home. There had been one uncomfortable afternoon when Grandma had found Molly teaching Abby how to blow smoke rings. She had grounded them and made them write to their parents, but apart from that, she hadn't even scolded anyone. She had barely raised an eyebrow.

They turned a corner Elizabeth remembered and she cast her mind back. What was missing that had been there last summer?

Laughter.

The things that had driven her crazy a year ago—Sheridan laughter and noise. They still laughed, and no one could accuse the Sheridans of being subdued. But it wasn't the same . . .

"We're here!"

Elizabeth brought her bike to a halt and her mind back to the present. The hedge looked the way she re-membered it, and the maple trees still towered above them . . .

. . . *but the light is all wrong.*

Elizabeth shook her head impatiently.

Just because it was sunny last year, there's no reason it should be today.

They left their bikes under one of the trees and made their way up a gravel pathway to a steep wooden staircase. Elizabeth shuddered.

I forgot about this.

Grandma gave her a quick glance and started up. Elizabeth took a deep breath and leaned forward. She climbed in fits and starts, holding both railings, certain there were more stairs than there had been a year ago. She reached the top and scurried away from the edge.

Oh.

The Japanese garden still looked like a painting. The lawn that sloped toward the stone wall was the same, and the ocean still roared. White spray rose into the air, although it didn't glitter the way she remembered . . .

The rocks are wrong.

She looked to her right.

The two triangular ones. Where are they?

As though she had read Elizabeth's mind, Grandma said, "The pointed rocks were knocked over by the same storm that took down our pine trees." She stepped forward and pointed. "They're down there."

Elizabeth bit her lip. The stones were lying sideways, as though discarded by an uncaring hand. They looked smaller than she remembered.

"Natalie thinks the view's been improved."

Natalie? Oh. The lady that owns this place.

Elizabeth looked past the rocks to the sea.

I don't.

"I'm not sure I agree." Grandma squinted at the water. "But I'm glad *she* thinks so. Because here it is."

True. It's not as though you could move them back . . .

Elizabeth glanced sideways.

Is she trying to tell me something?

"Shall we go below?" Grandma asked. "Or is one set of stairs enough for today?"

Elizabeth hesitated.

What does she want to do?

Grandma's expression was blank.

Heights don't bother her . . .

"Below, please."

Grandma led the way to the second staircase and began the zigzag descent to the tide pools. Elizabeth swallowed past a dry throat and followed her. The wind was less harsh than she remembered, and the trip down less frightening. She stepped through the space between two giant boulders and froze.

It's lovely!

Elizabeth's eyes swept from the high-water mark on her left, past the acorn barnacles to the floor of the enclosure, across the faintly-shimmering tide pools, and up the other side. The flat light of the overcast sky made everything look softly veiled.

It's like being inside a dream . . .

Her eyes retraced their path, slowly this time.

There's a sun star, and a kelp crab . . .

"Fair-sized jellyfish," Grandma called. "Want a look?"

Elizabeth followed the sound of her voice to the edge of a pool and cold prickles raced up her spine.

That's where I fell in!

A spasm knifed her middle. She jerked in a breath and tried to swallow. She hugged her arms to her stomach, but it was no use. Her lunch spattered onto the rocks.

I can't breathe!

She caught a glimpse of pale green seaweed, mermaid's cups against a mottled rock. Another spasm forced her eyes closed and she threw up again.

"Elizabeth?"

A strong arm held her upright. A quiet voice urged her forward. She swayed. Grandma tightened her grip and they took the stairs one at a time.

Go up. Get away . . .

Grandma eased her onto the grass. A seagull screamed close at hand, jerking Elizabeth into an awareness of her surroundings. The breeze was damp and cool, and the sound of the waves on the rocks was rhythmic and soothing.

"Elizabeth?" Grandma squatted down.

She's worried.

Elizabeth blushed and nodded. "I'm O.K."

How could I have done that?

"Maybe I'd better get the car."

"No! Please!" Elizabeth tried to slow her racing heart. "I can ride. Please don't leave me here."

"All right, sweetheart." Grandma smoothed her hair. "When you're ready."

A large, cold drop of rain splashed onto Elizabeth's thigh and she looked up. Dark thunderheads roiled above them.

"I'm ready."

Numbly, Elizabeth crossed the lawn and made her way down the stairs. Rain hissed against the maple leaf canopy, but the ground beneath it remained dry. They wheeled their bikes to the hedge and paused. Sheets of water blew across the puddle-lined road.

"Wait it out?" Grandma suggested.

Elizabeth shook her head and pulled on her helmet. Grandma leaned into the wind and pushed off. Elizabeth pedaled by instinct, aware of only the need to follow the bicycle in front of her.

We're already home?

They put the bikes away, plodded across the soggy lawn, and climbed the steps to the porch.

"Hot showers. You first." Grandma held the door open. "And then I think we should talk."

Elizabeth cast her eyes to the floor and shook her head hard.

Grandma looked out into the rain-soaked dusk. "It was an invitation, not an order." Her words were quiet and sad. "Please go take a shower."

Elizabeth slipped past her grandmother and ran up the stairs. She turned on the water, peeled off her wet clothes, and stepped into the tub.

We shouldn't have gone.

She had wanted to go back for a year, and the whole thing had been a disaster. She'd been disappointed, gotten sick, and been drenched. Worse, she'd made Grandma worry . . .

. . . and now I've hurt her feelings.

She stood under the water until tears no longer ran down her cheeks.

Chapter
Twenty

The road to the beach became blurry and the lump in Elizabeth's throat doubled in size.

Ten days till Dad and Mom know.

Around her, the tribe chattered brightly. Grandma walked to one side of the group, listening with apparent interest but without comment. When they reached the first corner, Petey dropped behind the others.

"The sky is *weird* today, isn't it, Turtle?"

Elizabeth looked up. It *was* weird—dotted with dark clouds that skittered across the sun. The light was bright, and then dim, and then extra bright.

Like a slow-motion strobe light.

"Are you mad at Grandma?"

What?

"No!" Elizabeth squinted at Petey. "Why?"

"You didn't look at her during lunch."

Elizabeth sighed. "I think I hurt her feelings yesterday."

Petey gave her a puzzled look. "Then tell her sorry."

It's not that simple.

"Want *me* to?" Petey asked.

Elizabeth shook her head.

That wouldn't help.

They crossed the stony ground to the sand. The dark clouds had been replaced by larger, paler ones, and the beach was bathed in an eerie, dull light.

"See you later, Turtle." Petey ran toward the water.

Elizabeth fought back her tears and dropped onto the sand. She was sick of making castles, sick of having to confront her failure twice a day, sick of being the only nonswimmer in the family.

I'm sick of thinking about it.

She combed the sand with her fingers, breaking shells as she found them. It wasn't just the water, either. She didn't have other people to talk to. She didn't play volleyball, or football, or soccer . . .

To her right, a few yards off, Molly was laughing with friends. Petey was carrying his pail along the water's edge. She watched him stoop down, poke the sand, and resume walking.

What's he collecting today?

Behind her, someone shouted. She looked over her shoulder in time to see Caroline give Sarah a high five, and Paul chase a ball past the towel that served as the goal line.

Even Sarah plays soccer . . .

Elizabeth watched her cousins and siblings scramble across the sand.

How do they know where the ball will go? And how fast to run?

She snapped another shell in half.

Another Sheridan thing you don't do.

She turned toward the water. The sky had grown darker and the wind was whistling.

When do I get to start feeling as though I really belong?

There was a sudden silence behind her and one high-pitched scream. Elizabeth spun around. Grandma was racing toward the soccer players. Caroline was easing Abby onto the sand, and Andrew was bending over Paul.

He's bleeding!

Jumbled loud calls for cold packs, for towels — strangers' voices. Grandma reached Abby and leaned down. Molly grabbed hold of Sarah and spoke to her sharply. People everywhere, sand flying from bare feet, legs blocking Elizabeth's view.

What happened?

Elizabeth started forward.

Something's wrong . . .

Caroline holding Abby's head. Grandma kneeling

next to Andrew and Paul. Molly with Sarah. No
Adam, of course . . .

Petey?

Elizabeth scanned the shore. No purple bucket,
no royal blue trunks.

He must be with the others.

Her heart thudded. Against her will, she turned
around.

He's not there.

Elizabeth spun back to the water. Sixty feet away,
twenty feet from the shore, a sandy head bobbed once
and vanished.

No!

She fixed her eyes to the spot and flew toward it.
She ran at an angle, faster and faster, her feet barely
touching the sand.

Petey!

She splashed through the shallows, eyes darting,
desperately seeking another glimpse of pink amid
gray. The water reached her thighs and she stopped.

Where?

Her eyes darted back and forth, up and down, but
found nothing. She waded forward, snapping her
head from side to side. If only the water would stop
moving!

There!

Elizabeth threw herself forward and caught a wave
in the face. She pedaled furiously, trying to touch
sand, to find bottom. The water seemed determined

to thwart her, tossing her backwards, buffeting her knees and her shoulders.

Petey!

She jerked her chest from the water, beat her way through another surge, and spotted him. Fighting to stay upright, she turned sideways. Brine spilled from her mouth. She spat, took a deep breath, and lunged. A wave washed Petey a few feet to her right and her fingers grasped only water.

No!

Panic burned her chest. She launched herself against another wave. Her scrambling fingers encircled a wrist and she pulled. She found her feet and grasped Petey under his arms. His skin was warm against her own. Free of the waves, his head lolled sideways.

Petey?

An undertow threatened to tear him from her arms.

Get to the sand!

Elizabeth turned toward the beach and Petey's face flopped into the water. She wrestled his head onto one shoulder and began to walk backwards, legs apart, heels sliding against sand.

Please!

She slipped sideways and another wave slapped her face. Water filled her throat and clouded her mind.

Somebody, help us!

If only she could catch her breath, she could *call* for help. Another wave loosened her grip. She dug her fingernails into Petey's skin and tried to hold her ground. Her stomach rocked with the horizon and she closed her eyes.

"Here! I've got him!"

Elizabeth frantically fought to maintain her hold.

"I've *got* him!" the voice said again. Petey slipped from her grasp, cold water rushed onto her chest, and she staggered backwards.

He's gone.

"Help the girl!"

Elizabeth lifted her head. Someone tall was running through the shallows, Petey limp in his arms.

No!

She sank into the water.

"Can you stand?"

What?

"Let me help you." An arm slipped around her and yanked upward. Her rescuer waded forward, holding her tightly. Elizabeth's screaming lungs longed to expand, and darkness washed through her.

Petey?

"Here you go." Elizabeth was ankle deep in water. A dark-haired woman gripped her shoulders and shook her. "Are you all right?"

Elizabeth tried to step sideways.

"Slow down!" Her rescuer continued to hold her. "Get some air." Elizabeth took two quick breaths and the woman released her. "Good thing you saw him."

With knees barely able to bend, Elizabeth staggered toward a new crowd.

"Petey?" A gust of wind carried Grandma's voice toward her.

"There's the ambulance!"

"Thank God for cell phones!"

A round-bellied man called for people to make way. A triangle opened and it grew suddenly quiet. Elizabeth heard someone retch.

The taller of two uniformed women dragged a stretcher across the sand. "How long was he under?"

"Two minutes," someone replied. "Maybe three."

"More than that," another voice argued. "That girl ran all the way from the rocks."

"He had a pulse when they pulled him out," the first person said. "Started breathing on his own a minute ago."

Breathing?

Elizabeth's knees buckled.

He's breathing?

"Elizabeth?"

Molly's lips were parted and beads of perspiration dotted her forehead. Sarah stood behind her, eyes wide and unblinking, as though she'd awakened from a nightmare.

"Can you get up?"

Elizabeth allowed herself to be pulled to her feet and the three of them walked toward the ambulance.

The others were gathered in a small knot, Abby and Paul holding makeshift bandages to their heads.

"Your *only* job is to drive safely." Grandma had Caroline's chin in her hand. "Molly and Andrew will take care of everything else."

Caroline nodded, and Grandma gave her shoulder a quick squeeze. Then she turned toward Elizabeth and her gray eyes filled with tears.

"Let's go!" Lights were flashing and one paramedic stood ready to close the back door. Grandma ran a finger down Elizabeth's cheek and climbed into the ambulance. No one moved until the siren started to wail.

Andrew took a deep breath. "C'mon, guys."

A silent trip home. Ice and oversized sweatshirts for Abby and Paul. Clothes and Mr. Hum for Petey. Clothes and wallet for Grandma. The Just-in-Case folder with its letters of permission for emergency medical treatment. Directions to the hospital. Keys. Andrew and Abby in the backseat, Caroline and Paul in front. Caroline's white knuckles grasped the steering wheel and the station wagon rolled forward. It jerked to a stop at the end of the driveway, turned right, and disappeared.

"I'm freezing," Molly mumbled. "I'm going to change."

The screen door banged and Elizabeth sank onto the swing.

Is Petey all right?

Her throat narrowed.

"You look cold."

Sarah was holding a comforter toward her. Elizabeth wrapped herself in the blanket and lifted one corner. Sarah crawled beneath it and nestled against her.

"You saved him," she whispered.

Elizabeth was suddenly chest deep in water, fighting for air, struggling to hold Petey.

I didn't save him. I couldn't!

A wave of terror swept through her.

If that man hadn't come . . .

Elizabeth wrenched her mind away from the ocean. "How did Paul and Abby get hurt?"

"They were trying to hit the ball with their heads, and they ran into each other." Sarah shuddered. "It made a *horrible* noise."

Chapter
Twenty-One

A black-and-red truck with blinking yellow lights roared into the driveway and pulled to a stop ten feet from the porch. Adam took the steps three at a time, spied them on the swing, and stopped short.

He's heard.

Sarah freed herself from the blanket, ran toward him, and leapt. Adam caught her and held her tightly. Over her shoulder, he gave Elizabeth a questioning look.

"They're O.K."

Adam's eyes closed, his neck convulsed, and he squeezed Sarah harder.

"The paramedics gave Petey oxygen." Elizabeth cleared her throat and continued in a voice that sounded almost like her own. "They said the hospital was just a precaution."

Adam swallowed again. "Abby and Paul?"

"They needed stitches. They might have concussions." Elizabeth took a quick breath. "But they could talk and they sounded O.K."

The screen door slammed open. "What are *you* doing here?" Molly demanded.

Adam lowered Sarah to the porch. "I just heard what happened."

"Like you *care*, Adam!" Molly spat the words. "Like you *care* if Abby and Paul bleed to death, or if Petey drowns!"

Sarah backed away from the chasm between Molly and Adam.

"Like you *give* a damn, about *anyone* in this family!" Molly's dark eyes blazed. "Don't come around now, pretending you care." Her voice shook. "You've already proven how much you *don't*!"

A muscle rippled along Adam's jaw. He dropped his gaze to a spot near his sister's bare feet, turned, and silently went down the steps. Seconds later, the truck and Adam were gone.

Molly emitted a guttural sound, an angry cross between disgust and despair, and stormed into the house. Sarah looked at Elizabeth with tear-filled eyes and darted through the door.

She's more frightened than I am.

Elizabeth followed her to the front bedroom. Sarah was curled up on her bed.

What will help?

Gingerly, she sat down. Sarah curled herself even tighter.

What would sound normal?

"We should probably wait till they're home to make dinner."

Sarah didn't move.

"But we could make dessert." Elizabeth tried again. "Brownies or something."

"Butterscotch?" Sarah whispered.

Elizabeth nodded. "But let's change first, O.K.?"

"O.K."

Sarah didn't speak again until Elizabeth put the brownies into the oven. "Why did Molly say that, Elizabeth?" Her hazel eyes shimmered. "Why did she *yell* at Adam?"

Elizabeth pictured the fury on Molly's face and the emptiness of her brother's expression.

What can I say that won't make her feel worse?

"Maybe because she was scared," Elizabeth suggested. "Sometimes that makes people say things they don't mean."

A glimmer of hope flickered into Sarah's eyes, but they quickly clouded over. "Sounded to me like she meant it."

Me, too.

Elizabeth tried to smile. "We'll feel better when the others get home."

They rummaged in a drawer for a deck with fifty-two cards and played go fish until Molly abandoned her book and suggested a game of hearts. Fortune smiled upon Sarah, and she grew more cheerful as she fattened her pile.

The station wagon pulled into the driveway at ten after seven. Sarah jumped to her feet and ran onto the porch.

"Oh, Abby—your hair!"

"They had to cut it." Abby grimaced and reached toward her bandage. "Talk about ugly!"

"Hands off!" scolded Andrew. "You, too, Paul."

"But it itches!"

Andrew put his hands on his hips. "You want to have to go *back?*"

Paul snatched his hand from his head.

"How is Petey?" Molly asked.

Caroline nodded. "He's O.K. They bent the rules and we got to see him for a minute." She smiled. "He kept asking for Abby and Paul. He wanted to be sure that *they* were O.K."

Petey's all right.

Heat flooded Elizabeth's chest.

"How long does he have to stay?"

"Just overnight. They're supposed to discharge him by eight."

"Taxi!" Andrew grinned and waved his hand. "Oh, *t-a-x*-i-i-i!"

"We got there, didn't we?" Caroline scowled. "I'll manage to do it again."

"You're a *good* driver, Caro," Abby said loyally.

"I'm hungry," Paul complained.

Details were shared en route to the kitchen. It had taken six stitches to close Paul's wound, Abby had needed nine, and the novocaine had been the worst part. The nurses continued to check Petey's pulse and respirations, but by the time they'd been allowed to see him, Grandma was having a hard time keeping him in bed.

Sandwiches were made and quickly consumed. Caroline was prying the last brownie from the pan when the telephone rang. Petey had spoken to his parents, eaten a few bites of dinner, and fallen asleep watching TV. Grandma was holding up; how were things at home? Caroline assured her that they were all fine, and promised to be at the hospital by quarter to eight. Would it be O.K. if, just this once, they got out the television and rotted their minds? Grandma said yes, and wished everyone a good night.

Molly made popcorn and they turned on a sitcom. *Petey's O.K.*

Elizabeth's eyes lingered in turn upon each of the others.

Or we wouldn't be watching TV.

When yawns began to outpace commercials, they

all stumbled upstairs. Elizabeth gratefully accepted Abby's invitation to sleep in her old bed and said good night. The lights had been off for twenty minutes before it dawned on Elizabeth that she'd been in the ocean.

No, I wasn't.

She pulled the blanket close to her ears.

I've just been dreaming . . .

Elizabeth awoke before dawn and crept up to the Crow's Nest. At seven-thirty, Caroline drove off. Elizabeth dressed and returned to the window. Forty-five minutes later, the station wagon pulled in and Petey climbed out.

He's home.

Elizabeth closed her eyes.

He's walking, and he's talking, and he's home.

She took another look and pushed herself away from the window. The screen door banged and there was a burst of applause in the front room. Elizabeth reached the second floor as Petey stepped onto the landing.

"Hi, Petey," she whispered.

He wavered for a moment. She bent down and reached out, and he scrambled into her arms. Elizabeth stood up, barely able to breathe, reassured by the painful strength of his embrace.

"You O.K.?" she asked softly.

His cheek slid up and down next to hers.

He's not going to let go.

Elizabeth carried him to the steps and eased herself down.

How frightened he must have been!

She gently began to rock back and forth.

He's so warm . . .

She closed her eyes.

Footsteps thundered up the back stairs. "Petey?" Paul shouted. "Your French toast is ready!"

Petey's hold did not loosen.

Has he fallen asleep?

"Petey?" Elizabeth tried to lean back. "Breakfast. French toast."

"Come with me?" His breath warmed her neck.

"Sure."

He climbed down from her lap and held out his hand. She took it, and they went down to the kitchen. Grandma looked up from the stove, smiled gently, and slid Petey's plate onto the table. Her eyes grew bright and she kissed Elizabeth's cheek.

Petey climbed onto a chair and picked up his fork. "*Sit,* Turtle."

The sounds of morning chores echoed above them.

The way they did yesterday. The way they do every day.

Elizabeth shook her head. Except for a redness where the sand had abraded his chin, Petey looked the way he always did.

"Finished?"

Petey nodded and Elizabeth rinsed his plate.

"All set?" Grandma came back into the kitchen wearing her bathing suit. "Then run and get changed."

"No." Petey's mouth became a tight little circle.

"You don't have to swim," Grandma said briskly. "But you can't stay home by yourself."

"I'd like to go to the library," Elizabeth stammered. "Can Petey come with me?"

Grandma studied her for a moment and turned back to Petey. His eyes were wide and the skin below them was white. "All right," she said quietly. "You may go. But this afternoon, you *both* come to the beach." She looked at each of them again. "Understood?"

Elizabeth nodded. Petey finally bobbed his head and Grandma left the room. They remained in the kitchen until the house was quiet. On their way into town, they spoke not at all. On the way home, they spoke only intermittently, and only of the things around them. Elizabeth read to Petey until the others returned.

Lunch was subdued and Elizabeth had to force herself to eat. When Andrew called to them to change, she carried her bathing suit to the bathroom. Petey did not appear in the hall, and she climbed the stairs to the Crow's Nest. He was running a car over hills in his bedspread.

"Petey?"

He did not look up.

"Everyone's waiting."

"I'm not going." His lips barely moved.

"Grandma said that we *have* to."

"I don't care."

Elizabeth's pulse quickened. When Grandma said, "Understood?" she meant business. If Petey didn't change, *now*, there was going to be trouble.

"You can bring your bulldozer." Elizabeth's eyes darted to Petey's car box. "And your airplanes. We'll build an airport, O.K.?"

Petey shifted restlessly and she quickly handed him a bathing suit.

"We'll make *two* airports, and the planes can fly back and forth." She turned around. "Go ahead. I won't look."

Petey's sneakers thumped onto the floor and Elizabeth slowly exhaled. A moment later, he handed her four little airplanes and picked up his bulldozer.

Downstairs, Grandma gave them each a penetrating look. She said nothing, however, and the throng teemed onto the lawn. Petey walked close to Elizabeth, his eyes on the road. When Elizabeth began to hear waves, she glanced down. Petey was noticeably paler and he was holding his truck in both hands. They reached the stony ground and his steps became slower. At the edge of the sand, he came to a stop.

Grandma's watching us.

"C'mon, Petey." Elizabeth pointed. "Let's put the first one over here."

Moving stiffly, he followed her.

"How many runways?" Elizabeth placed the airplanes next to him.

Petey set his truck's caterpillar wheels onto the sand
and deliberately lowered the shovel. "Three."

How long is Grandma going to stand there?

"Where do you want the observation tower?"

"Here." Petey placed a shell next to her and pushed
the bulldozer forward.

Elizabeth began to dig. She reached damp sand
before Grandma stepped past them. From the corner
of her eye, Elizabeth saw her drop her towel, speak
to Abby and Paul, and go into the water. Petey announced the need for a fourth runway and Elizabeth
returned her attention to the tower. They worked
steadily for twenty minutes before Grandma appeared
at the edge of the airport.

"Either of you ready for a swim?" Her voice
sounded strained.

Petey shook his head hard and resumed his exca-
vation. Elizabeth glanced up. Grandma was gazing at
Petey with worried eyes. Petey continued to dig with
brittle intensity, and she finally turned to Elizabeth.

You know I can't!

Elizabeth fixed her eyes on her tower and shook
her head.

"Maybe later."

Grandma withdrew and Petey began a new runway.
During the course of the afternoon, he resisted invitations to swim from Andrew, from Sarah and Molly,

from Caroline, and a second one from Grandma. As they walked home Elizabeth realized that, the whole time, Petey hadn't even *looked* at the water.

Elizabeth was leaning on the kitchen windowsill, gazing at the sky, when Grandma and Petey appeared at the side of the house. They walked to the barn, Petey lagging a yard behind his grandmother. They sat on the log benches for almost ten minutes before Petey abruptly jumped to his feet and ran toward the house. Elizabeth ducked away from the window, hurried into the front room, and accepted Andrew's offer to play chess. Her efforts to focus were unsuccessful, and he beat her soundly three times in succession.

At bedtime, Elizabeth collected her pajamas and brushed her teeth. When she returned to the Crow's Nest, Petey was dragging a red jeep along one of Mr. Hum's arms.

"Want me to read for a while?"

Petey nodded.

"The Rescuers?"

He nodded again. Three pages later, Grandma came up the stairs and kissed each of them. "Good night. Sleep well."

Elizabeth finished the chapter and turned out the light. "Good night, Petey." ·

"G'night."

Below them, a door slammed and Molly yelled, "Give it *back*, Paul!" Grandma said something short and sharp, and the second floor grew quiet. Petey's bed creaked.

"Turtle?"

Elizabeth heard him swallow.

"Let's make a racetrack."

He means at the beach. Instead of swimming.

"O.K.," she whispered.

"Big enough to sit inside. Big enough for both of us."

"Really big," she assured him.

"And nobody else can come in."

A little island, reserved for nonswimmers.

"Especially Grandma."

I can't take sides against Grandma!

The ache in her throat became a bitter liquid.

But I can't abandon Petey . . .

For the first time in almost a year, Elizabeth fell asleep wishing she were someone else.

Chapter
Twenty-Two

"Elizabeth?"

Grandma was standing in the hall doorway. Her arms were folded and her brow was furrowed. Elizabeth snapped her eyes back to the pile of breakfast dishes next to the sink.

"Can we talk for a minute?" Grandma tipped her head toward the back door.

She's not going to take no for an answer this time.

Elizabeth dried her hands, followed her grandmother to the picnic table, and perched herself on the edge of a bench. Grandma sat down across from her and spoke to the dew-covered wood.

"Petey says he's never going swimming again."

Elizabeth cringed.

"The longer he waits," Grandma whispered, "the harder it's going to be."

Elizabeth began to breathe faster.

Don't. Please don't.

"Will you help him?"

I can't!

"He knows that you're as scared as he is."

"He almost drowned," Elizabeth whimpered. "He's got a *reason!*"

"You must have one, too. Even if you don't know what it is." Grandma leaned forward. "Maybe helping Petey . . ."

"I can't!" Elizabeth dropped her face into her hands.

Don't you understand?

Blood screamed in her ears.

I want to, and I can't!

"Grandma?" Paul bellowed from the kitchen window. "Telephone!"

"I'm sorry, Elizabeth," Grandma said softly. "I shouldn't have asked." She stood up. "You'll swim, when you're ready. Petey will, too."

The door banged and Elizabeth sobbed.

All I do is disappoint people.

It had just happened again. And when her parents arrived, it would happen with them.

"Turtle?"

If you ask me why I was crying, I will scream.

"The van is back."

Elizabeth blinked and looked up from the sand.

"Can I come with you?" Petey begged. "Please?"

Elizabeth nodded. "If Grandma says."

Petey scampered off and returned with a grin. "She said O.K."

Elizabeth brushed the sand from the backs of her legs and sluggishly led the way to the van. Near the road, the reeds were still bent where the ambulance had driven over them. Elizabeth shivered.

How much does he remember?

She shook her head. Petey had said nothing—not one word, about any of it—and she wasn't about to ask.

"There's the boat!" Petey pointed. Oily smoke in its wake, the little craft chugged into view. Near the rocks, Pap was struggling to attach the black box to the tripod.

"What is that thing, Turtle?"

"Let's ask when she's done."

They waited patiently. When the box was secure, Pap abruptly turned toward them and swore. "Got no time to baby-sit!"

Petey looked at Elizabeth with frightened eyes.

"He doesn't need babysitting," Elizabeth said firmly. "He'll just watch."

"Never seen a four-year-old *watch*," Pap retorted.

"Petey's five, and he's different." Elizabeth folded her arms. "We both stay, or we both go." She looked pointedly at the cooler, heaped to its brim with collecting bottles.

There was a crackling noise and Pap pulled her

walkie-talkie from her pocket. "He *breaks* anything . . ." She snatched up her clipboard and lumbered toward the water.

"C'mon, Petey."

Elizabeth collected two boxes of test tubes and a box of syringes and settled herself next to the cooler. With a wary glance at Pap's broad back, Petey sat down beside her. "She's *mean*, Turtle."

Elizabeth shook her head. "Just grumpy." Pap was scribbling furiously on the clipboard. "She's worried. Somebody must have dumped something else bad in the water."

Petey's eyes widened as he watched her take the protective cap from a syringe. "How'd you learn *doctor* stuff?"

"Pap taught me." Elizabeth smiled. "If we work fast and do a good job, maybe she'll let you try."

Petey watched closely as she filled and labeled the first set of test tubes. He asked intelligent questions about everything she did, and she did her best to answer. At one point, Elizabeth had the feeling that they were being watched. She looked around, saw nothing, and shrugged.

Probably just Pap keeping tabs on Petey.

Pap glanced at them once or twice but remained at the tripod.

"She needs more hands," Petey whispered.

Elizabeth watched Pap for a moment and grinned. "You're right."

The sun was hot and high overhead when Petey announced that he was hungry. Elizabeth looked at her watch and almost dropped the test tube she was holding. "No wonder!" She scrambled to replace her supplies. "It's after twelve-thirty."

He helped her put things in the van and followed her to the tripod.

"We have to go," Elizabeth said. "But we'll be back later."

Pap squinted at Petey. "You *can* watch." She turned to face the water. "Sorry I barked."

"That's O.K." Petey gave her a small smile. "Turtle said you were worried."

Pap snorted. "Worried ain't the word for it . . ." The walkie-talkie crackled and she raised it to her ear.

"C'mon, Petey." Elizabeth took his hand. "We'll ask about the box later."

"I saw Adam this morning." Caroline's voice was casual.

"Paul, please pass the sandwiches." Grandma turned to Caroline. "Where?"

"Near the road. About ten-thirty." She shrugged. "He was just standing there."

"Nice of him to show a little concern," muttered Andrew.

Abby shrugged. "Maybe he doesn't know what happened."

"But he *does* know," Sarah protested. "That's why he came!"

Everyone turned toward her.

"When did Adam come, Sarah?" Grandma asked.

"When you were all at the hospital."

"Elizabeth?" Grandma tipped her head. "Molly?"

Molly was looking down at her plate. Her cheeks were flushed and her ears were red.

"Before Abby and Paul got home," Elizabeth said quickly. "He . . ." She faltered. "He was worried."

"Then why didn't he stay?" Caroline demanded. "Or call, or come back?"

Molly took a deep breath. "Because I told him not to pretend that he cares about any of us." Her voice dropped. "I said he'd already proven he doesn't."

The air grew still.

"Do you *believe* that, Molly?" Grandma asked very softly.

"I know I shouldn't have said it, but that's how it feels!"

"And the rest of you?" Grandma looked around the table. "Do you think that's true?"

A sea of uncertain eyes looked back at her.

He cares!

Elizabeth's temples pounded.

"I see." Grandma pressed her lips together. "I think you're wrong. All of you. But what I think doesn't matter." She stood up. "I'll be back as soon as I can."

She went through the door to the kitchen, the mudroom door banged, and the station wagon sputtered to life.

"Where is Grandma going?" Sarah asked.

"To Ron's," Petey growled. "To get Adam."

Chapter
Twenty-Three

"I seem to have a talent for making things worse," Molly said bitterly. "So I'll do my part by staying upstairs." She carried her plate from the room.

"Will Grandma *make* him come, Caro?" said Paul.

Caroline hesitated and then shook her head. "I don't think so."

Petey folded his arms. "I hope he says no!"

Abby sighed. "He has to come back *sometime*, Petey."

His eyes narrowed. "Why?"

Abby spread her hands. "He's part of the family!"

"She's right, Petey." Andrew reached for another sandwich. "Even if he's been a jerk lately, he is still our cousin."

Petey continued to scowl.

"Let's play something," Caroline suggested. "How about I Spy? Petey, you start."

They had guessed the pepper shaker, Sarah's shirt, and the dolphin on the fruit plate before the front door banged. Grandma stopped in the archway.

"Adam wasn't there." Her eyebrows drew together. "He asked Ron if he could borrow the truck and said he'd be back around five."

Caroline set down her sandwich. "Back from where?"

Grandma shook her head. "Adam didn't say, and Ron didn't ask."

"There are *two* boats now, Turtle!"

Elizabeth shaded her eyes. The black-and-white boat was farther from shore than it had been, and a small yacht bobbed a quarter mile to its left.

"The new one is fancy," Petey added. "It's got gold on it!"

Brass, anyway.

"Pap?" The radio crackled in her vest pocket. "You got those numbers?"

"Hang on, hang on . . ." She squinted and repeated the sequence into the radio.

Petey pointed to the black box. "What does this do?"

"Big ruler," Pap grunted. "Laser beam measures distance to the boats."

"So you know exactly where each sample was collected?" Elizabeth asked.

Pap nodded. "*Two* teams to keep track of today."

"Whose boat is that one?" Petey pointed to the yacht.

"Belongs to Mr. Checkbook." Pap snorted. "But it's needed. Two flushes last night."

Petey peered up at Elizabeth.

"I'll explain while we work."

"Finish those by four-thirty?" Pap asked. "They're bringing in two hundred more."

Elizabeth's eyes widened. "I'll try . . ."

Petey proved to be an able assistant. Whenever Elizabeth finished one task, he handed her the next thing she needed. "You must be awfully bored," she apologized as she filled another syringe. "But it's going a lot faster than it would by myself."

"I like helping you, Turtle." Petey smiled. "Besides, it's *important,* isn't it?"

She nodded. "Sure is."

They packed up the last test tubes at four-twenty, and Petey hollered, "We're finished!"

Pap checked her watch and gave them thumbs up. *She smiled!*

Elizabeth shook Petey's hand. "Thanks, partner!"

Petey beamed. "Can I help tomorrow?"

Elizabeth looked at Pap.

"He does Sheridan work," she grunted. "He can come back."

"What did she mean, Turtle?" Petey asked as they headed for home.

Elizabeth smiled. "That you did a good job."

"If *you* go," Grandma said, "there's a chance that he'll listen."

Elizabeth winced. If she went, it would be the fourth time she'd ridden to Ron's to deliver something to Adam. The other three times she'd only had to hand over an envelope—his pay from the bait shop, and two letters from his mother—but this would be different.

"Please?"

Elizabeth reluctantly nodded.

"Thank you." Grandma smoothed her hair. "Keep your eyes open. It's rush hour."

Elizabeth shuffled across the lawn, wrestled a bike from the shed, and put on a helmet.

"Hey, Turtle!" Petey called from the porch. "Where are you going?"

"Just on an errand."

If Adam won't come, there's no point in getting Petey upset.

She waved and turned the corner.

Or anyone else . . .

Elizabeth bit her lip. Keeping secrets was so exhausting, so unlike the Sheridans.

So unlike Grandma.

"Let's get it all on the table" was Grandma. A horn blared and Elizabeth swerved toward the side of the road.

Better pay attention, or you'll end up squished.

She shook her head. Grandma didn't need another trip to the emergency room. She paused at each of the stop signs in town and turned the last corner. Ron's black-and-red truck was parked in front of the garage doors.

Adam's back from wherever he went.

Gasoline fumes filled her throat. She coughed and put down the kickstand. "Adam?"

"What?" His muffled voice came from the far side of a dust-covered minivan. Elizabeth followed the sound into the oily darkness of the garage. Adam was squatting next to the right front wheel, tire jack in hand. A dented hubcap lay on the cement next to him.

"Hi."

"Hi." Adam spun the jack and a lug nut came free. "What's up?"

He doesn't sound angry . . .

"You're invited to dinner," she said quickly. "Tonight."

He repositioned the jack. "Why?"

Elizabeth shrugged and stammered, "We haven't seen you all summer."

"What's the hidden agenda?" Adam wrenched the tire free, cupping his hands to keep it upright as it bounced onto the floor.

Hidden agenda? What does he mean?

Elizabeth shook her head.

Adam studied her for a moment. Then he rolled

the tire to the back of the garage, put his hands in his pockets, and recrossed the floor.

He's showered. And shaved.

"Is everyone still coming this weekend?"

Elizabeth nodded.

"Tell Grandma I can't come now, but I'll come Saturday night." He selected a new tire from a rack. "And she shouldn't kill the messenger."

She shouldn't kill the . . . ? Oh. She shouldn't be mad at me because he can't come.

Adam checked his watch and turned back to the van. "You'd better get going."

Elizabeth examined him once more and slowly walked to her bike.

What's different about him?

She put on her helmet, watched Adam hoist the tire into place, and pushed off.

Did he seem older?

She shook her head. *Not exactly.*

The circles under his eyes weren't so deep, and he was cleaner.

Definitely cleaner. But . . .

He was calmer.

She brought her bike to a halt and pictured him again. *Not exactly friendly, but not hostile.*

Detached?

She shook her head again.

I delivered the message, and he's coming on Saturday.

Chapter
Twenty-Four

"Hi, Pap!" Petey chirped. "Happy August!"

Pap yawned, muttered an oath, and yawned again.

Petey tipped his head. "Why are you so tired?"

"Three hours' sleep," Pap mumbled. "My night for stakeout."

"What does *that* mean?"

"Fountain of questions, isn't he?" Pap glared at Petey and Elizabeth grinned.

"What's stakeout?" he persisted.

"Sit in a car. Watch for bad guys." Pap squinted at the water, pointed to the boats, and stepped toward the tripod. "Busy today."

They *were* busy. Elizabeth and Petey labeled one hundred fourteen test tubes before Caroline called them to go home. They left Pap at her tripod, still yawning.

Lunchtime conversation centered around the arrival of everyone's parents and plans for the weekend. Mr. Ciminelli was scheduled to take the family portrait Sunday afternoon.

"Will Adam come?" Sarah asked.

"I certainly hope so," Grandma said evenly.

Caroline looked at Molly, and back to her grandmother. "Does he know when it is?"

Grandma shook her head. "But we can tell him Saturday night." She handed the pickles to Andrew. "He'll be here for dinner."

A restless quiet settled over the table.

"The only other appointment this week is nine-fifteen Thursday," Grandma said briskly. "For Abby and Paul to have their stitches removed."

"Then we can go swimming!" hollered Paul. "Right, Grandma?"

She nodded.

"Finally!" Abby said. "I *hate* not being able to swim!"

Welcome to the club.

Elizabeth looked down at her plate.

I wonder how Petey feels.

She glanced at him. He had peeled apart his sandwich and was examining his peach jam. A moment later, he pressed the two sides together and took a small bite.

Does he miss the water?

Elizabeth sighed. They still hadn't talked about it.

Maybe there aren't words for some things.

So what was she going to say to her parents? Grandma *must* have told Kevin and Karen that she hadn't gone swimming. Why hadn't they said anything on the phone?

Will they pretend they don't know? Will they ask why?

Her stomach lurched.

What if they try to make me?

Her pulse raced for a moment.

Kevin and Karen wouldn't do that . . .

Her eyes watered.

. . . but they'll be so disappointed.

"Turtle?"

She blinked and looked up. The others had left the table. Petey was standing next to her, his eyes filled with concern.

"What were you thinking about?"

She shook her head. "Nothing."

"It wasn't *nothing*," Petey argued. "Nothing doesn't make someone *sad!*" He whirled away and stomped from the room.

Elizabeth followed him. Despite her efforts to apologize, Petey continued to sulk, and when they got to the beach, he chose to remain with the others.

Stay, then!

Little spurts of sand flew from Elizabeth's feet as she marched toward the van.

You're the one who wanted to come.

"Where's your helper?" Pap called.

Elizabeth yanked open a box of syringes. "Taking the afternoon off."

She threw herself into her task because Pap was counting on her, but she found the work tedious, and by midafternoon she had come to the conclusion that the Water Minders were overzealous and quite possibly hallucinating: every one of the eighty-eight test tubes she had labeled looked exactly the same.

"Save the *whales*, maybe," she muttered as she packed up. "Save the *plankton* doesn't quite cut it."

A shadow fell across the box she was taping. "No gun to your head." Pap's chin jutted forward. "Don't want to be here, don't come!"

Now I've got her *upset.*

"Sorry," Elizabeth mumbled.

"You show up tomorrow," Pap grunted, "you might learn something."

Huh?

Pap yawned. "Post office, then shut-eye, for me." She put the laser machine into the van, slammed the door, and drove off.

Elizabeth scowled.

Maybe I won't *come.*

Her feet pounded the sand.

Pap can fill her own stupid test tubes. Whole thing's probably just a waste of time anyway.

The others were putting on sneakers and shaking sand from their towels. She stood to one side of the

group, glowering at a seagull that was plucking something brown from the sand. Another bird tried to
snatch it, and the first bird made a threatening lunge.

Stupid birds.

Petey took a step toward her. She turned her back
and remained where she was until the others had all
reached the road.

Stupid birds, stupid beach, stupid Pap . . .

She kicked a small stone as she walked.

. . . stupid plankton, stupid chemicals . . .

She stomped up the driveway.

. . . stupid test tubes, stupid water . . .

She slammed up the steps to the porch.

"Elizabeth? Petey?" Grandma said. "May I see you
for a moment?"

What now?

Elizabeth glared at her grandmother's sneakers
until the others went into the house.

"Both of you." Grandma pointed to the swing.
"Sit."

Make it a short lecture. Please.

Elizabeth slumped onto one hip facing the far end
of the porch. Petey shuffled toward her and she felt
the swing rock. There were several long moments of
silence.

O.K., Grandma. Get on with it!

The screen door banged softly.

What's the big idea?

Elizabeth looked over her shoulder. Petey's eyes

were almost closed and his arms were tightly folded.
Grandma was gone.

Did the phone ring or something?

Elizabeth checked her watch and turned back to
her end of the porch. 4:48. She sighed and counted
the pinecones on the tree closest to her.

Sixty-eight. So what?

5:03. Elizabeth rolled her eyes.

Sitting here is just stupid.

Her hip began to ache and she shifted her weight.
Petey didn't move.

Sixteen per board, each board four by eight . . .

Elizabeth calculated the number of nails that held
the porch together and looked again at her watch.
5:12.

She's probably forgotten we're out here.

Petey began to swing his feet back and forth.

Stop it! You're making me seasick.

Molly came around the side of the house, trotted
up the steps, and grinned. "You guys had a fight,
didn't you?"

How did you know?

Molly smiled again. "Grandma used to make us
do that all the time."

"Do *what?*" Petey growled.

"Sit there, until we were friends." Molly shrugged.
"Until we laughed."

"Ha, ha." Elizabeth swung her feet to the floor.

Molly looked toward the house. "I wouldn't, if I were you . . ."

"There's nothing funny," Petey pouted.

"You have to *find* something." Molly shook her head. "One time Adam and I sat there for an hour!"

The screen door banged. 5:27.

Terrific. We have now been bored for thirty-nine minutes.

Petey began to bounce.

"Cut it out!" Elizabeth whispered sharply.

"I can't help it," Petey snapped. "I have to *go!*"

"Think about something else."

The bouncing stopped for a moment and then started again.

Oh, brother.

5:41.

"Four score and seven years ago . . ."

Elizabeth shook her head impatiently.

Too easy. Count *the words . . .*

5:54.

We've broken Adam and Molly's record.

"You guys still out there?" Molly spoke through the window. "Dinner's almost ready!"

Petey crossed his legs and bit his lip.

Poor kid . . .

Elizabeth cleared her throat. "You know any jokes?"

He shook his head.

"We have to think of something funny, or you're going to burst."

A moment of silence was followed by a muffled hiss. Petey grew pale.

Too late.

He looked at her with brimming eyes.

"I'm sorry, Petey."

They both looked down. A thin yellow line was wending its way from Petey's sneakers to the edge of the porch. A tear slid down his cheek. Then his shoulders fell and he started to giggle. A moment later, the two of them were doubled up with laughter.

The door creaked. Grandma stepped onto the porch, looked from the swing to the floor, and folded her arms. "Pigheaded, Sheridan *stubborn*. Both of you!"

Elizabeth blushed. Then her eyes met Petey's and they both giggled again.

"The others are still at the table," Grandma said softly. "Go around to the mudroom, and they'll never know." She looked at the ceiling. "I'll take care of the porch."

Petey whispered, "Thanks, Grandma!" and scurried down the steps. Grandma's eyes began to twinkle and Elizabeth scrambled after him.

Chapter
Twenty-Five

"Come on, Petey," Andrew pleaded softly. He glanced at his grandmother. Twenty feet from where they were standing, she was solemnly listening to a friend. Andrew turned back to his brother. "I'll *carry* you."

Elizabeth looked down at Petey and winced.

Don't pressure him, Andrew. It's not fair.

Petey's chin quivered.

"I promise I won't let go."

Petey looked at the water, closed his eyes, and shook his head.

"You're never going swimming?" Andrew put his hands on his hips. "Not *ever?*"

Petey stood very still.

Stop it, Andrew!

The skin around Petey's lips became white and Elizabeth stepped forward. "Coming, Petey?"

He looked down and nodded.

"Thanks a *lot*, Elizabeth!" Andrew turned on his heel.

Elizabeth's neck burned.

You don't know how he feels!

Petey wrapped his fingers tightly around hers and Elizabeth sighed.

Neither do I. Not about drowning . . .

The beach was crowded and noisy, and they picked their way among groups without speaking.

. . . but I know how it feels to let someone down. Someone you care about and look up to.

"Who is *that*, Turtle?"

Elizabeth stared. Pap's van was in its usual place, but the person beside it was dark skinned and slender, hatless and tall. He wore a brightly-colored shirt, and when he lifted the binoculars to his eyes, it was as though a bird had taken flight.

"You show up tomorrow, you might learn something."

Elizabeth shrugged. "Another Water Minder, I guess."

Still holding hands, they walked toward the man. He suddenly laughed, a rich melodious sound that seemed to float in the air.

"Isn't it a *glorious* day?" He raised his arms, closed his eyes, and beamed at the heavens.

Elizabeth blinked and looked around. Sunlight

glittered on the pale sand, the waves were postcard-blue and frosted with white, and the breeze was gentle and cool. Petey squeezed her hand.

It is glorious!

The man's dark eyes sparkled. "You must be Pap's helpers." A row of perfect teeth shone against mahogany skin. "The girl who knows how to keep silence, and the boy with ten thousand questions."

He laughed again and they looked at him in alarm.

"Both good workers, I'm told." He smiled.

"I'm Elizabeth," she stammered, "and this is Petey."

The man placed one hand to his chest and bowed. "And I am DaCosta."

"Do you help the water, like Pap?" Petey asked.

"I am learning." The man laughed again. "There is no one like her!"

That's true enough.

Elizabeth warily examined DaCosta.

But you've got to be one of a kind.

"Come, little ones!" The man raised his arms toward the sea. "Say 'Good day' to our mother!"

Is he going to pray or something?

Elizabeth glanced down. Petey wore a look of joy that threatened to erupt into laughter.

He hasn't smiled that way since . . .

DaCosta finished embracing the ocean and lowered his arms. "Mother returns our greeting." He winked. "And asks for our help."

Elizabeth followed his gaze. Three brimming coolers stood next to the van.

"Lack of sleep has caught up with Pap," the man said. "I assured her we would take care of these."

All of that? He's got to be kidding!

DaCosta laughed again. "Do not be afraid," he said. "The boats are elsewhere today, and six hands will do what four hands could not."

Elizabeth's eyes darted. The tripod was missing, and so were the boats.

"Come *on*, Turtle!" Petey tugged her arm.

When she resisted, he dropped her hand, trotted to the van, and pulled out her supplies. Elizabeth shook her head and followed him. Petey handed her a pair of test tubes and a collecting bottle and looked up at DaCosta.

He's as tall sitting down as Petey is standing up!

Elizabeth filled a syringe.

Some of his hair is gray . . .

"Where do you live?" Petey asked.

DaCosta's eyes twinkled. "Why do you ask?"

Petey tipped his head to one side. "Your words go up and down." He grinned. "Like music!"

DaCosta laughed. "A lovely description!"

"Where *do* you live?"

DaCosta pulled a piece of paper toward him and drew a rapid sketch. "Do you know what this is?"

Petey nodded. "The United States."

DaCosta's pencil moved again. "This island is Jamaica, my home."

Petey handed Elizabeth another collecting bottle. "What is it like?"

Too many questions, Petey . . .

"Parts of it are very beautiful," DaCosta replied quietly.

Two coolers were emptied as he held them spell-bound with descriptions of lush mountains, waterfalls six hundred feet tall, and the ocean around them, turquoise and translucent.

"Do you miss it?" Petey's brow was furrowed.

Elizabeth glanced at DaCosta. The box beside him contained twice as many test tubes as hers, and he had been talking!

"I do." DaCosta nodded. "But it is sometimes necessary for me to travel."

"Why?"

"To learn." He gazed at the water. "That is why I am here."

"What are you learning?"

Petey! That's enough!

DaCosta's eyes twinkled. "Right now, I am learning new ways to ask questions."

Petey's face fell.

"And I am learning from the Water Minders."

Elizabeth raised a test tube and sputtered, "You certainly know how to do this!"

DaCosta laughed. "*This* I have been doing since before you were born."

"Then . . . ?" Elizabeth faltered.

"There are large companies, with many resources,

that dump wastes into the waters near Jamaica. I need to learn how to *document* these events, so the courts may hold them accountable."

Elizabeth turned to Petey. "So he can prove the bad guys did it."

Petey nodded eagerly.

"And I need to learn how to recruit volunteers. People who will do what Pap does." DaCosta waved his hand in a circle. "What you are doing."

"What's a volunteer?"

"Someone who will work for the love of the ocean, instead of for money." He paused. "In Jamaica, finding such people is difficult."

"Why?"

DaCosta smiled sadly. "I told you parts of my island are very beautiful?"

Petey nodded.

"Other parts are very poor." DaCosta held up a test tube. "A man who is hungry has small interest in things he cannot even see."

Elizabeth caught her breath. She had lived in some awful foster homes, but she'd never been too hungry to *learn*, to be interested in things . . .

DaCosta suddenly smiled. "Perhaps you are the answer!" He looked skyward and laughed. "Perhaps I will find the help that I need among children!"

Petey bounced and grinned.

"I see you are restless." In one fluid motion, DaCosta got to his feet. "We have worked well. It

is time to refresh ourselves." He smiled at the water
and pulled his shirt over his head.

Elizabeth glanced to her right. Petey was staring
down at the sand.

"You do not wish to swim?" DaCosta's dark eyes
darted between them. "But you are wearing bathing
suits . . . ?"

Elizabeth mumbled, "We're just getting over sore
throats."

"Ah," DaCosta nodded vigorously. "Here, even in
the hottest months, the water is cold." He gestured to
the waves. "You do not mind?"

They shook their heads and DaCosta loped toward
the water.

"Turtle?"

Elizabeth finished writing a label. "What?"

"You didn't *want* to lie, did you?"

Elizabeth shook her head.

Petey sighed. "I don't want him to know, either."

They worked in steady silence until DaCosta returned, dripping and beaming. "On a day such as this,
it is difficult to believe that someone has poisoned the
water."

He resumed working at his casually rapid pace.

"What does the poison *do*?" Petey asked.

DaCosta considered. "Among the animals that
live in the sea, do you have a favorite?"

"Dolphins!" Petey said quickly. "And octopuses,
and crabs, and . . ."

DaCosta grinned and held up one hand. "One at a time, little one. Begin with the dolphin. Do you know what he eats?"

Petey hesitated. "Fish?"

"Fish." DaCosta nodded. "And are those fish smaller or larger than the dolphin?"

Petey squinted. "Don't animals *have* to eat things that are smaller?"

"Not always." DaCosta smiled. "But most of the time." He reached for the paper on which he'd drawn his map and Elizabeth leaned forward.

He's drawing a food chain.

"Here is your dolphin, and here is *his* dinner, and here is *his* dinner, and here is . . ."

"They keep getting smaller!" Petey sat very still. "Where does it stop?"

"With animals too small to see."

"But what do *they* eat?" Petey protested.

"Plants." DaCosta held up a test tube and raised one eyebrow.

Petey wrinkled his nose. "There are *plants* in there? Too little to see?"

DaCosta nodded.

Petey stared into space, then at the water, and again at the drawing. He began to breathe faster. Elizabeth's chest grew warm and she stole a glance at DaCosta. He saw her and winked. She smiled and turned back to Petey. His dark blue eyes were shining brightly.

He sees it! He sees the whole thing!

"The poison kills the plants."

Petey's grin vanished. "But if the *plants* die . . ." He looked with dismay at the waves.

DaCosta nodded slowly. "Something very small can be very important."

Petey's eyes filled with tears. "Will . . . *everything* die?"

DaCosta wagged one long finger at Petey. "Mother is stronger than that!"

Petey looked at Elizabeth. She glanced at DaCosta and gave Petey a tentative nod.

"But she will never be as she was."

Elizabeth's throat narrowed. "Never?"

DaCosta shook his head. "Even now, she is working to heal herself." He looked at the water. "But that, too, entails change."

"What do you mean?" asked Petey.

DaCosta pointed to the faint scars on Petey's legs. "You were hurt?"

Petey nodded. "I had poison ivy."

DaCosta's eyebrows drew together.

"He touched a plant that makes blisters," Elizabeth explained.

"It itched worse than spider bites," Petey said. "But it's mostly all better now."

DaCosta nodded. "The blisters have healed, and soon your skin will look as it did." He tipped his head. "But you have changed."

Petey wrinkled his nose and DaCosta grinned.

"Will you touch that plant again?"

Petey shook his head vehemently.

"If someone else gets the blisters, will you understand how it feels?"

Petey nodded.

DaCosta smiled. "Then you have changed."

Petey looked at the water. "How has the ocean changed?"

"The plants that have died are gone. Some of the animals that ate them will die, but others will not."

"Why?" Petey's brow grew furrowed. "Don't they *have* to eat?"

DaCosta nodded. "But some of them will find other plants."

"E-*liz*-a-beth!" Molly called. "*Pe*-tey! Time for lunch!"

DaCosta stood up and smiled. "It has been a pleasure."

"We'll come back," Petey assured him.

DaCosta shook his head. "I will finish these, and then I must go."

You're leaving?

"Are you going back to Jamaica?" Petey said sadly.

"First to Virginia, *then* home." DaCosta turned to Elizabeth and held out his hand. "Good-bye, Elizabeth-Turtle!"

She reached forward. His grip was gentle yet firm.

"Good-bye, Petey." Again, he held out his hand. Petey shook his head and wrapped his arms around his waist. DaCosta's eyebrows rose. Then he smiled and hugged him back.

"I will not forget this morning!" He laughed. "Or either of you."

"We won't forget *you*," Petey promised. He turned back to wave three times before they reached the road.

"I really liked him, Turtle."

Elizabeth smiled. "Me, too."

Chapter
Twenty-Six

Whooping loudly, Paul and Abby ran toward the water. They splashed through the shallows and dove, surfaced, and gave each other high fives.

At least they're back in the water.

Elizabeth looked down. Petey was gazing at the far end of the beach.

Maybe Andrew was right. Maybe I shouldn't let him go with me.

"Come on, Turtle."

Elizabeth stumbled after him. Petey's not swimming was a lot worse than her not swimming. He had *loved* the water. She had only wanted to please her parents and Grandma.

That's not the whole truth . . .

Elizabeth sighed. It hadn't *just* been wanting to please. She'd wanted to have something in common with the rest of the family.

"Pap is yawning again."

Another stakeout?

"Hi, Pap!" Petey trotted the last few yards to the van. "Were you watching for bad guys last night?"

Pap nodded. "Know who now. Just got to get it on tape."

Elizabeth's eyes grew wide. "You know who is dumping?"

Pap nodded again. "Bad news is, they know we're watching."

"They do?" said Petey.

"Led us on a goose chase last night." Pap pulled off her baseball cap, ran her fingers through her hair, and replaced it. "Headed for the marina, spotted us, and doubled back."

Just like on TV!

"Won't happen again, though," Pap said smugly.

Despite repeated questions from Petey, she would say nothing more. They labeled a cooler full of test tubes and headed for home. Midway up the beach, a shout drew Elizabeth's attention to the bank of reeds near the road.

The reeds are standing up again!

Her eyes darted back and forth, but she could no longer tell where the ambulance had crossed them.

"What are you looking at, Turtle?"

"I thought I saw something," she said quickly. "But I was wrong."

Friday dawned bright and clear. The breeze was strong, the sky was blue, and the sun cast a friendly primrose glow on everything. The walk to the beach was invigorating and full of cheerful chatter. The van was in its usual place, and Elizabeth and Petey hurried toward it. When they had caught their breaths, Pap handed each of them a paper cup.

What's this for?

Elizabeth traded puzzled glances with Petey and looked back to Pap. She was beaming.

"Champagne time!" She saluted them with a bottle of ginger ale. "We got 'em!"

Petey hopped in place. "You got the bad guys?"

Pap nodded and poured. "Ironclad! On tape and on paper." She finished pouring and raised her cup. "Here's to a *zillion* dollars in fines!"

Elizabeth grinned.

"Sprizzles!" Petey lowered his cup and rubbed his nose. "How did you do it?"

Pap shook her head. "Wish you could have been there!"

They sat down at her feet.

"Where?" Petey asked.

"Everywhere!" Pap laughed and clapped a hand against her thigh. "*Sixty* of us!"

Is she kidding?

"Please tell?" Petey begged. "Please, Pap?"

She nodded. "You've earned the right to the story."

Petey grinned and bounced.

"Remember I told you they knew we were watching?"

They nodded.

"We knew we wouldn't get anywhere trying to *follow* them." She chuckled. "So we set up a relay."

Elizabeth's eyebrows drew together. "You took turns?"

"Used the radios." Pap pulled a yardstick from the van and leaned forward to sketch in the sand. "Here's the factory, and here's the marina."

"How did you know which way they would go?" Elizabeth asked.

"Didn't. Staked out *all* the routes." Pap sketched again. "Soon as Joe spotted the truck, he got on the radio and told us all what to look for."

"Then what?" Petey asked.

"Tricky part was the marina," Pap admitted. "Pitch black. More'n two hundred boats." She grinned wickedly. "And a couple dozen Water Minders."

"Did you *see* the bad guys?"

Pap nodded. "Arrogant little cuss drove the truck." She scowled. "*Whistled* while he pulled barrels down!"

Petey looked at Pap with wide eyes and she nodded again.

"Got them down the dock and onto a launch.

Little thing. Rode low in the water once the barrels were on." Pap grimaced. "*Stupid* on top of it all. Served 'em right if they'd drowned."

Elizabeth shivered.

"Got the whole thing on tape," Pap added with satisfaction.

"But how?" Elizabeth sputtered. "You said it was dark!"

"Infrared film." Pap grinned. "Works with heat instead of light."

Cool!

"Then what?" Petey pleaded.

"Boat pulled off." Pap's voice dropped. "Not a light on, engine near silent."

"Did you follow it?" Petey breathed.

Pap shook her head and reached for the yardstick. "Our boats were already out there." She poked the sand in six places. "Each one with a camera."

Elizabeth held her breath as she watched Pap trace the boat's route.

"Got to here and cut the engine." Pap squinted at the sand. "Cameras rolling from both sides, they hauled the first barrel onto the stern." She pressed her lips together.

"Did they push it in?" Petey asked.

Pap shook her head. "Pulled the plug and just let the . . ." She looked at Petey.

"Bad stuff?" he supplied.

". . . bad stuff," Pap agreed, "into the water."

Petey's brow grew furrowed. "You couldn't *stop* them?"

"Had to get it on film first," Pap explained. *"Then the fireworks could begin!"* She leaned back and chuckled with glee.

"Fireworks?" Petey asked.

"You know the man with the fancy boat?" Pap pointed to the spot where they'd last seen the yacht. "He's got a few pals in the Coast Guard." She grinned. "We finished taping and grabbed the radios." She waved her arms. "And two cutters came out of no-where, with search lights and bull horns!"

"And caught them?" Petey hollered.

"Caught 'em good!" Pap nodded. "Brought 'em onto the dock in handcuffs!"

Elizabeth and Petey grinned.

"Gave 'em a Water Minders welcome, we did. Never *heard* such noise." Pap shook her head. "Like a party, it was!"

Chapter Twenty-Seven

Elizabeth cut two more beans and looked up.

It's going to be lemon.

Grandma set down a measuring cup and took the lemon extract from the cupboard.

All of Adam's favorites.

Elizabeth sighed against a tight chest.

I just hope he comes.

There was no reason to think that he wouldn't, but watching preparations for tomorrow night's dinner was making her stomach ache.

"Hi, Grandma!" Paul bounced into the room. "Hi, Elizabeth!"

Grandma smiled. "You look happy, Paul."

He pointed to the top of the dish cupboard. "I can have my rocket back, right? When Mom and Dad get here?"

Grandma nodded.

"Dad said he'd do it with me, right after dinner."

Elizabeth bit her lip and pictured her parents.

Never mind about Adam. What about Dad and Mom?

Elizabeth couldn't wait to see them—she even wanted to hug them—but she dreaded having to face them.

You'd better think of something. They'll be here tomorrow.

"Elizabeth?"

Paul had disappeared and Grandma was putting the cake pans into the oven.

"How do you feel about Adam's coming?"

Elizabeth's chest tightened a notch further.

Grandma carried the mixing bowl to the sink. "You don't have to tell me if you don't want to."

Elizabeth shook her head. "That's not it, Grandma. I'm just not sure how I feel."

Grandma ran some water into the bowl. "Some hopeful, some scared?"

Elizabeth nodded.

"I think that's pretty much how all of us feel. We've all missed Adam. But I think his not being here has been hardest on you."

What about Petey? And Caro? And you?

"You two were at odds most of last summer, and Adam hasn't been himself since the fall. You haven't had a chance to know Adam the way the rest of us do."

Elizabeth looked down at the beans.

"I don't know why he's coming tomorrow."

Grandma paused. "But I know I love him, and I know I love you."

Elizabeth looked up into warm blue gray eyes.

"I didn't want you feeling hopeful and scared by yourself."

Elizabeth managed a small smile. "Thanks."

"Now, if you would get going . . ." Grandma pointed to the cutting board. "Dinner is only an *hour* from now." She winked and went down the steps to the mudroom.

Elizabeth grinned and began to slice with a vengeance.

Petey moved one of his starfish a half an inch to the left, sighed, and moved it back. Elizabeth closed her book.

Something's really bothering him.

He turned a moon snail shell around, leaned on the trunk, and rested his chin on his arms. "I don't want tomorrow."

Because Adam is coming?

Elizabeth tried to sound casual. "How come, Petey?"

"Abby says Dad's gonna *make* me go swimming." His eyes filled with tears. "And if he does . . ." His voice broke. ". . . I'm running away!"

Oh, Petey.

Elizabeth sat down beside him. He scrambled onto her lap and buried his face in her chest. "I could *see* the light, Turtle." He began to breathe faster. "But I couldn't . . ." He choked.

Elizabeth put her arms around him. "Do you remember what happened?"

She felt him shake his head and then nod. "I was trying to find scallops." He took a quick breath. "And the ones on the sand were all broken, so I started wading." He shuddered. "And I stepped on a *big* one, and I tried to get it . . ."

Elizabeth drew him closer. "Did a wave come?"

His chest heaved sharply. "It *pushed* me," he sobbed, "and it wouldn't let *go!*"

"I'm sorry, Petey," Elizabeth whispered. "I'm so sorry."

The shadows lengthened and still he cried.

Should I get Grandma?

Petey finally grew quiet, but he continued to tremble. Twilight became dusk.

"Elizabeth?"

Someone touched her shoulder and she jerked her head up. The light was dim, and her arms and legs were covered with goose bumps. Petey's cheek was warm against her chest.

"I'll put him to bed," Grandma whispered.

Thank you.

By quarter inches, in waves of burning pain, Elizabeth unfolded her legs and straightened her arms. Grandma tucked in Petey's blanket, recrossed the floor, and ran a hand down Elizabeth's cheek. "Are you O.K.?"

She nodded and awkwardly got to her feet.

"We called you for dinner. Sarah said you were both asleep." Grandma glanced toward Petey's bed. "How about something now?"

Elizabeth shook her head. "I'm not really hungry, Grandma."

"Some juice, at least," Grandma said. "And a hot bath."

Elizabeth allowed herself to be led to the bathroom. She leaned against the sink and watched the water rise in the tub.

"In you go." Grandma turned off the taps. "When you're finished, please come to my room."

Elizabeth spent fifteen minutes soaking, put on her pajamas, and walked down the hall. Grandma wrapped a quilt around her shoulders and handed her a steaming cup of raspberry-colored liquid.

"Thank you." Elizabeth took a small sip. "This is good. What is it?"

"Cranberry juice and chamomile tea." Grandma sat down, rested her elbows on her knees, and twisted her wedding ring. "What happened upstairs?"

Elizabeth shook her head. She couldn't remember.

"Why was Petey in your lap?"

Elizabeth closed her eyes.

The starfish. The moon snail . . .

"He's scared that Uncle Tim will *make* him go swimming."

"What did he say?"

"That if he does, he'll run away."

Grandma's eyes shimmered.

"I wouldn't let him, Grandma. Not for real."

Grandma shook her head. "I'll talk to Tim," she said softly.

Thank you.

"And to Kevin." Grandma mustered a very small smile. "No running away for you either."

Elizabeth blushed.

Grandma pointed to the cup. "All of it, before you go up?"

"Promise."

Grandma kissed her cheek. Elizabeth listened to her footsteps go down the stairs, drained her cup, and tiptoed up to the Crow's Nest. The faint light of a crescent moon outlined the room. Her bed creaked as she slipped under the blanket.

"Turtle?"

I thought you were asleep.

"What, Petey?"

"I can't *really* run away, can I?"

"It's probably not such a good idea," Elizabeth admitted.

The silence resumed and lasted nearly ten minutes.

"Turtle?" There was a pause. "How do you stop being scared?"

Elizabeth's eyes filled with tears. "I don't know, Petey."

"When you came to get me, were you scared?"

"Really scared."

"Of the water?"

Elizabeth swallowed hard. "That you were going to drown."

Petey slipped from his bed and padded across the floor. Elizabeth lifted the blanket and he curled up beside her. Moments later, they were both asleep.

"Petey?" Elizabeth called. "They're here."

He pulled Mr. Hum from his pillow and wrapped his arms around him. Elizabeth sighed and turned back to the window. Andrew, Abby, and Sarah were bouncing between their parents, hugging and laughing and talking thirty words to the dozen. Caroline and Paul joined the fray, and were quickly followed by Grandma and Molly.

"C'mon, Petey. Let's go down."

He shook his head hard.

"Sheridan stubborn" is right!

Elizabeth got to her feet.

"Stay, Turtle?"

"Petey?" his mother called. Two sets of footsteps came up the stairs.

"Hi, Aunt Rachel," Elizabeth said quickly. "Hi, Uncle Tim."

Aunt Rachel looked at Petey as though to memorize

him. Then she turned to Elizabeth and pulled her close. Uncle Tim's eyes grew bright and he hugged her, too.

"Hello." Aunt Rachel gently took Petey's face in her hands. His eyes remained glued to his father.

Please . . .

Uncle Tim shook his head. "You don't have to swim, Petey."

He looked at his mother. She shook her head, too. "You don't have to swim."

Petey threw himself into his mother's arms. Uncle Tim stepped toward them and Elizabeth quietly crept down the stairs.

Thank goodness.

Feeling dizzy, she pushed open the door to the porch.

They're here!

Elizabeth's heart zigzagged as she watched her parents climb out of the car.

Dad and Mom!

Something warm rushed into her ears. Paul and Caroline raced across the lawn. Feeling suddenly shy, Elizabeth clumsily trotted after them.

"Hello, sweetheart!" Karen opened her arms. Elizabeth breathed in her mother's clean scent and felt her legs tremble.

Hello, Mom!

Karen tightened her grip and released her. Kevin's eyes twinkled above his Sheridan smile. "How's my favorite mathlete?" He wrapped his arms around her and squeezed.

I've missed you!

"Mom! Dad!" Paul hollered. "You ready to swim?"

Elizabeth let her arms fall.

"Give us a *minute*, Tiger!" Kevin groaned. "We'd like to say 'Hello' first." He grinned and gave his mother a hug.

"Grown-ups always take forever," Paul grumbled.

."Then help! Grab the suitcases," his father suggested. "How *are* you, Mom?"

"Fair to middling." Grandma winked and turned to hug Karen. Petey came onto the porch with his parents and a new round of hugs began.

Now, while they're busy . . .

Elizabeth slipped through the screen door and flew up to the Crow's Nest. Then she stood still and scowled.

That was stupid.

She looked at her watch. How much time had she bought herself? Five minutes? Certainly no more than ten.

Get on with it.

She wrestled herself into her bathing suit, sat at the top of the stairs, and listened to the rise and fall of voices below her. A door opened.

"Elizabeth?" Karen called. "Ready?"

Has Grandma talked to them?

"Coming."

No one spoke until they reached the porch. The others teemed onto the lawn and Karen gently led her to the swing. Kevin sat on the railing.

"We hear you haven't spent much time in the water," he said quietly.

Don't tease, Dad! It isn't funny.

"It happened the first morning, didn't it?" Karen put an arm around her. "When you got so cold."

Elizabeth nodded.

Kevin leaned forward. "What frightened you?"

Elizabeth shook her head.

"Was it the waves?" Karen asked.

I don't know!

Elizabeth burst into tears.

"All right, sweetheart," Karen pulled her close. "We won't press you."

"I'm sorry," she sobbed.

Kevin crouched beside the swing. "You went into the water when you needed to." He rubbed her cheek. "There's no way to thank you for that." He hesitated. "But if you never want to go swimming, that's O.K."

Elizabeth's eyes filled again. "No, it's not."

Karen tipped her head. "Why?"

"Because everyone *else* swims!"

Karen looked at Kevin and back to Elizabeth. "Do you think we love Paul any less because he doesn't play chess?"

Elizabeth shook her head.

"Then why would we love you any less if you don't swim?"

That's different! Chess isn't important.

"We're sorry it's worried you so much." Karen gave her a squeeze and offered her a towel. "Here. Mop up." She smiled.

Elizabeth dried her eyes.

At least I don't have to worry about telling them anymore.

"Come on." Karen stood up. "We want to hear all about the dumping."

"And this friend of yours — Pap?" Kevin asked. "Who is she? The James Bond of South Wales?"

Elizabeth pictured Pap's barrel-like figure, her oversized vest, and her baseball cap, and smiled. "Not exactly, Dad."

Chapter
Twenty-Eight

He's not coming.

Elizabeth set down her plate and looked at her watch. It was 6:17.

He knows dinner's always at six.

Uncle Steve forked the last steak from the grill and Elizabeth stole a glance at his mother. Grandma was cutting Petey's meat. Over the quiet conversation around her, Elizabeth heard a familiar rattle.

He's here!

Adam backed Ron's truck around to face the road and turned off the ignition.

Thank goodness.

Aunt Elena crossed the lawn. Adam gave his mother a quick hug and said something brief. As he walked toward them, Elizabeth examined him carefully. He was wearing a dark green polo shirt, clean jeans, and new sneakers. His hands were spotless.

"Rare, Adam?" His father pointed to the steak platter.

Adam came to a halt between the picnic tables and shook his head. "Nothing, thanks. I'm not staying."

What?

"I just came to tell everyone that I'm leaving tomorrow."

"Leaving?" Uncle Steve repeated.

"For Montana."

"Montana?" Aunt Elena gasped.

Uncle Steve set the serving fork on the platter. "What's all this about, Adam?"

"I've changed my mind about going to college this year," Adam said evenly. "I've decided to do some work for the environment instead." He pulled a brochure from his pocket and handed it to his father. "Conservation work, in national parks. They have programs in Oregon, Maine, and Montana." He shrugged. "I picked Montana."

Elizabeth longed to look at the others, but she couldn't take her eyes from Adam.

"Why this sudden interest in the environment?" his father asked quietly.

Adam shrugged again. "I just felt like doing something different from school for a while. Something that mattered."

"How long will you be gone?" Aunt Elena had grown pale.

"They required a six-month commitment."

Six months!

"What about college?" his father asked.

"I asked them to defer my acceptance for a year." Adam lifted his chin very slightly. "And they agreed. I didn't even lose the deposit."

"What will you do for money?" his mother demanded.

"They cover insurance and provide food and lodging." Adam took a deep breath. "To get there, I'm using the money I'd saved for the kayaking trip."

"You seem to have thought this through," Uncle Steve said.

Why isn't he angry?

"Thought it through?" Aunt Elena protested. "The first we *hear* of it, and he's leaving tomorrow?" Her voice squeaked. "You can't *do* this, Adam!"

"I signed an agreement." He pulled another piece of paper from his pocket and offered it to his mother.

She waved it away. "Tell him, Steve!"

Uncle Steve looked at the contract. "He not only can, Elena, he *must*." He refolded the paper and handed it back to his son. "Legally, Adam is an adult. His signature is binding."

Aunt Elena's black eyes glittered brightly. "Just like

that!" She threw up her hands. "Just like *that*, our son is going off—to who-knows-where? In Montana!"

"He's got a level head, Elena. And he knows how to reach us." Uncle Steve put his hands on her shoulders.

She wrenched herself free. "A level *head?* Going halfway to Alaska on no minutes' notice?"

"It's my fault, Mom." Molly's cheeks became flushed. "It's because of what I said. The day everything happened."

"No, it isn't, Molly." Adam pointed to the date on the contract. "I'd already decided."

Uncle Tim cleared his throat. "What will you be doing, Adam?"

"Whatever's needed." He shrugged. "Building bridges, clearing trails, planting trees."

"What are the living circumstances like?" asked Kevin.

"Cabins. Outhouses."

"What's an outhouse?" Paul whispered to Caroline.

"Bathroom outside," she whispered back.

"No telephones," Adam added.

His mother put both palms on the table. "And how is your family supposed to get in touch with you?" She trembled as she pushed herself to her feet. "By carrier pigeon?"

"They deliver mail once a week." Adam put his hands in his pockets. "In an emergency, they send someone out with a message."

His mother stared at him. Then she abruptly

turned and walked away. A moment later, the screen door banged.

"I promised Ron I'd finish two jobs, and I've got some packing to do." Adam's eyes swept the group. "My bus leaves at 7:20 tomorrow morning, so I'd better get going."

This isn't happening.

"Here's the address, and all that." Adam tucked an index card under a pepper shaker, nodded once, and headed for the driveway.

Without even giving his parents a hug?

Petey was staring at his plate and Sarah was looking at her mother. The others were all watching Adam. The truck door slammed softly and Elizabeth's eyes jerked toward the sound.

Don't go! Not like that!

Her heart thudded as she watched the truck turn onto the road.

Now what?

"Steve?" Karen got to her feet and looked toward the house.

Uncle Steve followed her gaze and nodded. "Thank you. Right now, you're a much better bet."

Karen crossed the lawn and climbed the steps.

"He could've eaten dinner," Andrew mumbled.

"His loss, Andrew." Uncle Steve offered the group a tight smile and sat down. "It all looks delicious. Come on, everyone." He raised his fork in his mother's direction and speared a slice of cucumber.

How can he eat?

"It's a little hard to pretend that Adam wasn't here, Steve," Kevin said. "That he didn't just announce he'll be gone for six months."

Uncle Steve's head snapped up. "And what am I supposed to *do*, Kevin?" His eyes shimmered. "If it were Caro, what would *you* do?"

"If I were going," Caroline said quietly, "I'd be really scared."

"Adam didn't look scared," Sarah said.

"But I bet he is." Molly sighed. "Especially having to meet people." She turned to her father. "You know what he's like, outside of the family."

Uncle Steve nodded.

"If you were scared, Caro," Kevin asked, "what would help?"

She broke a carrot stick into pieces. "A proper good-bye, I suppose."

"Adam didn't give us much chance for *that*," Molly said glumly.

He's not gone. It's not too late!

Elizabeth's heart pounded as she slipped from her place. "Be right back." She trotted around the side of the house to the mudroom and up the steps to the kitchen.

Bus station, bus station . . .

She flipped the pages of the thin South Wales directory.

There.

She copied the number, made a list of questions to ask, and dialed. Three minutes later, she handed a piece of paper to Kevin.

"What's this?"

"It's the only bus he could be taking," Elizabeth explained. "It leaves at 7:20 and goes to a city." She swallowed. "We could say good-bye in the morning . . ."

Kevin turned to his brother. "How about it, Steve?"

Uncle Steve glanced around the table and let his eyes come to rest on his mother.

"You need to eat something, Petey," Grandma said softly. She handed him a roll and watched him take a small bite.

She knows Uncle Steve's looking at her. Why won't she look back?

"Please, Dad?" Molly said. "I've been mad at him the whole summer. I don't want him to go without a chance to make up."

"He may not want us." Her father picked up the index card. "He's said good-bye."

"We could *try*, couldn't we, Uncle Steve?" Abby pleaded.

Uncle Steve examined the faces around him and nodded.

"The family portrait!" Caroline sat up very tall. "Grandma? Do you think . . . ?"

Grandma turned her spoon over twice. "Alberto gets up early." She folded her napkin. "I'll call, if you'd like."

"Let's give Adam a good-bye present!" said Paul.

"How about the stuff we got him for graduation?" Andrew suggested. "He never opened anything."

"Perfect, Andrew!" Aunt Rachel beamed. "Congratulations, good-bye, and good luck!"

"Can we make him some brownies or something?" Abby said. "To eat on the way?"

Grandma nodded.

"What's going on?" Karen asked from the porch. "Are we having a party?"

"A *good-bye* party," Paul hollered. "For Adam!"

Karen's eyebrows drew together. "The guest of honor appears to be missing."

Caroline laughed. "Not *now*, Mom. In the morning, at the bus station!"

Aunt Elena came through the screen door, red eyed and clearly confused by the cheerful faces before her.

"Good news, Elena." Karen put an arm around her shoulders and smiled. "You'll get to say good-bye after all."

Chapter
Twenty-Nine

"Mom?" hollered Paul. "How do you spell 'fantastic'?"

Karen spelled it and he shouted his thanks. Elizabeth reread what she'd written and winced. *Dear Adam, I hope you like Montana.*

Elizabeth bit her lip. She had been trying for twenty minutes, and she couldn't think of anything better to say.

"Everyone put something in?" Uncle Tim asked.

There was a chorus of affirmative replies. Elizabeth sighed, added her name to what she had written, and put it into the envelope.

"Wait, Uncle Tim!" Paul said. "I want to draw him a picture."

"No problem!" He turned to his mother. "You finished, Mom?"

Grandma shook her head. "I think, perhaps . . ."

She looked at the floor for a moment and went through the archway. When she returned, she slipped something small and metallic into the envelope.

She didn't write anything. And she's not talking . . .

Elizabeth followed her grandmother to the kitchen. Caroline and Abby were wrapping brownies in foil. "Think they'll be O.K. like this, Grandma?" Caroline asked. "If we put them on top?"

Grandma nodded and carried the pan to the sink. "They smell delicious."

"I still have to write something." Abby followed Caroline to the front room.

"Grandma?" Elizabeth ran a finger along the edge of the counter. "Are you O.K.?"

Her grandmother reached for the detergent. "I'm O.K."

You don't look like it.

Grandma's voice was soft. "Thanks for asking."

Elizabeth nodded and made her way to the second floor. She had started up the steps to the Crow's Nest before she remembered that the sleeping arrangements had all changed.

Crow's Nest: Andrew, Petey, and Paul. Back room: Aunt Elena, Aunt Rachel, and Mom. Middle room: Uncle Steve, Uncle Tim, and Dad. Front room: Caro, Molly, Abby, Sarah, and me . . .

She sighed.

. . . and Grandma, all by herself.

"I don't see him," Caroline said anxiously.

"It's only five to," Kevin assured her. "And he probably already has his ticket."

They were waiting near a blue-and-silver scenic cruiser. It was parked beneath a rusty sign bearing the number "8" and the word "outbound."

"*Buon giorno, buon giorno!*" Mr. Ciminelli hailed them from the corner. Andrew hurried toward him and relieved him of a camera bag the size of a pup tent. "Thank you!"

"You're a good sport, Alberto!" Uncle Tim set his tripod against the building. "You should charge extra for portraits at dawn."

Mr. Ciminelli shook his head. "Been up for hours." His eyes twinkled and he wagged a finger at Grandma. "But you're making a habit of changing appointments!"

He means last year . . .

Elizabeth stole a glance at Kevin and Karen.

. . . the day I said I wanted to be part of the family.

Grandma gave Mr. Ciminelli a small smile. "We'll try to do better, Alberto."

"There's Adam!" Abby whispered.

Mr. Ciminelli spun around. "The traveler has arrived!" He beetled toward Adam and pumped his hand. "My felicitations, Adam! The scenery in Montana is *truly* magnificent!"

Adam hesitantly looked from Mr. Ciminelli to the others. "Thanks, Mr. C."

He looks as though he hasn't slept.

"Now where . . . ?" Mr. Ciminelli looked around, nodded vigorously, and pointed to the bus. "Not beautiful, perhaps, but appropriate." He waved the others toward him. "Come, come!" He squinted at the sky, muttered something about the light, and reached for his camera bag.

"Good morning, Adam." Aunt Elena kissed his cheek and stepped back to look at him.

What is he thinking?

"Come!" Mr. Ciminelli pulled Adam's duffel bag from his shoulder and set it on the ground. "In the middle, on one knee." He moved Adam into place. "Petey, right here. Sarah and Abby, there, please." He shook his head. "No, better here . . ."

Elizabeth took her place and looked at her watch. Before the second hand had completed one revolution, the sixteen of them had been arranged to Mr. Ciminelli's satisfaction.

Good thing he's talking. No one else is.

"Good, good . . ." Mr. Ciminelli peered through the camera. "And now smiles . . ." A moment later he stood up and frowned. "You wish to ruin my reputation?" He spread his arms wide. "My unbroken string of Sheridan *masterpieces?*"

Several people giggled nervously.

"Then SMILE!" He ducked down and took four pictures in rapid succession. The bus roared and black exhaust filled the air. Mr. Ciminelli mopped his forehead with a spotted handkerchief and beamed. "Just in time!"

The group broke formation and milled around quietly. Grandma stepped toward Mr. Ciminelli. "Thank you, Alberto."

He kissed her hand. "My pleasure, Martha." He gave his camera an expert twist and freed it from the tripod.

"Here, Adam." Abby thrust a black nylon bag toward him.

"What is it?"

Abby wrinkled her nose. "Stuff for the trip. From everyone."

Adam accepted the bag and mumbled, "Thanks."

The announcer's voice crackled above them and Adam shouldered his duffel.

"Adam?" Molly stepped toward him and spoke very softly. He nodded and turned to his mother.

"Bye, Mom."

Aunt Elena's eyes filled with tears and she took his face in both hands. "*Vaya con Dios,*" she whispered and kissed him.

"Bye, Dad." Adam offered his father his hand. Without saying a word, Uncle Steve shook it.

"Bye, everyone." Adam quickly walked to other side of the bus. Elizabeth followed his sneakers until they disappeared.

No one's talking . . .

The tribe migrated toward the building. A strident horn blared and Grandma and Mr. Ciminelli hurried out of harm's way. The bus slowly moved backwards. Its dark windows glinted as they caught the early morning light. Gears shifted and the cruiser lumbered onto the street.

He's gone.

"So quiet, everyone!" Mr. Ciminelli scolded them. "Do you have a funeral to attend?"

Feet shuffled restlessly and Uncle Tim shrugged. "Good-byes aren't easy, Alberto."

"Good-bye to another country, perhaps!" Mr. Ciminelli puffed. "Good-bye to be a soldier, to fight in a war! Good-bye to freedom, to *honor!*" He waved his arms. "These are reasons for sadness!"

But . . .

"But good-bye to Adam?" he sputtered indignantly. "Who is going off to give service, to *help?*" He shook his head and muttered something in Italian. "My friends the Sheridans have gone crazy."

He's got a point. It's not like Adam died.

Uncle Steve squared his shoulders. "Mr. Ciminelli is right. There are lots of families saying much harder good-byes." He smiled bravely and put his arm around Aunt Elena. "So let's count our blessings."

"Turtle?" Petey drove his jeep across the sand bridge she had made.

"Hmmm?"

"Grandma's still sad."

Elizabeth looked up. Their grandmother was

sitting alone, apparently watching the water. "I know."

"How come?" he asked. "Mr. Ciminelli said we're supposed to be happy about Adam."

"I'm not sure, Petey." Elizabeth's eyebrows drew together. "Do you think it would help if you gave her a hug?"

Petey shook his head. "Not yet. Her shoulders aren't down."

Elizabeth looked at her grandmother again.

He's right. How does he know *things like that?*

"Adam didn't hug anybody," Petey mumbled. "Not even his mom."

Elizabeth combed the sand with her fingers. "Are you still mad at him?"

"No." Petey sighed. "I wish I never crossed him off the painting."

If only Grandma would let me make her a new one . . .

She had offered, but Grandma had firmly declined. "Thank you, Elizabeth, but please don't. It wouldn't be the same."

Nothing's the same.

Elizabeth's eyes moved from Petey to Grandma.

He isn't swimming. She isn't talking.

She looked at the waves and suddenly recalled something DaCosta had said.

"Even now, she is working to heal herself. But that, too, entails change."

Elizabeth squinted at the water. "Petey? Do you remember one time last year? When you asked me how come I never went swimming?"

He nodded.

"Did you want me to swim?"

He nodded again.

"Why?"

He turned away and flopped onto his stomach. "Leave me alone!"

"Petey?"

He wrenched himself onto his elbows and looked at her with shimmering eyes. "I wanted to share!"

Elizabeth nodded slowly and turned toward her grandmother. Petey followed her gaze. "I *hate* you, Turtle!" He threw himself back onto the sand.

Elizabeth leaned close. "I'm still scared, Petey."

There was no response and she forced herself to her feet.

Keep your eyes on the sand.

Her chest throbbed as she lurched toward her grandmother.

Just think about . . .

Her throat felt full, but when she tried to speak, she found her tongue dry. "Grandma?" she croaked. "I think I'll go swimming. Would you like to come?"

Her grandmother's eyes remained on the water as she got to her feet. Slowly, they started forward.

It's just water.

Elizabeth's chest contracted and burned.

We won't go very far.

The first shallow wave came to meet them.

It's just water!

"Wait!"

Petey hurtled toward them, legs stiff and eyes streaming. He stopped behind them and sobbed. Grandma held out her hand.

Please, Petey.

He grasped his grandmother's fingers and Elizabeth turned back to the ocean. Grandma's other hand was waiting for her.

Tears spilled down Elizabeth's cheeks as the three of them waded into the waves.

Chapter
Thirty

"We went in, didn't we,
Turtle?"

The swing creaked as
Petey turned toward her.
In the tangerine light of
the setting sun, his dark
blue eyes looked black.

Elizabeth nodded. "Both of us."

And Grandma.

"Are you still scared?"

Elizabeth hesitated, and then nodded again.

Petey swung his legs and the swing rocked gently.
"We helped Grandma, didn't we?"

"I think so."

At least she talked some during dinner.

The humming of insects grew louder as the light
faded from the sky.

"Nobody's said anything," Petey mumbled.

"I think they're afraid to," Elizabeth whispered.

"That it would jinx us or something, and we might not go in again."

Petey nodded.

"Elizabeth! Petey!" Caroline called through the window. "Time for dessert."

And bed. I'm sleepwalking now.

They slid off the swing and went through the screen door.

"Come on, Mom!" Uncle Tim teased. "Be a sport. Show the kids the pictures that aren't in the albums."

Grandma lifted her chin. "Those are not for public consumption."

"We're not public, Grandma," Abby argued. "We're family!"

"Hmmph!" she replied. "A group that relishes humor at my expense."

"Please, Grandma?" Molly said. "We won't laugh."

"Baloney!" She glared at her sons.

"We're going to roar our heads off," Kevin admitted. "You'll just have to be brave."

Grandma folded her arms. "You'll roar anyway, after my funeral. I suppose I might as well *see* the hilarity." She pushed back her chair.

"I'll go, Grandma," Elizabeth offered from the archway. "Where are they?"

"Second shelf of my closet. The square box."

Elizabeth hurried through the kitchen and up the stairs.

They must be pictures of when she was little!

Elizabeth smiled. It was hard to imagine Grandma at her age, or Petey's.

Second shelf, square box . . . oh!

On the top shelf, next to the box that held their stocking presents at Christmas, was her painting. Impulsively, Elizabeth pulled it down.

Grandma shouldn't have to look at this every time she gets dressed.

Her heart pounded as she tiptoed down the hall. Moments later, the painting lay at the bottom of her suitcase. It looked worse than she remembered. It couldn't be fixed, but she would take it away . . .

Hurry! They're waiting.

She raced back down the hall and pulled the square box from its shelf.

"Elizabeth?" Kevin called.

"Found 'em!" She trotted down the stairs and handed the box to her father.

"Wait'll you see these!" Kevin grinned wickedly. He went through the door to the dining room and held up the box in triumph.

"Hand 'em over, Kevin," Grandma said. "They're silly enough, and they won't be enhanced by cake crumbs and frosting. *After* dessert, you may look."

The throng assembled in the front room. As the photographs were passed around, conversation and laughter approached Sheridan noise, a volume painful to the ears.

Thank goodness.

Elizabeth looked at the pictures of Grandma with interest: as a toddler, her face obscured by a sunbonnet; wearing a Brownie uniform at age seven or eight; in an athletic jersey, number "18"; with an armload of books in front of an iron gate.

She looks like Adam in this one.

"Who is this, Grandma?" Andrew held up a snapshot.

"Someone I dated before I met your grandfather."

"What was his name?" Sarah asked.

"Joel," Grandma said. "Joel Weingartner."

"*Weingartner!*" Paul yelped. "What a name!"

"He was a very nice man," Grandma said sadly. "He was killed in Korea."

Elizabeth contemplated her grandmother.

She's had to say a lot of good-byes.

The last of the photographs was returned to the box, and everyone agreed that it was time for bed. Elizabeth kissed her parents and her grandmother good night, mechanically brushed her teeth, and pulled on her pajamas.

"Those pictures were cool," Abby said.

"I *loved* the one where Grandma was sulking," Molly said. "Nice to know she wasn't perfect as a child!"

Caroline nodded. "But my favorite was the one with the ringlets."

"I want to do that to *my* hair," Sarah said.

"No, you don't, Sair," Molly warned. "Grandma

told me it takes forever to wrap it up, and it's all lumpy to sleep on. She *hated* having to do it."

"Oh." Sarah yawned. "Then I won't ask."

Caroline turned off the light. "Wasn't it weird how, even when she was little, you could still tell it was Grandma?"

That's true!

"Yeah," Abby said. "She's changed, but she hasn't!"

There was a chorus of good nights and the room grew quiet. Although she was tingling with exhaustion, it took Elizabeth more than an hour to fall asleep.

"Petey?" Elizabeth waited until he looked up from the hole he was digging. "What's different about me from last summer?"

"Lots of stuff, Turtle!"

"Like what?"

"You talk more, and you smile a *lot* more." He grinned. "And sometimes you laugh and let people hug." He tipped his head. "You don't sit on the rock anymore . . ."

Elizabeth looked at the water and brushed some damp sand from her knees.

". . . and now you're friends with Grandma!" Petey finished proudly.

Lawson to Sheridan. "Iron Woman" to Grandma.

Elizabeth swallowed hard. "What's the same about me?"

"Why are you asking this stuff?"

"Please, Petey," Elizabeth stammered. "It's important."

"You *look* the same, 'cept you're taller." He shrugged. "You're still smart, and still shy."

A soccer ball rolled toward them. Elizabeth picked it up and tossed it toward Andrew. It thudded onto the sand ten feet short of its mark, and Petey's cobalt eyes danced.

"And you still stink at sports!"

Elizabeth grinned back at him. *"That* much, I knew!"

Elizabeth carried her suitcase across the lawn and quickly put it into the car.

Warning: contains stolen property.

She sighed and let her eyes wander from the fence to the porch and the flowers below it.

How can it be time to go home when we just got here?

Karen lumbered down the steps carrying two suitcases and a duffel bag. Elizabeth hurried to relieve her of the last item.

"Thank you, sweetheart." Karen hoisted the suitcases into the back of the station wagon. "Would you grab a few paper towels? The glove compartment's empty, and we're sure to spill something."

In the kitchen, Elizabeth found her grandmother packing snacks.

"Hi, Grandma. Mom asked me to get some paper towels."

"Good idea." Grandma smiled. "Help yourself."

Elizabeth did so, folded them carefully, and bit her lip.

I've said enough good-byes this summer.

She would probably never see DaCosta again, and she might not even see Pap. She had promised to let Grandma know when the dumping case came to trial, but who knew when *that* would be? And their farewell to Adam had been awful . . .

"There's a terrific new invention," Grandma whispered. "It's called a *telephone.*"

Elizabeth blushed.

"Although I'm partial to your letters . . ." Grandma shrugged. "All right. I'm greedy. I want both!"

Elizabeth grinned. "Promise."

Grandma tipped her head. "I hate to push my luck, but . . ." She opened her arms. Elizabeth smiled shyly and nodded. They hugged, long and hard.

"You got your birthday wish, Mom!" Kevin grinned at them from the doorway.

Grandma kissed her granddaughter and turned to glare at her son. "*Honestly*, Elizabeth—your father can't keep secrets for beans!"

Chapter
Thirty-One

Elizabeth's attention was briefly engaged by a few golden leaves against a purple November sky. Then her stomach resumed its uneasy protest against the train's motion and she sank back onto the seat.

Why does everything have to be such a mess?

For starters, there was the fight she'd had with her parents. Kevin and Karen had urged her to attend the fall dance at school, and she had refused. They had gotten Andrew to say he would take her. They had offered to buy her something special to wear, if she wanted, and to pay for her ticket. Kevin had promised to wait outside the school and to bring her right home if she'd stick it out for an hour. Elizabeth had finally cried and been allowed to retreat to her room. She hated being in conflict with her parents, and the matter had not been resolved.

I don't need to worry about being teased at some stupid dance. Family stuff's more important, and I'm confused enough about that.

She sighed. Within the extended family, there had been friction about where to hold Thanksgiving. Adam, of course, wouldn't be with them — and that was the problem. Should they celebrate at Uncle Tim and Aunt Rachel's as usual, or try something different? That, too, was unresolved.

Finally, there was the painting. It had haunted Elizabeth since their return from the ocean and she had begun to dream about it. She didn't know what to do with it, but she couldn't bring herself to throw it away. It continued to stand at the back of her closet, a daily reminder of unsettled tensions among Grandma and Adam and Petey.

Maybe I shouldn't have taken it.

Grandma must know it was missing, but she might not know who . . .

Please don't let her ask.

The train sped past the water tower.

Eight minutes.

Elizabeth lifted her suitcase onto the seat and counted the number of times she had been to South Wales.

One. The train, a year ago June, with Caro and Molly and Paul.

She hadn't spoken a word the whole trip.

Two. Grandma's car, a year ago October.

Elizabeth winced at the memory. She had been suspended from school for carving an obscenity into an art-room table. When they had reached South Wales, the whole story had come out, and Grandma had suggested she tell her teacher she was sorry. Elizabeth had written an apology to her art teacher, but more than a year later, she was still too embarrassed to *talk* to her.

Three. The train, at Christmas.

Elizabeth had gone ahead of the others, to help with preparations. Grandma had tried to explain about Adam while they'd trimmed the tree. That he had lost his closest friends. That they had been drinking and driving. That he had planned to be college roommates with Jimmy, and had saved for two years to go kayaking with Nate . . .

Four. Karen's car, with the family, at Easter.

When it had seemed as though Adam was better.

Five. Kevin's car, on Paul's birthday, the start of summer vacation at Grandma's.

The train slowed and Elizabeth reached for her suitcase.

Six. Today, November 18.

Elizabeth spied Grandma and waved. It wasn't

possible she'd been here only six times. She scrambled onto the platform, dropped her suitcase, and gave her grandmother a hug.

Grandma set the flour next to the mixer. "Where do *you* think we should have Thanksgiving?"

Elizabeth felt her back stiffen. Last night they had spent a happy evening playing Scrabble. They had gotten up early, decided to be lazy and remain in their pajamas, and lingered over their waffles. Their conversation had been friendly and light, and Elizabeth wanted to keep it that way. She shrugged and continued to grate orange peel.

"It doesn't matter to you, one way or the other?"

I want it to be like last year, at Uncle Tim and Aunt Rachel's. But with Adam there, and not depressed, and everyone friends!

Elizabeth spoke to the table. "What do *you* want to do?"

Grandma shook her head. "Your opinion should be your own."

"I don't have one." Elizabeth turned the orange and tightened her grip on the grater.

"Why not?"

"I don't know." Elizabeth scraped harder. "I just don't."

"What about Christmas?"

Elizabeth looked up in alarm.

Christmas has to be here!

Grandma raised one eyebrow. "Just because we're used to doing things a certain way doesn't mean that we have to."

Yes, it does!

Grandma took the sugar canister from its place. "Hanukkah begins on the twenty-second this year. Maybe we should celebrate the December holidays at Tim and Rachel's, and have Thanksgiving some-where else."

But you've had Hanukkah here other times—Abby told me!

"It doesn't really matter where we go," Grandma added. "I just wish we could settle things and every-one could stop fussing."

Elizabeth's chest pounded.

"Please grate a little more." Grandma pointed to the oranges. "We need three tablespoons."

They worked in silence until Elizabeth had pro-duced the required quantity.

"Thank you." The mixer whirled one last time and Grandma put the dough into a cookie press. "Flowers or stars?"

"Stars."

"You want to do it?"

Elizabeth shook her head and Grandma began to press cookies onto the tray. "Your mom says you don't want to go to the dance."

Elizabeth's cheeks burned.

"Any special reason?"

Elizabeth shook her head.

"It's hard to try new things when you're shy," Grandma said quietly. "I admire Adam for having gone to Montana when it meant meeting so many new people."

There was a long pause.

"Grandma? What did you put in his envelope?"

"The dolphin from a key chain he's always liked." Her eyebrows drew together. "Why?"

Elizabeth looked down. "How come you didn't write anything?"

Grandma reached for a new pan. "I didn't think he'd want me to."

Oh, Grandma . . .

"You wouldn't have to dance." Grandma returned to the previous topic. "I bet lots of kids won't, and you might make some friends."

"I don't need any friends. I have all of you."

"Adam needed other people in *his* life."

"It's different for him." Elizabeth shrugged. "He *belongs* to this family."

Grandma's eyes flashed.

Ow!

Elizabeth reached for her backside. "What was *that* for?"

"Figure it out." Grandma gave her a pointed look.

I didn't do anything!

Elizabeth spun away and scrubbed a tear from one

eye. It hadn't hurt all that much, but it had surprised her, and there hadn't been any reason.

All I said was, "It's different for Adam."

"You have belonged to this family, Elizabeth, since the day Kevin and Karen brought you home."

That's not what I meant.

"But if you need *additional* grounds for belonging, I can think of three off the top of my head."

Elizabeth turned halfway around.

Like what?

Grandma set down the cookie press and held up one finger. "You kept Petey from drowning." She raised a second finger. "You were the only contact Adam had with this family for most of last summer." She unfolded a third finger. "And you gave me a hug when I desperately needed one. When nothing else would have helped."

Elizabeth swallowed hard.

"So if you ever again suggest, even *hint*, you don't belong to this family, I will paddle your bottom into next week." She raised one eyebrow. "Understood?"

Elizabeth nodded.

"Even if you're all grown up." Grandma's eyes began to twinkle. "And I have to escape from the old folks' home in order to do it."

The telephone rang. Grandma gave Elizabeth a quick kiss and handed her the cookie press.

"Hello?" There was a brief pause. "Steve!" Grandma's voice softened and brightened. "How are you?"

There was a chilling silence.

Something's happened to Adam.

Elizabeth looked over her shoulder. Grandma's eyes were closed and she was holding the receiver with both hands.

"Poor Elena . . ."

It's not Adam.

Elizabeth slowly exhaled.

"Of course, Steve." Grandma reached for a piece of paper, scribbled something, and looked at her watch. "It's Elizabeth's turn to spend the weekend. Give us half an hour to pack, and three to get her home. . . . I should be there by two-thirty."

There was another brief silence.

"No." Grandma shook her head. "Just give her my love. The rest can wait."

Elizabeth set the cookie press on its end and began to scoop dough from the tray.

"You will, Steve," Grandma said softly. "If you listen, you'll know how to help."

How to help Aunt Elena?

"All right. I'll call if I'll be later than three." She paused. "I love you, too." Grandma gently replaced the receiver and stared at the phone.

"What happened, Grandma?"

"Elena's mother died very suddenly." She took a

deep breath. "Steve and Elena are flying to Barcelona tonight, and they've asked me to stay with Molly." She smiled sadly. "I'm sorry, Elizabeth."

"That's O.K., Grandma. I understand."

"I'll tell you more in the car." Grandma looked at her watch again. "Right now, I'd better call *your* parents, and then we'd better get dressed."

She turned back to the phone and dialed. "Karen? It's Martha." She shook her head. "No, no— Elizabeth's fine. But I'm afraid there's some bad news . . ."

Chapter
Thirty-Two

"It's a long story," Grandma warned as they pulled onto the highway. "You sure you want to hear the whole thing?"

Elizabeth nodded.

"Two days ago," Grandma began slowly, "Aunt Elena's mother came down with the flu. She went to bed assuring everyone that she would be fine. The next day her daughters decided she might have pneumonia. They rushed her to the hospital, but four hours later, she simply stopped breathing and died."

Elizabeth winced.

"Unfortunately, her mother's death isn't the only reason Aunt Elena is sad," Grandma continued. "And in order to explain the rest of it, I need to backtrack a little."

Elizabeth waited patiently until Grandma finished merging onto the highway.

"At the end of his sophomore year in college," Grandma continued, "Steve decided to spend his junior year in Barcelona." Grandma gave Elizabeth a quick smile. "Twenty minutes after he met Elena, he was in love."

Elizabeth grinned.

"He returned home in June, but the following spring, he went back and asked her to marry him."

Elizabeth wrinkled her nose. "But that doesn't sound sad at all!"

Grandma shook her head. "The *sad* part is that Aunt Elena's parents were furious that she would even *consider* marrying someone who wasn't Catholic. Her three sisters were even angrier when she announced that she and Steve would make their home in the United States. They felt that Elena had turned her back on God, family, and country—and they wanted nothing more to do with her."

Elizabeth's eyes widened in horror.

"Not even when she and Steve got married," Grandma added softly. "Not even when her father died."

"How *awful!*"

"Elena didn't learn that he had died until she received a sympathy note from a friend." Grandma shook her head. "She was *devastated . . .*"

Elizabeth bit her lip.

". . . but it made her determined to renew contact with the rest of the family. Her two older sisters remained adamant in refusing to see her, but her mother and Esther, the youngest, invited Elena to visit. She took Adam and Molly with her." Grandma signaled and changed lanes. "That was six years ago, and it was the only time they ever met their maternal grandmother."

"But," Elizabeth protested, "weren't Aunt Elena and her mother friends again?"

Grandma nodded. "They were. Since the trip, Elena has written, and called, and sent pictures of Adam and Molly at least twice a year. Another visit was scheduled for next spring."

Elizabeth shifted restlessly. "Does Adam know yet?"

"Steve tried to reach him, but he wasn't able to do more than leave a message." Grandma's eyebrows drew together. "And Elena doesn't want to leave the country without talking to him."

They drove in silence for several minutes before Grandma turned on the radio. Elizabeth found the classical music soothing, and she drifted to sleep.

"Elizabeth?" Grandma patted her shoulder. "You're home."

The driver's door thunked open and Elizabeth shook herself awake.

"Hi, Mom." Kevin kissed Grandma.

"Have you talked to Steve?"

Kevin nodded. "Adam called, and that helped." He smiled at Elizabeth and opened his arms.

"Hi, Dad." She hugged him tightly.

"I'm sorry your weekend was cut short, but I'm glad you're home."

Me, too.

Kevin turned back to his mother. "Can you come in?"

Grandma shook her head. "I told Steve two-thirty."

"Call later?"

Grandma nodded and Kevin kissed her again. "Drive safely."

Elizabeth pulled her pajamas from her suitcase, put them on, and restlessly pulled back her blankets. She wasn't surprised, but she wasn't sure she was glad, when her mother knocked and pushed open the door.

"Hi." Karen sat down next to her. "You O.K.?"

Elizabeth nodded.

"You've been awfully quiet." Karen gave her a small smile. "Even for you."

Elizabeth shrugged. "Just thinking."

"About . . . ?"

"Aunt Elena. Uncle Steve. What Grandma told me." Elizabeth shrugged again. "Everything."

Karen nodded. "It's a lot to take in, and a lot to sort out."

"How could they not even *tell* her when her father died?"

"I don't know, sweetheart." Karen shook her head. "Sometimes when people are really angry, or hurt, they get stuck in their thinking."

"I feel so *sorry* for her."

Karen nodded. "But Uncle Steve's there. And she knows that we love her."

Elizabeth sighed and Karen rubbed her back.

"Dad talked to Uncle Tim. They think it might be easiest for Molly if we have Thanksgiving where we usually do."

Elizabeth nodded.

At least that's settled.

"It's late." Karen kissed Elizabeth's cheek.

"Good night, Mom."

"By the way." Karen paused in the doorway. "You don't have to go to the dance."

How come?

"Dad and I decided it isn't important enough to be fighting about." Karen smiled gently and closed the door.

So that's settled, too.

Elizabeth felt relieved, but uncomfortably certain that the decision was somehow connected to Aunt Elena and her mother's death.

"Come on, everybody!" Caroline called. "The turkey's in the oven. It's ornament time!"

At least one thing's the same.

Elizabeth smiled as she watched Abby take ribbon-covered balls from a box.

Sarah's eyes grew wide. "You made so *many* this year, Grandma!"

"Molly's a fast worker." Grandma smiled. "And the more we make, the more money they'll raise for the shelter."

"Turtle?" Petey held up a Styrofoam ball. A piece of green velvet ribbon had worked itself free. Elizabeth refastened it and helped Petey choose sequins to add.

As the smell of the turkey grew stronger, they caught up with each other. Petey had found kinder-garten boring—his classmates were working on letter recognition and he was reading at a second-grade level. Sarah loved her teacher and had two best friends. Abby had been elected president of her class and had started in goal for six soccer games. Andrew was finding high school classes harder than expected, but he was managing, and he'd made the chess team. Molly's only comment about *her* freshman year was, "It's school."

The turkey came out of the oven just as the telephone rang. Uncle Steve and Aunt Elena insisted on wishing every member of the family a "Happy Thanksgiving." Molly asked to be last, and when it was her turn, everyone tactfully left the kitchen.

"They'll be back Saturday night," Molly announced as she came back into the dining room.

Dinner was delicious and conversation pleasant, albeit lopsided in favor of football. Aunt Rachel's pies were magnificent and all four were consumed in short order. Molly began to clear the table and Elizabeth got up to help.

She looks pretty O.K., but she sure isn't talking much.

They loaded the dishwasher and followed the others to the living room. A debate began, one part of the family in favor of charades, the other in favor of a trivia challenge.

Molly turned to Elizabeth. "I need some fresh air," she said casually. "And everyone'll have a fit if I go out by myself. Would you mind taking a walk?"

Elizabeth shook her head. They collected permission and coats and stepped into a crisp, starry night.

"We don't have to go anywhere," Molly said. "I just wanted to ask you something."

Elizabeth nodded.

"How old were you when your parents died?"

"Five."

Molly stared at her for a moment, and then looked out into the night. "Do you remember them?"

Elizabeth watched Molly's breath swirl in the light of the porch lamp and fade into the darkness. "A little. Mostly bits and pieces." She hesitated. "Why?"

Molly shrugged. "I met *Abuela* Rosa when I was eight. We were with her for six days. We did all sorts of things, went places she thought children would like." She took a deep breath. "But my only strong memory is how disappointed she was that I didn't speak better

Spanish." Molly shivered and turned up her collar. "Maybe we *should* walk."

Elizabeth followed her down the steps.

"And it's really kind of sad," Molly continued, "because now that she's gone, that's the only memory I'll ever have."

That is *sad.*

"And I feel like I ought to cry or something, because she was my grandmother." Molly spread her hands. "But I didn't know her. It's not like it would be with Grandma. If *she* died, I'd cry for a month, but I'd never forget her."

Elizabeth nodded.

"And there are Mom's sisters." Molly's eyes narrowed and her breathing became rapid. "I feel like I ought to get to know them, but except for *Tía* Esther, I don't want to." Her voice broke. "They hurt Mom too much."

Elizabeth winced.

It must have hurt even more, because Uncle Steve is so close to his family.

"And it was all so stupid," Molly said crossly. "Grandma didn't care that Mom is Catholic, or that Aunt Rachel is Jewish. Why did it have to matter to *them?*"

They walked in silence for half a block.

"I guess it bothers me more than I want it to." Molly's voice was soft. "I guess that's why I needed to talk about it."

Has talking helped?

Molly scooped a frost-covered stick from the side-walk and began to break it into small pieces. "I hate not having them here." Molly's face was an eerie silver in the light of the street lamp, and her eyes were black and bright. "And I really miss Adam."

"Did you get to talk to him?" Elizabeth asked.

Molly shook her head and tossed the stick onto a pile of leaves near the curb. "I went shopping with Dad. He called while we were gone."

Poor Molly.

"It was bad enough imagining that he'd be away at college, but I always thought I'd be able to *call* him. That he'd be home for Thanksgiving and every-thing." Mist whirled from her mouth as she sighed. "And Christmas is gonna be a killer. Especially for Mom."

They rounded the corner and climbed the steps to the porch.

"Thanks for listening, Elizabeth."

"I wish I could help," she stammered.

Molly gave her a small smile. "You have."

Sure doesn't feel like it.

Chapter
Thirty-Three

Elizabeth looked again at the grade at the top of her paper, reread, "A very moving portrait," and sighed.

It's better than nothing . . .
Her chest grew tight.
But what if it isn't? What if it's worse?

The first draft of "My Family" had run twenty-six pages. Elizabeth had labored over it and gotten it down to eleven. She had earned an A+, but the grade was irrelevant.

Should I send it?

At Thanksgiving, they had drawn names for the Christmas present exchange among cousins. After a lengthy discussion, they had decided to leave Adam out: he wouldn't be there to receive a gift, and it was unlikely he'd be able to shop where he was. Instead, they would each write him a letter and send them all in a gift-wrapped box. Elizabeth's envelope was the only one missing, and Karen wanted to mail the package today.

But what else could I write?

She shook her head. She had no idea. Caroline's footsteps came down the hall. "Mom's ready to go."

Elizabeth quickly folded her essay in thirds, shoved it into an envelope, and sealed it.

"You write a *book* or something?" Caroline hefted the wad of paper and grinned. "You just doubled the cost of the postage!"

Elizabeth gave her a weak smile.

"We're going Christmas shopping on the way back. If Mara calls, tell her we're working Special Olympics on Friday, O.K.?"

Elizabeth watched her mother back onto the street.

The house is empty. What are you waiting for?

She walked to her closet.

At least look at it.

Her heart pounded.

You're going to do more than that, and you know it.

She carried her painting to her desk and slowly turned it over. It looked hopeless.

You have to try.

Elizabeth sighed. Fixing the painting would take expert advice. Fixing it would mean talking to her art teacher.

"Mrs. Kilgore?" Elizabeth stammered. "Can I please ask you something?"

"Certainly, Elizabeth." She continued to alphabetize portfolios. "What is it?"

Elizabeth pulled the painting from a large plastic bag and edged it onto her teacher's desk. "Could you tell me how to fix this?"

Mrs. Kilgore's eyes flickered across the painting. She stood very still for a moment, and then picked it up. "You . . . made this?"

Elizabeth nodded.

Mrs. Kilgore laid the painting flat on her desk and lightly ran her fingers over its surface. "Watercolor?"

"Mostly," Elizabeth apologized. "The white and some of the gray is acrylic."

Mrs. Kilgore flipped the painting over, flipped it back, held it up to the light, and peered at the scar. She shook her head. "Water-based marker. It's going to bleed."

Elizabeth's throat was instantly full.

It can't be fixed.

Mrs. Kilgore carefully examined the edge of the painting. "I think . . ." She looked up. "How much time did it take you to do this?"

Elizabeth calculated. "About twelve hours."

"It'll take at least that to fix it." The words were a challenge.

Please?

Mrs. Kilgore looked at her watch. "I've got a faculty

meeting in ten minutes, but if you can stay late to-morrow, we'll start."

"Thank you!" Elizabeth fumbled her back-pack onto one shoulder. "Thanks a whole lot, Mrs. Kilgore!"

"Start by tracing the design in this corner."

Elizabeth sharpened a pencil and carefully did so.

"Ready to perform a little surgery?" Mrs. Kilgore placed a new blade into a matte knife and twisted the screw tight.

Huh?

Elizabeth looked down at her painting and at a piece of cardboard of identical thickness. Mrs. Kilgore handed her a jar of rubber cement. "The cardboard goes up as well as down where it's gouged. You need to replace this section."

Under her teacher's direction, Elizabeth brushed rubber cement on both sheets of cardboard. When they were dry, she pressed them together.

"You've got to keep the knife *absolutely* vertical," Mrs. Kilgore explained. "Or there will be gaps when you glue the pieces together."

Elizabeth held her breath and began. Mrs. Kilgore had said the seam would be less visible if it followed a crooked path, and she inched her way among the geometric shapes of the mosaic. She stopped several times to rest her cramped hand and to breathe. She finished at last and allowed her shoulders to fall.

"Peel them apart, and let's see how you did."

Elizabeth separated the two pieces, rubbed the rubber cement from them both, and slid them together.

Mrs. Kilgore inspected the seam. "Beautiful!"

Elizabeth blushed.

"I found this and trimmed it." Mrs. Kilgore pulled a piece of tagboard from a shelf. "You can use it for backing."

"Thank you," Elizabeth stammered.

She's being so nice!

"Use this." Mrs. Kilgore handed her a bottle of bonding material. "It should be dry enough to work on tomorrow."

"Color matching is part science, part art," Mrs. Kilgore announced. "You're going to have to experiment."

Elizabeth nodded.

"The *moment* a painting is finished, it starts to change."

Elizabeth squinted at her mosaic. "How?"

"The paper ages. So do the pigments. And particles in the air settle on the surface." Mrs. Kilgore pointed to a bit of white. "Where was this hanging?"

"Over a fireplace."

"I would have guessed it was something like that. Or in a kitchen." Mrs. Kilgore shook her head. "That's made it harder . . ."

Elizabeth looked up in alarm.

". . . but you can *do* it." Mrs. Kilgore pointed to

sienna and ochre. "You may have to mix in one of these. The tiniest bit."

Elizabeth nodded.

"Do one color at a time, and make more than you think you'll need. You'll have to do test strips, and let them dry overnight, before you know if you've got a good match."

Elizabeth nodded again and reached for her brush.

"How are you doing?"

Elizabeth shook her head.

"Let me look." Mrs. Kilgore leaned over her shoulder. "I think you've done an *incredible* job."

"But this one, and this one." Elizabeth pointed to one shade of blue and one shade of gray. "I can't get them." She offered the test paper to her teacher.

Mrs. Kilgore looked back and forth. "You're close. *Really* close . . ."

"But they don't match," Elizabeth protested. "And it'll *look* like this part is new!"

Mrs. Kilgore examined the six triangles and three hexagons that remained to be painted. "There's a way around it . . ."

Elizabeth sat up.

"Use what you've mixed," Mrs. Kilgore said slowly, "but use it here, and here, too." She pointed to spots on the original painting. "That way it will blend, and everything will be balanced."

Elizabeth stared.

It might work . . .

Elizabeth pulled a carefully-wrapped package from her backpack, set it in the middle of her teacher's desk, and tiptoed to the filing cabinet.

Please . . .

She bit her lip, reached up, and slowly pulled the painting toward her. The overall effect was slightly darker than it had been, but it was one painting, a unified whole.

"You do know how to smile!"

Elizabeth jumped. "Hi, Mrs. Kilgore."

"You should be very proud, Elizabeth. It turned out even better than I had imagined it would." Mrs. Kilgore set her satchel on the desk. "What's this?"

"Fudge," Elizabeth said quickly. "I made it. To say thank you . . ." She lifted the painting with both hands.

"You're welcome." Mrs. Kilgore tucked the gift into her bag. "And thank *you.*"

Elizabeth smiled.

"Have you got something to wrap it in?" Mrs. Kilgore nodded toward the sleet-covered windows.

Elizabeth pulled a large plastic bag from her pocket and, together, they secured the painting against the weather.

"May I ask you something?" Mrs. Kilgore said at the door.

Elizabeth nodded.

"Who is MWS?"

"My grandmother."

Mrs. Kilgore turned off the light. "She must be pretty special."

Elizabeth nodded. "Thanks again, Mrs. Kilgore. Have a great vacation!"

Chapter
Thirty-Four

It's so pretty . . .

The others clamored up the steps to the porch. Elizabeth remained near the car, drinking in the softness of the snow drifts around her, blue-shadowed in the light of the moon, faintly orange where the glow from the windows spilled onto the lawn.

And peaceful.

The drive to Grandma's had been exceptionally quiet, each person lost in his or her own thoughts, the hum of the engine interrupted only by an occasional question from Paul.

"Elizabeth?" Kevin called.

She stamped the snow from her feet, slipped through the door, and hung up her jacket. Her pulse quickened as she listened to the boisterous exchange of holiday greetings.

Will it look the way I remember?

Elizabeth stepped into the front room. The tree looked the same. And the holly on the mantelpiece, and the sixteen red-and-white stockings, and the candles . . .

That must be the menorah.

"Hi, Turtle!" Petey threw his arms around her.

Elizabeth squeezed him back. "Happy Hanukkah, Petey!"

"Andrew!" Uncle Tim scolded. "Where are your glasses?"

"Give me a break, Dad," Andrew complained. "It's *vacation.*"

"First night," Grandma said lightly. "No fighting allowed!"

"And where are *your* glasses, Mom?"

Grandma blushed.

"Some role model *you* are!" Uncle Tim thundered, and everyone laughed.

"I'll get them, Grandma!" Petey scampered up the stairs.

Uncle Tim put his hands on his hips. "Andrew?"

He rolled his eyes and followed his brother, and the clan resumed its exchange of greetings and hugs. By the time Elizabeth reached Grandma, she was wearing a pair of silver-rimmed glasses. Elizabeth stared for a moment. Then she grinned and gave her grandmother a hug.

"Trifocals," Grandma admitted. "I hate them."

"How come?"

Grandma shook her head. "Can't get used to wearing them."

"But don't they help you *see* better?"

"My sewing glasses were fine." Grandma scowled. "These make me feel old!"

"Quit complaining, Mom," Uncle Steve said. "You got away without them for sixty-six years."

"Yeah, Grandma," Andrew grumbled. "How'd you like to have had them at my age?" He glowered at his father from behind tortoise-shell frames. "Bad enough I play chess. These things put my 'geek-quotient' into the stratosphere!"

Uncle Tim folded his arms. "Your headaches have stopped and your grades have improved."

"They look *good*, Andrew!" Elizabeth stammered.

"You mean now that I've got them . . ." Andrew lifted his chin, ". . . you wouldn't be embarrassed to take me to a dance?"

Everyone laughed.

"*That* wasn't it!" Elizabeth's face burned. "I just didn't want to go."

"Easy." Uncle Tim put an arm around her shoulders. "Andrew was joking."

Oh.

Elizabeth's breathing slowed.

"Come on, everyone," Uncle Steve called. "Let's get the suitcases upstairs."

Grandma headed for the kitchen, the younger kids

tried to guess the contents of brightly wrapped packages, and the older ones began to collect luggage.

"Sorry, Elizabeth." Andrew's smile was gentle. "I was just teasing. You know how fragile the male ego is." He collected three duffel bags and followed the others.

No, I don't.

Elizabeth bit her lip.

And I still can't tell when someone is joking.

"Elizabeth?" Aunt Elena kissed her cheek. "Thank you for your sympathy card." She smiled very briefly. "What you wrote was very special."

"You're welcome." Elizabeth offered her aunt a shy smile. "Thanks for choosing to have Christmas and Hannukah here."

Aunt Elena shifted her gaze to the fireplace and nodded. "This is where we belong."

"Elena?" Grandma called. "Would you work your magic with the flan?"

Elizabeth wrinkled her nose. "What is that?"

"A Spanish dessert. An egg custard." Aunt Elena shook her head. "Your grandmother can make flan that would have pleased my father." She smiled sadly. "But it is kind of her to make me feel needed."

Deep in thought, Elizabeth made her way to the second floor. Caroline, Molly, and Abby were chattering in the front bedroom. The sounds of a pillow fight came from the Crow's Nest, and the Sheridan uncles were laughing together at the end of the hall.

The painting!

Elizabeth's shoulders fell. The only logical thing to do was to put it back in Grandma's closet. But in a house with fourteen other people, when would there be a chance?

The question gnawed at her until dinner was over and everyone moved to the front room.

"I love it when Christmas and Hanukkah happen together," Sarah confided. "It's more exciting that way!"

"I dunno," Abby said thoughtfully. "I kind of like it when there's time in between. It makes each one more special."

"I'm with Abby," Andrew said. "I like my latkes separate from my eggnog."

Latkes?

"All you *think* about is food!" Abby said sharply.

"Abby." Aunt Rachel shook her head. "Not now."

Elizabeth listened with interest to the story of the victory of Judas Maccabeus and the rededication of the temple in Jerusalem. A vial containing oil enough for one day had somehow burned eight, a miracle commemorated by the lighting of candles on the menorah. Elizabeth wasn't sure she believed in miracles, but when the shammes was lighted, her heart began to beat faster. Aunt Rachel chanted in Hebrew and Andrew repeated the prayers in English. There was a still pause, and then Aunt Rachel nodded at Petey. He pursed his lips and leaned forward to light the first candle.

Elizabeth shivered.

He's doing something people have done for thousands of years . . .

Petey looked at his mother. Aunt Rachel nodded and smiled.

Everyone's smiling.

The room felt suddenly warm. The two new pairs of glasses reflected the flames. Aunt Elena's black eyes did, too, as they suddenly filled with tears.

I wish Adam were here.

Elizabeth pulled her pajamas from her suitcase, caught a glimpse of her mosaic, and fell into a restless sleep. She dreamed that all of the names had disappeared and only the geometric figures remained.

The next two days were busy and full and presented no opportunity for Elizabeth to return the painting. She discovered that latkes were a sort of potato pancake fried in oil, and that they were delicious. She participated in her first snowball fight and vowed that, in the future, she would heed Grandma's warnings: Abby's aim was deadly. She walked along the beach with Kevin, marveled at how much sand remained uncovered by snow, and wondered about the plankton. An envelope addressed to *Water Minders, Junior Division*, contained a terse but cheerful greeting from Pap, long-distance regards from DaCosta, and the news that the preliminary hearing in the dumping case would take place in February.

The light was fading from a gray sky when the Sheridan uncles began to organize people and cars for the annual Christmas Eve tour of outdoor lighting displays.

They'll be gone for two hours . . .

"Mom?" Elizabeth asked. "Would it be O.K. if I stayed here?"

Karen's face fell. "I'd really hoped you'd come with us this year."

"My stomach's a little funny," Elizabeth stammered. "Even if I took my pills, I'm not sure . . ." She looked toward the archway. "And Grandma might need help with dinner."

Karen looked doubtful, but nodded. "All right." She gave Elizabeth a quick kiss. "We'll be back in a couple of hours."

Elizabeth headed for the kitchen.

Her bedroom's right overhead. She'd hear me . . .

"Hi, Grandma."

Her grandmother jumped. "Heavens, Elizabeth!"

"Sorry," Elizabeth said quickly. "I didn't mean to scare you."

Grandma shook her head and pointed to a list on the counter. "We brought home nineteen bags of groceries the day before yesterday, and we're *out* of things I need to make dinner!" She crossed her eyes and Elizabeth grinned.

She can do that even with her new glasses!

Grandma looked at her watch. "I'd better hustle. Christmas Eve, the grocery store closes at five."

She's leaving . . . ?

Elizabeth held her breath.

Grandma scooped up her wallet and keys. "Want to come?"

Elizabeth pointed to a ten-pound bag of potatoes. "How about if I peel those instead?"

"That would be terrific!" Grandma grinned. "Thank you, sweetheart."

Elizabeth watched the car turn onto the road and then raced up the stairs.

Please let it be O.K. to have fixed it.

On the top shelf of Grandma's closet, fifteen paper bags bulged with small parcels wrapped in red-and-green paper.

Merry Christmas, Santa.

Elizabeth slid the painting behind the bags and quickly closed the door. By the time Grandma got home, she had peeled twenty-one potatoes.

They lit the menorah's third candle. It burned down amid quiet conversation, and Santa's believers were sent off to bed.

"I think I'll go to midnight mass," Aunt Elena said.

"I'll go with you, Mom." Molly hesitated. "Unless you'd rather go alone."

"I would love to have you come." Aunt Elena smiled. "Does anyone else wish to go?"

"I'd like to," Elizabeth stammered. "I've never been to a mass."

Molly grinned. "Christmas is *definitely* the place to start!"

As they drove, Aunt Elena and Molly speculated about what Adam might be doing. Alone in the backseat, Elizabeth contemplated the religious perspectives held by her parents. On their application to adopt, Kevin had described himself as "Christian by tradition; no parish affiliation." Karen had written, "Protestant upbringing. Currently agnostic."

We are a mixed group.

Elizabeth shook her head.

All we need is a Muslim, a Buddhist, and a Hindu or two!

Snow squeaked underfoot as they climbed the steps of Blessed Sacrament Church, a small building made of dark red stone. Elizabeth's eyes widened as Aunt Elena and Molly dipped their fingers into little dishes of water and crossed themselves. They chose a pew halfway to the altar. Aunt Elena lowered the knee rest and knelt, folded her hands, and bowed her head. Molly did the same.

I didn't even know this part of Molly existed . . .

Aunt Elena crossed herself again, sat back on the pew, and took a small package from her purse. "*Feliz Navidad*, Magdalena."

Molly unfolded the paper and stared.

"It belonged to *Abuela*," her mother said softly. "Your aunts wanted you to have it."

Molly ran a finger over the dark wooden beads and gently traced the cross. "All of them?" she whispered.

Her mother nodded. "*All* of them."

A high-pitched chime drew Elizabeth's attention to the altar. Poinsettias, some bloodred, some ivory, sat amid large white candles held aloft by gleaming brass sticks. Men in white robes with intricately embroidered scarves walked down the aisle. Elizabeth watched them, drinking in the details—the yellow cast of the chalice, the pale gray smoke of the incense, the worn black boots of an elderly man who looked too frail to support the cross that he carried. Aunt Elena prayed in Spanish, and Molly in English, but their inflections were identical.

It sounds as though they're saying the same words.

Elizabeth's mind drifted and she was startled when Molly nudged her to her feet. A moment later, everyone reached forward and back and sideways to shake hands. "Peace be with you," people murmured over and over. Elizabeth shook hands with her aunt and her cousin and five perfect strangers.

I don't like this part.

Aunt Elena and Molly slipped past her to the line for communion.

People have been doing this for thousands of years, too . . .

"So, Elizabeth," Molly said en route to the car. "What'd you think of your first mass?"

"It was beautiful," she said quietly.

"The church was, anyway," Molly agreed. "But the homily wasn't anything to write home about."

"We have heard worse." Aunt Elena's black eyes twinkled. "Remember two Easters ago? The padre who whispered?"

Molly groaned. "You wouldn't have believed this guy, Elizabeth. He *mouthed* the words, and he was *up* there for an hour!"

The ride home was filled with memories of other masses and other things that had gone wrong.

It's nice that they're laughing.

Elizabeth contemplated the figures in front of her, black silhouettes against the curtain of snow lit by the headlights.

And it must be O.K. to make jokes about church if Aunt Elena is doing it.

The car rocked through a snowdrift and into the driveway.

Everyone's asleep.

Except for one light in the front room, the house was dark.

No wonder. It's almost one-thirty.

Elizabeth quickly slipped off her jacket. "I'll turn off the light."

Aunt Elena nodded and whispered, "Good night."

Elizabeth tiptoed past the table near the front hall.

Why didn't Grandma leave on the lamp closest to the door?

She reached the table near the archway.

And why'd she move the holly?

Her eyes darted to the fireplace. Sixteen stockings were overflowing with presents. Her painting was hanging above them.

Chapter
Thirty-Five

"Come *on*, Turtle!"

Petey climbed onto Elizabeth's cot and tugged the blanket away from her face.

Come back when the sun is up.

"Hurry up, Molly! It's Christmas!"

"Go away, Petey!" she groaned.

"You *guys*," Petey wailed. "*Santa* came!" He yanked on Elizabeth's pillow. "Please, Turtle?"

She opened one eye into darkness and sighed. "All right. I'm coming."

"Molly?" he pleaded.

"Peter Allen Sheridan, you are a world-class pest!" Molly lifted her head from her pillow. "I'm going to *get* you for this." She threw back the blanket. "But I'm up!"

Petey grinned and scampered through the door.

The late-night churchgoers splashed their faces with water, pulled on sweatshirts, and stumbled down the stairs.

"Merry Christmas!" bombarded them from every corner of the room.

"Next year," Molly yawned, "*vigil* mass."

Kevin handed them their stockings and they found places to sit. Grandma gave them each a kiss and a cup of hot chocolate. "Santa was busy last night."

Elizabeth glued her eyes to her cup.

"Can we *go?*" shouted Paul.

Uncle Steve grinned wickedly.

"Have a heart, Steve," Uncle Tim chided.

Uncle Steve winked at Petey. "Go!"

Sheridan noise filled the room and wrapping paper filled the air. The opening of stocking presents was followed by breakfast and showers in two shifts. By ten-thirty, the cars were loaded and fourteen Sheridans were on their way to the Bread & Fishes food pantry in Brockport. They helped to cook for and serve three hundred people. Then they polished the kitchen and headed for home.

"Did Adam call?" Aunt Elena asked as they came through the door.

Grandma shook her head. "But he wouldn't have tried when he knew you were at the food pantry." She gave her daughter-in-law an encouraging smile. "He'll call, Elena."

They ate sandwiches and drifted off to play board

games, to re-examine stocking presents, or simply to talk. Elizabeth decided that she needed a nap and curled up on her cot. She had barely pulled up the blanket when she heard the door open.

"Turtle?" Small feet crossed the floor. "Are you asleep?"

"Sort of." Elizabeth opened her eyes and smiled. "What's up, Petey?"

His dark blue gaze was intense. "Thank you."

"For what?"

"For fixing the painting."

"You're welcome." Elizabeth propped herself on one elbow. "Did Grandma say anything about it?"

Petey shook his head. "When we got up this morning, it was just *there*."

Maybe she won't ever say anything.

"How did you *do* it, Turtle?"

"My art teacher helped me." She smiled. "Does it look O.K.?"

Petey nodded vigorously. Then his brow furrowed. "Santa brought Adam's presents here." He tipped his head. "Doesn't he go to Montana?"

"Well, sure, Petey." Elizabeth swallowed. "Maybe he was extra rushed, or something. Santa would know we'd make sure Adam gets them."

Petey's forehead relaxed, but he sighed. "I hope he calls soon. Aunt Elena's getting all twitchity."

The phone rang once before dinner—a wrong number. It rang twice while they ate—both calls from

Grandma's friends. It rang once more during the present exchange—a classmate of Kevin's in town for the holiday. The pile of presents under the tree dwindled to three identical rectangles.

The family portraits.

"Well, Mom?" Kevin said with forced cheer. "Aren't you going to let us have a look?"

Grandma nodded. "Abby? Please?"

Abby handed one package to her father and the other two to her uncles.

"It's going to be hard to top last year's portrait." Uncle Steve smiled at Elizabeth. "But let's see." He tore the paper from his package and his brothers followed suit.

"It's not *too* bad," Abby said.

"It's not bad at all," Karen argued gently. "It's just *different*. We're used to seeing everyone on the porch."

Elizabeth looked at Grandma and followed her charcoal gaze to the sofa. Uncle Steve was whispering to Aunt Elena. She nodded and continued to stare at the picture.

Just how diplomatic are they being?

Elizabeth leaned over her father's shoulder. The only resemblance this portrait had to last year's was the number of people in the picture. The blue stripe on the bus made several heads look disconnected from bodies, and such smiles as were present were strained. Adam looked like a sphinx.

A sphinx with a toothache.

The telephone rang again and Grandma slipped through the archway.

Aunt Rachel looked at her watch. "Petey? Time for pajamas."

Petey nodded and went up the stairs.

"It's a little early for the rest of us." Uncle Tim smiled bravely. "How about playing something?"

Four or five people made suggestions and they settled on a trivia game. Elizabeth knew that butter-flies belonged to the order Lepidoptera and her team-mates applauded. The game moved around the room and her thoughts wandered.

Where is Grandma?

She checked her watch.

Still on the phone?

An argument began about the spelling of "fluores-cent" and Karen reached for the dictionary. Something made her turn her head, and Elizabeth looked over her shoulder. Grandma was standing in the archway. She was smiling, but behind her new glasses, her eyes were bright.

Who is that?

A bearded lumberjack took a step forward and smiled.

"*Adam!*" The color drained from his mother's face. He nodded.

"*Dios mio!*" Aunt Elena's chest heaved and her eyes filled with tears.

"Merry Christmas, Mom."

The room was suddenly full of movement and noise. Adam embraced his parents. Aunt Elena babbled in Spanish while Uncle Steve quietly beamed.

"Hey, Mol." Adam wrapped his arms around his sister. When he released her, the questions resumed.

"But you were in Montana!"

"How did you *get* here?"

"Hugs first," Adam insisted. "Everybody."

When at last he turned to Elizabeth, he raised his eyebrows. She nodded and her feet were no longer touching the floor.

"Take it *easy*, Adam!" Kevin said. "She's still new at this!"

Adam set Elizabeth down amid gentle laughter. "You O.K.?" he asked gravely.

She nodded again and looked toward the front hall.

Petey.

Adam opened his arms. Petey's chin quivered and he shot forward. Adam caught him and held him tightly.

"Sktchee!" Petey's protest was muffled.

Adam loosened his hold. "What did you say?"

"It's scratchy!" Petey pointed to his beard.

"Sorry about that." Adam grinned. "Helps keep me warm."

"That's O.K., Adam." Petey rubbed his cheek. "I don't mind."

The room erupted into laughter and again into questions.

"One at a time," Uncle Steve finally said. "Or we'll *never* get the story."

"Thanks, Grandma." Adam accepted a plate full of food and a tall glass of eggnog.

"We've been hoping all day . . ." Aunt Elena gave him a bewildered look. ". . . for a call from Montana."

"You almost had one from Maine." Adam grinned. "That's where I've been for the past six weeks."

"Huh?" said Paul.

"What were you doing in Maine?" Andrew asked.

"Same thing," Adam admitted. "Tagging trees, cutting trees, planting trees, *counting* trees . . ."

"But why did you leave Montana?" Caroline asked.

"I told you they have programs in three states?" Everyone nodded.

"Well, they had some problems in Maine. Turns out not everyone had the same motive for joining." Adam took a sip of eggnog and shook his head. "Probably more accurate to say that *no one* had the same motive."

"What kind of problems?" Kevin asked.

"Lots of nasty interpersonal stuff, including some practical jokes that went way too far. Four people finally packed up and walked out."

"They didn't have enough volunteers left . . ." Aunt Rachel tipped her head. ". . . so you got transferred?"

Adam nodded. "That's about it. They asked who was willing to go, and I raised my hand."

"Didn't you *like* Montana?" Petey asked.

"Mr. Ciminelli was right. The scenery is beautiful." Adam shrugged. "But I hadn't really made any friends, so it wasn't too hard to leave."

"Is Maine better?" Molly asked quietly.

"It is." Adam grinned. "I even have a girlfriend of sorts!"

Sarah bounced. "What's she like, Adam?"

"You'd steer clear of her in a dark alley." He chuckled. "Crew cut, studded shirts, leather boots— the works. More earrings, in more places, than this whole family combined."

Aunt Elena's eyes grew wide. "Are you *serious*, Adam?"

"Yeah. Wears nothing but black." He grinned again. "And swears like a sailor!"

Uncle Steve smiled nervously. "And what is it you find *attractive* about her?"

Adam grew sober. "She's the only other person, in either place, who likes to read." He paused. "And she was as appalled as I was about the way people had treated each other."

"Is that what you meant?" Karen asked. "About people having different motives for joining?"

Adam nodded. "A few guys on power trips. A few guys looking for a free ride. Lots of people running away."

"From what?" Abby asked.

"Different things." Adam paused. "Some from

girlfriends or boyfriends. Some from situations at home. One guy didn't think the credit card people would find him in Montana." He made a wry face. "He was wrong."

"You've certainly met some interesting people!" Uncle Tim teased.

"I have," Adam said solemnly.

The room grew quiet for a moment.

"Let's give Adam a breather." Kevin added another log to the fire and handed Adam his stocking.

"Santa knew!" Petey's sapphire eyes became saucers. "He *knew* that you'd be here!"

"Remember, he's *magic.*" Adam winked. "But if it's O.K., I'll open these later. I've got a little sack of my own." He went through the archway and returned with a mud-stained backpack. The first thing he took from it was the gift-wrapped box of letters.

"But we sent those to Montana!" Caroline sputtered. "How did you get them?"

Adam grinned. "Part of my deal for going to Maine. Phone calls relayed within the hour, and mail forwarded overnight." He looked at his mother. "No carrier pigeons, Mom."

She smiled and shook her head.

"Thank you all for these," he pointed to the box. "And for my graduation presents. Caro's sweater *saved* me once it started snowing!"

Caroline smiled. "I'm glad, Adam."

"And now, the results of two other gifts." He pulled

a handkerchief from his bag. It was filled with small objects covered in aluminum foil. "Sorry about the wrapping paper—it was all I could find."

Everyone sat very still as he distributed the tiny bundles.

Whatever it is, it doesn't weigh very much.

"Go ahead, everybody." Adam grinned. "Merry Christmas!"

Elizabeth carefully teased apart the foil. Inside lay a tiny snake, carved from what she guessed was pine, and exquisitely detailed with tiny scales.

But why did he give me a snake? I'm terrified of snakes!

"Ohhh, Adam!" Sarah squealed and held up a butterfly. "You *made* this?"

He nodded and smiled at Kevin and Karen. "That knife came in handy!"

"*Look* at this swallow!" Aunt Elena exclaimed. "It's beautiful, Adam."

"What did you get, Mom?" Uncle Steve asked.

Grandma's glasses glinted as she lifted the little figure from her lap. "A dolphin." She smiled. "Thank you, Adam."

He kissed her cheek and whispered, "You're welcome."

Chapter
Thirty-Six

At breakfast, Adam explained that his borrowed truck had to be returned the next morning. He was sorry, but he would have to leave right after lunch.

But it will be O.K. this time.

Elizabeth hovered on the fringes of conversation, refilling coffee cups, doing housework, unwilling to be alone with anyone for too long. She had too much to think through, too much to sort out, to add any new thoughts to her brain.

Midmorning, Adam found her in the mudroom. "Mind if I watch?" he said. "Haven't seen an iron in months."

Why'd he close the door?

Elizabeth clumsily pressed a wrinkle into a table-cloth. "You haven't missed much."

"You're wrong, Elizabeth. I've missed a lot."

She tugged on the cloth and pressed the steam button.

Adam hoisted himself onto the dryer. "I'd like to apologize," he said simply.

Elizabeth looked up. "For what?"

Adam gave her a small smile. "Lousy timing."

What is he talking about?

"For disappearing when you were still figuring out how to be part of a family."

How to be . . . ?

"When I met you, I was pretty sure about a lot of things." Adam looked at the floor. "Things my family had taught me."

Like what?

"That if you play fair, you get fair. That if you work hard, you can change things for the better. That if you show people you care, they'll believe you."

Elizabeth's hands trembled as she moved the tablecloth.

"Then Jimmy and Nate died." Adam paused. "And everything I'd looked forward to wasn't going to happen. And all the rules I'd ever learned, everything I'd ever believed was important . . ." He shrugged. ". . . none of it rang true anymore."

There was a long silence. Elizabeth finally set down the iron and met Adam's dark gaze.

"I felt betrayed," Adam continued in a soft voice. "So I got angry. At the wrong people."

Elizabeth looked down.

"And especially at Grandma. Because for my whole life, for the whole family, it had always seemed as though she had the answers."

Elizabeth bit her lip.

"I didn't want to be a Sheridan anymore." He spoke to his sneakers. "I wanted to be just Adam, and figure out my own rules."

Elizabeth picked up the iron.

"Believing my family was nuts was easier than believing that *I* was." Adam snorted. "But the people in Montana set me straight. They told me I was nuts all the time."

Elizabeth's eyebrows drew together. "Why?"

"Because I didn't think it was funny to get drunk, or do less than my share on the job, or steal food from other crews, or try to look when the girls showered." He pressed his lips together. "I didn't *want* to do any of those things. And it had nothing to do with family rules."

Adam sat very still.

What is he thinking?

Elizabeth folded the tablecloth.

"Anyway." Adam smiled briefly. "When the whole Maine thing came up, I jumped at the chance. Then I got to know Kala . . ."

"The girl with the black clothes?"

Adam nodded. "When *Abuela* Rosa died, I told Kala about Mom's family, and about Jimmy and Nate. She told me some stuff about *her* family, and a friend of hers who had died . . ." He faltered. "She helped me put things in perspective."

Elizabeth reached for a napkin.

"So did your essay."

Elizabeth pressed down hard on the iron.

"It's pretty much your fault I'm here." Adam smiled. "Yours and Grandma's. She sent me a copy of the portrait at the bus station. I was so awful all summer." Adam shook his head. "But there you all were. Still trying. Still standing behind me."

Elizabeth's eyes watered.

The way everyone kept trying with me.

"We're not the people we were eighteen months ago," Adam said softly. "Are we, cousin?"

Not even close.

Elizabeth shook her head.

Adam slipped down from the dryer and grinned. "Heard a rumor you swim now!"

Elizabeth nodded.

"And I'm not nuts anymore. I've changed, but I'm back to being proud of my family." Adam's eyes twinkled. "Even if we *are* all Sheridan stubborn." He put his hands on his hips in mock indignation. "Grandma says you and Petey broke our sit-till-you're-friends record!"

Elizabeth grinned.

Adam checked his watch, looked around the room, and then frowned. "How did this . . . ?" He

pulled Petey's birthday present from behind a box
of detergent.

"He didn't want to open it," Elizabeth stammered.
"Because you weren't here."

Adam's dark eyes grew bright. "I knew I'd hurt
Grandma pretty badly . . ."

He doesn't know about the painting.

Elizabeth tried to smile. "You could watch him
open it now."

Adam contemplated the box. "I wasn't on the
beach when Petey needed me, Elizabeth." He took
a deep breath. "I'm sure glad Turtle was there."

He kissed her cheek and opened the door. His
footsteps faded and Elizabeth picked up the iron.

I'm so glad you're back.

Caroline folded her napkin. "What's next, Adam?"

"Finish my commitment in Maine," Adam said.
"And then find a job till September." He looked at
his father. "I'm still going to college, Dad."

Uncle Steve's eyebrows shot up. "I'm relieved to
hear *that!*"

Everyone laughed.

"But I'm thinking about a different career," Adam
added.

Molly grinned. "Woodcarving?"

Adam blushed. "Close enough." He glanced at his
father and mumbled, "Forestry."

Uncle Steve set down his silverware and contemplated his son. "You've talked about journalism for so long," he said slowly, "that I suppose we'd begun to take it for granted." He smiled. "But if forestry is where your heart lies, you certainly have *my* blessing."

"*And* mine." Aunt Elena rolled her eyes. "I worried *enough* when your father was in the wrong job!"

Amid laughter, they rose from the table and reassembled in the front room. Adam squatted down in front of Petey.

"Pals?"

Petey nodded, hugged Adam tightly, and stepped back. "But are you gonna *shave* when it's summer?"

Laughter echoed from the walls.

When Adam turned to her, Elizabeth pulled her snake from her pocket. "How come . . . ?"

"Snakes are quiet creatures. Hard to appreciate, at first," Adam explained. "But they play a critical role in an ecosystem."

He winked and hugged her tightly.

That beard does scratch!

Elizabeth smiled.

But I don't mind either.

Adam grinned at his sister. "Promise you'll miss me some more?"

"Yeah, stupid." Molly opened her arms. "I promise." When they released each other, she wiped her eyes.

She called him "stupid." That means they've made up.

Adam freed himself from his father's embrace and

turned to Grandma. They hugged each other for a long time, Sheridan noise swelled, and Adam was gone. The rest of the family wandered off. Elizabeth stood by the fireplace, watching small flames dance among logs that were nearly ashes.

Grandma came through the archway. "Can we talk for a minute?"

Elizabeth nodded.

Grandma folded her arms and looked up at the painting. "I was really, really angry with you for taking it."

Elizabeth winced.

"I didn't say anything because I assumed it was gone for good."

It almost was.

"When I went to fill the stockings, I almost fell over." Grandma glanced at her. "Then I was hurt because I'd asked you *not* to make another one."

"But . . ."

Grandma held up one hand. "Then I looked at it closely." She tapped her glasses. "And I realized that it was the original. That you had *repaired* it."

Elizabeth swallowed hard. "Are you still upset?"

Grandma slowly shook her head. "It was an incredibly generous and loving thing to do, an even greater gift than it was the first time. I don't know how to say thank you."

Elizabeth gave her grandmother a small smile.

"Not just for me, but for Petey. And Adam."

"You're friends again, aren't you?" Elizabeth pleaded.

Grandma nodded. "We talked for a long time before breakfast. About grasping at straws when things change too quickly."

Adam's not wanting to be a Sheridan . . . Elizabeth's pulse quickened.

. . . and my not being able to swim!

"We probably should have checked with you first." Grandma hesitated. "I hope you don't mind, but he asked me to read the essay you sent him."

Elizabeth's cheeks burned.

"Am I still 'Iron Woman'?"

Elizabeth shook her head.

"Why not?"

"That was when I only knew you from the outside," she stammered. "When I knew you were strict, but I didn't *understand* anything."

"When did 'Iron Woman' disappear?" Grandma asked softly. "What changed?"

Elizabeth looked at the floor. "At the tide pools. The first time you took me, and I fell in." Her voice dropped. "I was too scared to breathe."

"I remember," Grandma whispered.

"You came right into the water, and helped me get out." Elizabeth swallowed. "You promised you'd catch me if I slipped." She looked at the fire. "And I suddenly knew that you would."

Grandma contemplated her for a long moment.

"You're something else, Elizabeth." She smiled and tipped her head. "What else happened that day?"

Elizabeth's cheeks grew pink again. "You made me say it."

Grandma's eyes began to twinkle. "Made you say *what?*"

"'I want to be part of this family.'"

Grandma took Elizabeth's chin in her hand. "And what's *changed* since then?"

"I want to." She grinned. "And I *am!*"

V. M. CALDWELL is the author of *The Ocean Within,* which won the Milkweed Prize for Children's Literature in 1999.

If you enjoyed this book, you'll also want to read
these other Milkweed novels.
To order books or for more information, contact Milkweed at
(800) 520-6455 or visit our website (www.milkweed.org).

The $66 Summer
by John Armistead
Milkweed Prize for Children's Literature

By working at his grandmother's general store in Obadiah,
Alabama, during the summer of 1955, George Harrington figures he can save enough money to buy the motorcycle he wants,
a Harley-Davidson. Spending his off-hours with two friends, Esther
Garrison, fourteen, and Esther's younger brother, Bennett, the
unusual trio in 1950s Alabama—George is white, and Esther and
Bennett are black—embark on a summer of adventure that turns
serious when they begin to uncover the truth about the racism in
their midst.

Gildaen, The Heroic Adventures of a Most Unusual Rabbit
by Emilie Buchwald
Chicago Tribune Book Festival Award, Best Book for Ages 9–12

Gildaen is befriended by a mysterious being who has lost his
memory but not the ability to change shape at will. Together they
accept the perilous task of thwarting the evil sorcerer, Grimald,
in this tale of magic, villainy, and heroism.

The Ocean Within
by V. M. Caldwell
Milkweed Prize for Children's Literature

Elizabeth is a foster child who has just been placed with the boisterous and affectionate Sheridans, a family that wants to adopt
her. Used to having to look out for herself, however, Elizabeth
is reluctant to open up to them. During a summer spent by the
ocean with the eight Sheridan children and their grandmother,

who Elizabeth dubs "Iron Woman" because of her strict discipline, Elizabeth learns what it means—and how much she must risk— to become a permanent member of a loving family.

No Place
by Kay Haugaard

Arturo Morales and his fellow sixth-grade classmates decide to improve their neighborhood and their lives by building a park in their otherwise concrete, inner-city Los Angeles barrio. The kids are challenged by their teachers to figure out what it would take to transform the neighborhood junkyard into a clean, safe place for children to play. Despite their parents' skepticism and the threat of street gangs, Arturo and his classmates struggle to prove that the actions of individuals—even kids—can make a difference.

Business As Usual
by David Haynes
from the West 7th Wildcats Series

In Mr. Harrison's sixth-grade class, the West 7th Wildcats must learn how to run a business. Kevin Olsen, one of the Wildcats as well as the class clown, is forced out of the Wildcat group and into an unwilling alliance working in a group with the Wildcats' nemesis, Jenny Pederson. In the process of making staggering amounts of cookies for Marketplace Day, the classmates venture into the realm of free enterprise, discovering more than they imagined about business, the world, and themselves.

The Gumma Wars
by David Haynes
from the West 7th Wildcats Series

Larry "Lu" Underwood and his fellow West 7th Wildcats have been looking forward to Tony Rodriguez's birthday fiesta all year—only to discover that Lu must also spend the day with his two feuding "gummas," the name he gave his grandmothers when he was just learning to talk. The two "gummas," Gumma Jackson and Gumma Underwood, are hostile to one another, especially when it comes to claiming the affection of their only grandson. On the action-packed day of Tony's birthday, Lu, a friend, and the gummas find themselves exploring the sights of Minneapolis and St. Paul—and eventually enjoying each other's company.

The Monkey Thief
by Aileen Kilgore Henderson
New York Public Library Best Books of the Year:
"Books for the Teen Age"

Twelve-year-old Steve Hanson is sent to Costa Rica for eight months to live with his uncle. There he discovers a world completely unlike anything he can see from the cushions of his couch back home, a world filled with giant trees and insects, mysterious sounds, and the constant companionship of monkeys swinging in the branches overhead. When Steve hatches a plan to capture a monkey for himself, his quest for a pet leads him into dangerous territory. It takes all of Steve's survival skills—and the help of his new friends—to get him out of trouble.

The Summer of the Bonepile Monster
by Aileen Kilgore Henderson
Milkweed Prize for Children's Literature
Alabama Library Association 1996 Juvenile/Young Adult Award

Eleven-year-old Hollis Orr has been sent to spend the summer with Grancy, his father's grandmother, in rural Dolliver, Alabama, while his parents "work things out." As summer begins, Hollis encounters a road called Bonepile Hollow, barred by a gate and a real skull and bones mounted on a board. "Things that go down that road don't ever come back," he is told. Thus begins the mystery that plunges Hollis into real danger.

Treasure of Panther Peak
by Aileen Kilgore Henderson

Twelve-year-old Page Williams begrudgingly accompanies her mother, Ellie, as she flees her abusive husband, Page's father. Together they settle in a fantastic new world — Big Bend National Park, Texas. Wild animals stalk through the park, and the nearby Ghost Mountains are filled with legends of lost treasures. As Page tests her limits by sneaking into forbidden canyons, Ellie struggles to win the trust of other parents. Only through their newfound courage are they able to discover a treasure beyond what they could have imagined.

I Am Lavina Cumming
by Susan Lowell
Mountains & Plains Booksellers Association Award

In 1905, ten-year-old Lavina is sent from her home on the Bosque Ranch in Arizona Territory to live with her aunt in the city of Santa Cruz, California. Armed with the Cumming family motto, "courage," Lavina deals with a new school, homesickness, a very spoiled cousin, an earthquake, and a big decision about her future.

The Boy with Paper Wings
by Susan Lowell

Confined to bed with a viral fever, eleven-year-old Paul sails a paper airplane into his closet and propels himself into mysterious and dangerous realms in this exciting and fantastical adventure. Paul finds himself trapped in the military diorama on his closet floor, out to stop the evil commander, KRON. Armed only with paper and the knowledge of how to fold it, Paul uses his imagination and courage to find his way out of dilemmas and disasters.

The Secret of the Ruby Ring
by Yvonne MacGrory
Winner of Ireland's Bisto "Book of the Year" Award

Lucy gets a very special birthday present, a star ruby ring, from her grandmother and finds herself transported to Langley Castle in the Ireland of 1885. At first, she is intrigued by castle life, in which she is the lowliest servant, until she loses the ruby ring and her only way home.

A Bride for Anna's Papa
by Isabel R. Marvin
Milkweed Prize for Children's Literature

Life on Minnesota's Iron Range in 1907 is not easy for thirteen-year-old Anna Kallio. Her mother's death has left Anna to take care of the house, her young brother, and her father, a blacksmith in the dangerous iron mines. So she and her brother plot to find their father a new wife, even attempting to arrange a match with one of the "mail order" brides arriving from Finland.

Minnie
by Annie M. G. Schmidt
Winner of the Netherlands' Silver Pencil Prize as
One of the Best Books of the Year

Miss Minnie is a cat. Or rather, she *was* a cat. She is now a human, and she's not at all happy to be one. As Minnie tries to find and reverse the cause of her transformation, she brings her reporter friend, Mr. Tibbs, news from the cats' gossip hotline — including revealing information that one of the town's most prominent citizens is not the animal lover he appears to be.

The Dog with Golden Eyes
by Frances Wilbur
Milkweed Prize for Children's Literature

Many girls dream of owning a dog of their own, but Cassie's wish for one takes an unexpected turn in this contemporary tale of friendship and growing up. Thirteen-year-old Cassie is lonely, bored, and feeling friendless when a large, beautiful dog appears one day in her suburban backyard. Cassie wants to adopt the dog, but as she learns more about him, she realizes that she is, in fact, caring for a full-grown Arctic wolf. As she attempts to protect the wolf from urban dangers, Cassie discovers that she possesses strengths and resources she never imagined.

Behind the Bedroom Wall
by Laura E. Williams
Milkweed Prize for Children's Literature
New York Public Library Best Books of the Year:
"Books for the Teen Age"

It is 1942. Thirteen-year-old Korinna Rehme is an active member of her local *Jungmädel*, a Nazi youth group, along with many of her friends. Korinna's parents, however, secretly are members of an underground group providing a means of escape to the Jews of their city and are, in fact, hiding a refugee family behind the wall of Korinna's bedroom. As Korinna comes to know the family, and their young daughter, her sympathies begin to turn. But when someone tips off the Gestapo, loyalties are put to the test and Korinna must decide in what she believes and whom she trusts.

The Spider's Web
by Laura E. Williams

Thirteen-year-old Lexi Jordan has just joined The Pack, a group of neo-Nazi skinheads, as a substitute for the family she wishes she had. After she and The Pack spray paint a synagogue, Lexi hides from her pursuers on the front porch of elderly Ursula Zeidler, a former member of the Hitler Youth Group, who painfully recalls her ugly anti-Semitic Nazi activities and betrayal of a friend that she bitterly rues. When her younger sister becomes enthralled with Lexi's new "family," Lexi realizes the true meaning of The Pack and has little time to save herself and her sister from its sinister grip.

Milkweed Editions publishes with the intention of making a humane impact on society, in the belief that literature is a transformative art uniquely able to convey the essential experiences of the human heart and spirit.

To that end, Milkweed publishes distinctive voices of literary merit in handsomely designed, visually dynamic books, exploring the ethical, cultural, and esthetic issues that free societies need continually to address.

Milkweed Editions is a not-for-profit press.

JOIN US

Milkweed publishes adult and children's fiction, poetry, and, in its World As Home program, literary nonfiction about the natural world. Milkweed also hosts two websites: www.milkweed.org, where readers can find in-depth information about Milkweed books, authors, and programs, and www.worldashome.org, which is your online resource of books, organizations, and writings exploring the ethical, esthetic, and cultural dimensions of our relationship to the natural world.

Since its genesis as *Milkweed Chronicle* in 1979, Milkweed has helped hundreds of emerging writers reach their readers. Thanks to the generosity of foundations and individuals like you, Milkweed Editions is able to continue its nonprofit mission of publishing books chosen on the basis of literary merit—of how they impact the human heart and spirit—rather than on how they impact the bottom line. That's a miracle our readers have made possible.

In addition to purchasing Milkweed books, you can join the growing community of Milkweed supporters. Individual contributions of any amount are both meaningful and welcome. Contact us for a Milkweed catalog or log on to www.milkweed.org and click on "About Milkweed," then "Why Join Milkweed," to find out about our donor program, or simply call 800-520-6455 and ask about becoming one of Milkweed's contributors. As a nonprofit press, Milkweed belongs to you, the community. Milkweed's board, its staff, and especially the authors whose careers you help launch thank you for reading our books and supporting our mission in any way you can.

Typeset in Electra 11.5/15.5
by Stanton Publication Services, Inc.
Printed on acid-free, recycled 55# Frasier Miami Book
Natural paper by Friesen Corporation